NOTES OF
A MEDIOCRE MAN

STORIES OF INDIA
AND AMERICA

ESSENTIAL PROSE SERIES 130

NOTES OF
A MEDIOCRE MAN

STORIES OF INDIA
AND AMERICA

Bipin Aurora

**GUERNICA
EDITIONS**

GUERNICA
TORONTO—BUFFALO—LANCASTER (U.K.)
2017

Michael Mirolla, editor
Cover design: Allen Jomoc Jr.
Interior design: Jill Ronsley, Sun Editing & Book Design
Guernica Editions Inc.
1569 Heritage Way, Oakville, (ON), Canada L6M 2Z7
2250 Military Road, Tonawanda, N.Y. 14150-6000 U.S.A.
www.guernicaeditions.com

Distributors:
University of Toronto Press Distribution,
5201 Dufferin Street, Toronto (ON), Canada M3H 5T8
Gazelle Book Services, White Cross Mills, High Town,
Lancaster LA1 4XS U.K.

First edition.
Printed in Canada.

Legal Deposit—First Quarter
Library of Congress Catalog Card Number: 2016930158
Library and Archives Canada Cataloguing in Publication
Aurora, Bipin, author
Notes of a mediocre man : stories of India and America /
Bipin
Aurora.—1st edition.

(Essential prose series ; 130)
Issued in print and electronic formats.
ISBN 978-1-77183-141-3 (paperback)

I. Title. II. Series: Essential prose series 130
PS3601.U7N68 2016   813'.6   C2016-900113-X
                                        C2016-900114-8

To Joel Aurora, John Robbins,
and Rajive Aurora

Contents

Munnu Shunnu   1
The Dance   23
Krishna   37
My Father Is Investigated by the Authorities   57
A Small Market   75
The Servant   95
Gurmeet Singh   111
Mother of Gulu   127
Raghavendran Ramachandran   141
D.K. Choudhary   159
Notes of a Mediocre Man   177
The Boy   197
Ahmed   207
My Daughter   227
The Lovers in Bengal   241
Ajay Bhatt   259
The Bill   279
Pranab Roy   303

Acknowledgments   325
About the Author   327

Munnu Shunnu

The two brothers in school, how can one forget them? Their ranks were the lowest in class. In sports they were the worst. But the stories they came in with, always the stories.

"A camel has been found, sir, found dead in the sand."

"A madwoman has been found, sir: in her right hand is a bag of burlap, in her left hand a red brick."

"A submerged temple has been found, sir—the water dry, the temple has risen to the ground. In the inner shrine the picture of God is still intact."

The teacher would grow angry at them, he would ask them where they had heard these stories.

But the boys would grow silent.

"Tell me."

The boys would not answer. And then:

"There is a nice woman, sir."

"A nice woman?"

"She can read in her sleep, sir. She can pray in her sleep. She can cook food in her sleep, sir, she can even knit sweaters."

The teacher would be furious at their words, he would slap them.

"Useless boys," he would say. "Foolish boys. Have you no shame?"

But this is the way they were. This is just the way they were.

The boys would return to their desks—they would sit there in silence.

But then, a few minutes later (only a few)—or at least the next day:

"We saw a cricket match, sir."

"What is this?"

"The ball hit the bat, sir, the bat hit the ball. But this was not all. A crow came, sir (a black crow): it took the ball away."

"What is this?"

"The crow, sir, it was a black crow. It took it to the temple, it took it to the market. Even to Dubai, sir (they were having a fair there, a nice fair)—it took it there as well."

The teacher would look at them, look in amazement. Was it in awe as well?

***

The two brothers—no, we had never seen anyone like them. Where they came from, no one knew. Who their father was, no one knew. One day they had come to school—just like that they had come.

"I am Munnu."

"Yes."

"This is my brother—he is Shunnu."

"Yes."

And like that—just like that they had come.

There was a green bag—it was over the shoulder of Munnu. There was a red bag—it was over the shoulder of Shunnu. And like that—just like that they had come.

They were different, so different from the rest of us. We had never seen anyone like them.

We were fair-skinned; they were dark. We had hair on our heads; their heads were shaved (only a small tuft at the back). We wore shoes. They came in their bare feet. We wore shorts (and sometimes pants); they came in their white pajamas.

And yes, here they were.

The teacher would walk down the rows of the class, he would stop at their desk.

"Five and five?" he would say.

"Nine."

"How many grams in a kilogram?"

"Three."

"The highest mountain in the world?"

Silence.

"Useless boys!" the teacher would shout. "Foolish boys. Have you no shame?"

Useless boys, yes, foolish boys, yes. But this is the way they were. This is just the way they were.

The teacher would recite a lesson, they would try so hard to follow it. The teacher would recite a lesson, they would recite with everyone else in return.

"And Rangoon is the capital of Burma."

"And Rangoon is the capital of Burma."

"And eight times nine is seventy-two."

"And eight times nine is seventy-two."

"And water becomes water vapor and goes to the sky."

"And water becomes water vapor and goes to the sky."

The teacher would recite a lesson, how hard they would try to follow it. But when the lesson was over, did they retain any of it? Ask them five minutes later (or even one), did they remember—remember anything at all?

"The capital of Burma?"

"Sir?"

"Eight times nine?"

"Sir?"

"What happens to water ..."

"Water from the fridge, sir, it is nice and cold. The poor people do not have it. But water from the fridge, sir, is it not a good thing?"

Water from the fridge—what kind of answer was that? But this is the way they were.

***

The teacher was a strict man, he tried to make an example of the boys. Sometimes he slapped them. Sometimes he made them come to the front of the class. In front of the others, he pulled on their ears (the ears turned red). In front of the others, he asked them to extend their hands. The cane was in the air; the cane made a slice through the air and it came down.

But do you think it helped?

"We are stupid boys," they said.

"We are the worst boys," they said.

"You punish us—is it not right that you punish us?" they said.

The boys felt that they were being punished. They felt that they were being rightly punished. But the lesson to be learned, did they learn that?

The school session ended, the report cards came out. And their ranks—was it any surprise?—were the lowest in the class. There were thirty-seven students in the class. Sometimes Munnu was thirty-six, Shunnu thirty-seven. Sometimes it was the other way around.

Their ranks were the lowest, yes. But the brothers—and this was also a part of their strangeness—did not seem concerned. In fact when the report cards came out, they asked, "So Praveen, what rank were you?"

"I was eight."

And then Munnu would say, "I was thirty-six."

And Shunnu would add, "I was thirty-seven."

They asked their questions matter-of-factly. They offered the information about themselves matter-of-factly as well.

One time the brothers were asked, "Are you not jealous that the others finish ahead of you?"

"Oh no," they said.

"But the others finish ahead?"

"We are so happy for them." "How intelligent they are." "How proud their parents must be of them."

Perhaps the boys were telling the truth, perhaps they were pretending. But in this way they spoke.

***

The teacher was a strict man—from Sialkot he came. When partition had come, he had left his home, he had come to Delhi.

Sometimes the teacher would walk around the room, he would tell a story. And how the brothers would come to life!

"It is a good story, sir."

"Tell us another story, sir."

"The story, sir, is it not a good thing?"

Their ranks were the lowest. They had trouble following their lessons. But when the teacher told a story (and sometimes he did—even he), how their minds came to life!

Sometimes the teacher would walk around the room, he would say to the children: "You children, you do not listen." Or else: "You are too spoiled." Or else: "You do not know the meaning of discipline." And then he would tell a story about the time that he had been a child. The teachers had been so strict that if you made any noise in the class—if you so much as sneezed or dropped an eraser to the floor—you would be punished.

The other students thought that the teacher was silly, old-fashioned, too strict; and behind his back they laughed at him.

Only the brothers did not laugh: "We like the teacher," they said. "He is a *good* teacher," they said.

"In the days of old," said the teacher, "the boys showed respect for the teacher. They swept the teacher's house, they did the shopping. They chopped the wood and they brought daily offerings—offerings of milk and curd, of vegetables and fruit."

Again the other children sneered at the teacher, they laughed. "So students were not students," they said, "they were *slaves* in those days."

Only the brothers did not laugh. With rapt attention they listened to the teacher. "Tell us more," they said. "Tell us more."

They had trouble following the lessons. (What trouble they had!) But now the teacher was telling a story. And could they just refuse?

The teacher told the children stories about the past. The brothers walked around the grounds of the school repeating the stories.

The teacher spoke of the days in Sialkot when he had been a child.

The brothers spoke of the days in Sialkot as well.

He spoke of the times when he had been a student.

They spoke of the times when he had been a student.

They would stand on a mango crate (or on the top of the steps). "Listen children," they would say. "Listen." And then they would tell the story that the teacher had told.

Sometimes they would repeat the story of the teacher word by word. Sometimes they would add to the story. And sometimes they would come up with a new story of their own.

The bell would ring, it would be time for the children to return to class.

But the boys would be there, still there, telling a story—waving or gesturing with their hands.

The teacher was a busy man, he must return to the lessons.

"But the lessons, sir, are they really important?"

"What is this?"

"The lessons, sir, are they really the key?"

"What is this?"

The brothers would stand there, nodding their heads. They would stand there, rocking back and forth.

"A story, sir, is it not a good thing?"

"A story, sir, is it not the best?"

"A story, sir—one more story (just one)."

They were strange words—what strange words they were. (Were they insolent words as well?)

But this is the way the boys were. This is just how they spoke.

***

One time the teacher told all the children to read the newspaper. There was news in the world, important news, they must keep up with it.

Some of the children ignored the teacher, others did the minimum work required (and did it as a duty). But with what eagerness the boys read the news. The next day the boys came in, they came in bursting with the news!

"A horse has been found, sir, lying flat on its back. There was no food in the house, the mother killed it. What else could the mother do?"

"A boy has been found, sir, he was walking in the streets. His father has kicked him out, said he was not a good son."

"A man has been found, sir, eating the roots of trees. He used to live on the second story, eat carrots and peas. The monsoon rains came, sir (or was it the bad people?). They took his house away."

The teacher just looked at the boys. He looked at them aghast. He had asked them to read the news, to keep up with the news of the world. Was this the news?

"A boy has been found, sir, a tear in his eye. He does not have a fridge, he does not have a flush toilet. He must go to the back, he must use the public latrines."

"A man has been found, sir, an Assistant (a small man) in the government. He thinks he is no one, he should have been more. He hits himself in the forehead, and sometimes he hits his wife."

"A cricket player has been found, sir, he was out on the first ball. He sits in the dark room, his face to the wall. He rocks back and forth, sir, he rocks back and forth."

Again the teacher just looked at them. He looked at them in silence. Was it in awe as well?

"A blind man came, sir, he took the sun away."

"What is this?"

"In a horse carriage he came, sir, he took the sun away."

"What is this?"

"Our father, sir, he tells us."

"Your father?"

"He is a good man, sir, a good man's son. And he tells us—he tells us about the world."

The teacher just looked at the boys, he looked at them in wonder. The boys were orphans (so the teacher knew). A father who was a good man—who told them all about the world—how could it be?

"This father," he said, "show me this father."

But the boys were silent.

"This father," he said, "take me to this father."

But the boys were silent. And then:

"He is busy, sir."

"He is away, sir."

"One day, sir, you will meet him. And then all will be made clear (is it not so?). All will be made clear."

They were strange words—what strange words they were. But this is the way the boys were. In this way they spoke.

***

The teacher sat at his desk, he thought about the boys. He thought about them for some time. They were strange boys—what strange boys they were. They told these stories—*why* did they tell them? They spoke about their father—this father who did not exist. *Why* did they do it?

The teacher went and talked with the principal. Do you think it helped? He went and checked the school records that were kept for the boys. Do you think it helped? He checked the money that was received for the boys' tuition and books. Quietly the money came, anonymously.

Many times the teacher went up to the boys, he spoke to them directly. But was it of any use?

"Your father," he said.

They did not answer.

"Your father," he said.

They did not answer.

"Your father," he said.

"But God, sir, *God* is our father."

"What is this?"

"But God, sir, *God* is our father."

There was truth, of course, there was truth to the words. But could the words be enough—could they really be enough?

"In the assembly each morning we say our prayers. We say the words 'Our Father Who Art in Heaven.' And God *is* our father, the father of all of us. But on earth, I mean, who is your father on earth?"

The boys were silent.

"On earth?"

Still the boys were silent. And then: "But God, sir, *God* is our father."

They were strange words—what strange words they were. Did the boys believe the words—did they actually believe?

One day the teacher tried to take a slightly different approach. He went up to the boys again.

"Where do you live?" he said.

"There, sir."

"Where?"

"There." And the brothers pointed into the distance, in a general direction.

"Do you live alone?"

"Oh no, sir, we live with each other."

"But you are so small. Who takes care of you? Who cooks your food, who washes your clothes?"

The boys smiled sheepishly.

"Well?"

"Each other, sir. Munnu cooks for me, I cook for Munnu. Munnu washes for me, I wash for him."

The teacher smiled. "And this God that you speak of, this Father, doesn't *he* cook for you, doesn't he do the wash?"

The brothers looked at each other.

"And this God that you speak of …"

The brothers looked at each other. And then:

"But God, sir, he is a busy man. He has so many children; he must listen to their prayers, he must tell them stories. Time to cook, to wash—how can he have time for that? To cook, to wash—how can he have time for that?"

The teacher was amazed (was he even impressed?). There was truth to their words (they were not without merit). Were they really so stupid, were they really so mad?

The teacher shook his head—he shook it in acknowledgment. He shook his head—was it in frustration as well?

***

And so the days passed. The boys came in, they told their stories. Each day they came, they told their stories. The teacher told them to be quiet. Do you think it helped? He told them not to disturb the class. Do you think it helped? He told them to concentrate on their studies. After all, isn't this what they were there for? There were exams to be taken, tests to be passed. If they did not make an effort, would they ever be able to do it—to pass?

"A story, sir, a story."

"A story?"

"A story, sir, is it not a good thing?"

"A story, sir, is it not the best?"

The boys came in—each day they came. "There is shame in the world, sir."

"Shame?"

"There is shame in the world, sir, so much shame. But who will come, sir—who will come and take the shame away?"

And then they would talk for days and days—talk about nothing but the shame.

"There is sadness in the world, sir."

"Sadness?"

"There is sadness in the world, sir, so much sadness. They are looking for someone—someone to take the sadness away."

And then they would talk for days and days—talk about nothing but the sadness.

"We saw an old man, sir."

"An old man?"

"He is trying, sir, he is trying. But he is not sure that even he can do it—that even he can take all the sadness away."

They were strange words, they were astounding words. But this is the way the boys were. This is just the way they spoke.

"There is a nice man, sir."

"A nice man?"

"He has three heads, sir (or is it three eyes?). One to drink tea, one to read the newspaper. One to cast upon his neighbors the evil eye."

"We saw a dead pigeon, sir."

"A dead pigeon?"

"He lay on his stomach, sir, a twig (a small twig) on his face."

"We saw a green tiger, sir."

"A green tiger?"

"It roared and it roared, sir (we were so afraid). But then his mother called him in. It was dark, it was late—it was time for him to eat his food. It was dark, it was late—it was time (was it not?) to pull on his ears: to pray, to pray."

***

The days passed. The behavior of the boys, it was widely discussed. The teacher spoke about it, the other teachers spoke about it. The other children spoke about it—they spoke as well.

But do you think it helped?

The boys came in—they told their stories. Each day they came. Their supply of stories, it seemed, was endless. Their supply, it seemed, would never end.

One time the other children said, "Where do these stories come from?"

The boys did not answer.

"But these stories, they must come from somewhere."

Silence.

"A story," said the children. "Another story."

The boys would suddenly smile. They would go stand on a mango crate (or on the top of the steps). They would hold hands, they would gesture. And they would tell a story. Another story.

The sun would rise in the sky. The sun would move to the west, near the Quaker Center; the shadows would grow long. And there the boys would be (the two boys): they would still be telling a story.

Some said that the stories came from a bag, some said they came from a tin box. Some said that they came from a tin trunk—from a tin box inside the trunk. But wherever they came from, the boys brought these stories—these stories without end.

Sometimes the boys would *perform* the story as well. Munnu would begin the story, Shunnu would encourage him along. He would nod his head, he would cry. At the appropriate place, he would clap; he would begin to shed tears.

At some point Shunnu would pick up the story. Now Munnu would do all the things that the other had done.

The other children would listen, they would watch. They would listen to the words of the first, they would follow the actions of the second. Sometimes— many times—the other children would be moved. They would clap. They would cry. Sometimes it was such a good story—they would do both. Yes, they would clap and cry at the same time.

"There is sadness in the world."

"Yes yes."

"There is shame in the world."

"Yes yes."

They would clap and they would cry—they would do both at the same time.

***

But the things of the world, they do not last forever. The things of the world—do they not come to an end?

And so it was—so it was here as well.

One time the boys did not come to school—not come to school for several days (or was it even for a whole week?). There was no note for their absence (how could there be?), there was no letter or phone call from home.

Then one day they came walking in—the same dark skins, the same shaved heads—they walked in as if nothing had happened.

The teacher was curious, he asked them where they had been.

The boys were silent.

Again he asked them.

The boys were silent.

And then:

"We were with our father, sir."

"Your father?"

"He was teaching us, sir—he was teaching us about the world."

"He was teaching you—what was he teaching you?"

But the boys were silent.

"He was teaching you—what was he teaching you?"

But the boys were silent.

And then:

"There are ants in the world, sir, there are so many ants."

"What is this?"

"There are trees in the world, sir, there are so many trees."

"What is this?"

"We must go away, sir (is it not so?), we must go away for a few days."

"Go away—where will you go?"

"We must go away, sir, we must go away for a few days."

The brothers did not come to school—they did not come for several days.

One day they came back.

Again they did not come for several days.

One day they came back.

And then one day—was it not inevitable?—they stopped coming to school. They *stopped coming altogether*.

Some people said that they had seen the boys the day before (only the day before). They had walked out of the gate, walked into the distance. They had grown smaller and smaller—and then they were only a speck, a speck on the horizon.

Was this really possible? Could it be?

Some people said that the boys were the children of God—they really were—and now they had returned to their Father.

Was this really possible? Could it be?

Some people said that the boys liked to tell stories. They had moved to another town (that is all); they were now telling their stories there.

Was *this* really possible? Could it be?

But whatever really happened, one thing was clear. The boys were gone. And would we ever see them again?

The brothers were gone, were gone. And would we ever see them again?

***

It was a cold afternoon, there were clouds in the sky. It was a grey afternoon, there were birds there as well (a sparrow, a crow).

And there we saw them—was it in our imagination, only there? There we saw them—was it for the last time?

The dark skins, the shaved heads. The white pajamas—the pajamas as well.

There was a mango crate, they stood on the crate. There were some steps—they stood on the steps.

"A story, sir, is it not a good thing?"

"A story, sir, is it not the best?"

"A story, sir—one more story (just one)."

Munnu was there—he shook his head. Shunnu was there—he joined him.

"A man has been found, sir, a turban on his head. He says that we all have to die. He says that one day we all have to go—go to the other side."

"The other side?"

"A woman has been found, sir, she is blind in one eye. She has lived on air for three years, on water for five. She says she has seen many things. And now she is ready—ready to go to the other side."

"To the other side?"

"A woman has been found, sir, lying dead on the sand. She wanted to go to the cricket match, see the great players. A lion came, sir, he took her on his back. He took her away."

"He took her away?"

"To the Red Fort, sir, to the Jumna River. To the special place, sir—the special place where stories are made."

"The special place?"

"It is a nice place, sir. It is a nice place."

The teacher asked the children to tell him about this place.

But they would not say.

Again he asked them.

But they would not say.

It began to rain—so hard it rained. It began to pour—how hard it poured. But the boys did not stop (how could they?).

"A story, sir, is it not a good thing?"

"A story, sir, is it not the best?"

"A story, sir—one more story (just one)."

Munnu was there, he shook his head. Shunnu was there, he joined him.

They were here, they were not. They were in the other place (they were not). But one thing was the same (always the same).

"One more story, sir."

"One more story, sir."

"One more story, sir. Just one. *Just one.*"

The Dance

There was a dance. It was called the "Sway." There was another dance. It was called the "El Paso." There was a short woman with greying hair. She was about fifty-five years old. She introduced herself. "I am Edna," she said. "And this group, it is PWP—Parents Without Partners."

She asked me if I was a parent. I said no. She asked me if I was looking for a partner. I said no. She asked me why I had come.

"There was a flyer," I said. "It said there was a dance at the fire station. I came to see what it looked like—the fire station."

"You came for that—the fire station, not the dance?"

"Yes," I said.

She was surprised at my words, and perhaps a little peeved. I was being flippant and she could tell. I was lonely, lost, no better than the others there. I was just pretending to be better.

Edna was the head of the organization. She spoke to people and she answered a lot of their questions. It was important work—or at least it made her feel important. My answer seemed to make light of all that.

Someone was in line behind me. Edna turned away from me to that person. "Welcome," she said. "I am Edna," she said, holding out her hand. "And you?"

***

Edna did not want me around. I left her and walked a few feet. There was a door there, a man sitting at the entrance behind a wooden table. "Seven dollars," he said.

I reached into my pocket, took out the seven dollars.

The man gave me a blue paper stub. "Don't lose it," he said. Then the man took a rubber stamp and pressed it on the back of my left hand.

I continued on my way. There was a long hall with simple aluminum chairs and a few small tables along the edges. In one corner, to the right, was a long table with a plastic tablecloth and with things on top. I approached the table, noticed there were refreshments. Beer: two dollars. Punch: one dollar. Wine: two-fifty.

A man brushed against me from behind, apologized. "Peace be with you," he said. He was a tall man, nicely dressed in a tan jacket and a tie. I thought that the man was joking but then I was not so sure. I had been to church a few times. I had heard the words in church.

"Peace be with you," I began to say as well. But the man was long past me and headed to the other end of the hall. He was a handsome man. Perhaps he was a successful man as well. He had places to go, people to meet.

I bought some punch. They served it in a white Styrofoam cup. The cup was small and the punch overly sweet. But I did not say anything. I stood in the corner and I observed the scene. There were grown men and women, all there for a social gathering. The youngest were in their thirties, the oldest even more than sixty. Most of the people had made an effort to look nice for the occasion. There were no jeans or tennis shoes. The men wore collared shirts, some of them wore jackets and sometimes even a tie. The women wore dresses or nice slacks, often white or tan. Many of the women wore high heels—it must be hard to dance in the high heels but perhaps it was more important to look nice than to dance. Or perhaps if you did not look nice to begin with—that is, you were without the high heels—how would you even be asked to dance?

The room was dimly lit with some strobe lights flickering against the wall and the floor. Speakers were spread throughout the hall and the sound, coming from some machine in the corner, was of reasonable quality. Not good, not bad.

A man came and stood beside me. He was a tall man with white skin. He looked pale to me—perhaps too pale. He was balding as well, with some brown hair spread across his scalp. The hair belonged to one side but he had combed it all the way across so it could cover most of the head. If they turned on a fan, the man would be in trouble.

The man wore pants that came almost to his chest. He wore a blue short-sleeve shirt. He said that he had lived in Richmond, Virginia, for ten years.

"Richmond?" I said. I asked him what was special about Richmond.

"Rich people live there," he said. "It is their world—their *monde*. That is French, you know."

I nodded at his words, I acknowledged them. "I never knew that," I said. "I never thought of it that way."

The man was impressed by his words. He was impressed that I was impressed.

We went to a nearby table and sat there to rest our feet.

"You like this place?" he said.

"My first time."

"You like to dance?"

"I'm not very good."

The man began to speak again but the music came on, the new dance began. It drowned out his words.

***

The man had brought some kind of thermos with him. He opened the thermos, poured some liquid into a cup. He began to drink.

"Soup," he said.

I asked him what kind of soup it was.

"Chicken noodle," he said.

"Is it homemade?"

"Oh yes," he said.

Later that evening I went with the man and a few others to a place where he said that he had gotten the soup. The waitress came, I ordered the same soup. It was salty—overly so. It tasted like something from a can. When the waitress came back I asked her if it was homemade.

"It is from a can," she said.

I lost my faith in the man. Yes, from that moment—you can understand why—I lost faith in him.

A new dance was going on. People were in line, a couple at a time, dancing together. It was the "El Paso Line Dance." Some of the dancers were good, some not so good. But they tried.

Tip-toe front, tip-toe back; sometimes a turn to the side. Sometimes a twirl. And so on. A few people were not in line but stood a few feet away. They were watching the dancers, trying to imitate their steps. They were new to the dance, trying to learn. But they would join the line in a few minutes or next time.

When they grew confident. Yes, that.

Most of the couples in line were a man and a woman. But in one or two places were two women together. Perhaps no one asked them to dance. Perhaps they didn't want to dance with a man. Which was true, it was hard to say.

The minutes passed. People danced, they clapped. They made hooting noises. They laughed—sometimes at others, sometimes at themselves. I sat at the table on the side. The man with the soup was beside me. Sometimes he left me to join the dancers—to become one of them. Sometimes, but less and less frequently, he came back.

A man came, stood to my left. A woman came, sat at the table two seats from me.

"Join the fun," she said.

"Soon," I said.

"Can't be a wallflower."

"Soon," I said.

Tip-toe front, tip-toe back. Sometimes a turn to the side. Sometimes a twirl. How ingenious it all was.

After forty-five minutes or so, I decided to give it a whirl and to join the dance myself. I saw a woman against the wall. I gathered the courage, I went up to her. I asked her if she wanted to dance. "Not right now," she said. I asked a second woman. "I'm waiting for my boyfriend," she said. "He just went to get a drink." I asked a third: "Maybe in a bit."

I walked back to my seat, but it was taken. Someone else was sitting there now. The man with the soup was back at the table, running his hand over his bald head.

"Great dance," he said.

"Yes," I said.

"I love the soup," he said.

"It must be good," I said.

"Homemade. The best—the very best."

***

The people were dancing, I was not. They were having a good time. And I? But why think of these things? I decided to go outside.

A few people were already in the courtyard, scattered throughout. Inside it was warm, but outside it was cool with even a nice breeze. Some people stood in a circle. I went to their circle, tried to insinuate my way in. One of them looked at me.

"Nice night," I said.

The man did not answer me.

They stood there and they chatted. Were they looking for something? I stood there and I watched them.

One woman was covered in sweat, her dress soaked. She took her handkerchief and fanned herself. "Boy, that was something," she said. It was not complaint, but exultation.

Another woman puffed on a cigarette. "I love it," she said. "But I just needed to get out. Get some fresh air."

The sky was overcast, but here and there you could still see a few stars. Even the moon—a crescent sliver—went in and out from behind the clouds.

A man stood in the distance away from the group. He was of medium height, a little on the thin side. He stood near the bushes, his arms folded across his chest. He was deep in thought. Thought of what?

The sounds of the music wafted outside. Every so often some clapping was heard—no doubt the end of some song had been reached.

There was a cigarette between the man's index and middle fingers. Every so often he lifted his hand to his mouth and puffed from it.

The man stood apart. Who was he, why did he do it? I began to walk back inside. Then matter-of-factly—very matter-of-factly—I called out to the man: "Nice to be outside," I said.

The man did not answer. Perhaps he had not heard me.

This was my chance and I walked not inside but towards him. I stopped but a couple of feet from him. "You like the dance?" I said.

He did not answer me.

I did not think that he was being particularly friendly. But I did not let that dissuade me. "Good to stretch the legs, get some fresh air."

The man still did not answer me. He puffed on the cigarette and watched the smoke rise in the air.

Some gnats circled around the nearby bushes. "The gnats do not bother you?" I said.

"I've seen worse."

He had spoken at last. But he spoke curtly and it was obvious that he did not want to be bothered. Yet I did not leave him alone. I persisted.

"I am Nadeem," I said, holding out my hand.

The man leaned forward. "Didn't catch that," he said, leaning forward even more and straining his ear.

I repeated the name.

"*Neem. Mister Neem*," he said. He finally held out his hand. *Mister Neem*: was he being serious, was he mocking me, I could not say. But there was no joy in the effort. His hand was weak and limp. The cigarette was still between his lips.

I spoke again about the weather. No answer. I asked him about the dance. No answer. The man did not want to be bothered. But I lingered, lingered. At last, perhaps, the man had had enough of me.

"Don't take this the wrong way, but I'm really not in a talking mood. I came out to get away, have a smoke."

The man did not want to be bothered—he had made that clear more than once. But something drove me, intrigued me. What was it?

"Well, I guess I'll see you inside."

No answer.

"Enjoy the evening."

No answer.

I knew when I was beaten. (Or did I?) I continued on my way. One step and then the next. One step and then the next. I made my way inside.

***

I walked past the man at the door. He stopped me as I went past, gently holding my wrist. Realizing what he wanted, I turned over my hand so he could see the stamp on top of it.

I continued walking. The hall was much more crowded now. It was ten-thirty and many more people had come in. A few were outside trying to get fresh air. "They must do good business here," I thought. But was it really a "business"? Who organized it? Parents Without Partners (PWP). Who kept the money? Perhaps they did. But they had the hall to rent, the refreshments to buy, the music to pay for. It did not look easy.

A new dance was going on. People were in line—a couple at a time—dancing together. It was the El Paso Line Dance again. Some of the dancers were good, some not so good. But they tried. The line dance ended, a new dance began.

The time passed. I saw a few people, I talked to them. I saw a few people, I asked them to dance. Most said no, one finally said yes. But the song ended less than a minute after we began. There was no second dance.

People danced, I leaned against the wall and watched them. There was an empty seat; I rushed to the seat. Taken. More minutes passed, I saw another seat. I rushed to it, even faster this time. The seat was all mine.

A man was sitting next to me. "You like this place?" he said.

"My first time."

"You like to dance?"

"I'm not very good."

I had had the conversation before—of course I had. But some things repeat themselves. They repeat themselves again and again.

The time passed. Slowly it passed. Later that evening some of the people went to a diner to get something to eat. How, I do not know, I was asked to go along as well. Perhaps the others liked me. Perhaps they had seen me sitting by myself and felt sorry for me.

At the diner we sat at a long Formica table. One man—the same tall pale man I had met first at the dance—was again drinking soup. He had brought it in his thermos.

Also at the table was the man from outside with the cigarette. It turned out that he was an engineer— a mechanical engineer of some kind. How different he sounded now, a completely changed person. He sat at the middle of the table, perhaps the head of the group. He spoke about the search for energy throughout the country. For the car engine that gives one hundred miles to a gallon; for free energy; for the perpetual energy machine. Some said that these things had already been invented but that the government, or rich people in industry, were not letting them get to the public. Too much money, the loss of too much money, was at stake.

Others said that this was just nonsense, that there were always these conspiracy theories floating around. Others said that they were just not sure.

The conversation turned to dance. The engineer was also a good dancer, in fact a dance teacher. He spoke about different dances, about the different ways of doing the same dance. He spoke about the Lindy: "Too athletic," he said. "Not subtle like the waltz." He spoke about the Sway, the El Paso.

The others at the table listened to him, deferred to him. He was the leader. He certainly thought of himself as the leader. And perhaps they were in accord as well.

There was another man who worked with computers. He said he was tired of his job and he wanted to work with people.

"People?" someone said.

"More people," he said, "and preferably women. At least sixty percent—seventy percent—women."

There was always a cigarette between his lips. He puffed on his cigarette and watched the black smoke rise in the air.

He said that he had thought about working on a cruise. As a waiter perhaps or as a bartender— "at a poolside with a Tiki bar." He had also thought about working at a store in the mall—maybe even a Victoria's Secret.

"Are you serious?" I said.

"Sure," he said. "The pay may not be much but the women will be there. Many of them young. And I will be with people—mostly women."

I did not know if he was being serious or if he was pulling my leg. But his demands, his expectations, seemed perfectly reasonable. Who was I to disagree?

There was another man there. He was tall and slim with blond hair, not bad-looking. He spoke to two girls. They ignored him. He spoke to another girl. "Not right now," she said. He left us for a few minutes, came back with some things in a bag. Vegetables. Apparently he had gone to the grocery store and bought them to take to some other girl's place. The girl had a juicer at home that she had bought recently; he would try the vegetables in the juicer equipment.

He walked away to use his cell phone, called the girl. When he came back, the people at the table asked him what the girl had said.

"She says it is late in the evening, not a good time for me to come over."

He sat in his chair at the end of the table for a few minutes. But he did not look happy. He sulked and looked as if it caused him pain to sit there. After a few minutes he rose; he took the vegetables and left for the girl's place anyway.

When he was gone the others talked about him.

"He is desperate," they said.

"He is lonely," they said.

"Sometimes he embarrasses himself—makes a fool of himself. You try to stop him, but what can you do? People are people. What can you do?"

***

The hours passed, it was time to go home. I had forgotten my keys at the fire station—I had my car keys but not the second set, the one for home. I said goodbye to the others at the diner. They were polite to me, but formal. After all, we hardly knew each other.

I drove again to the fire station. They were cleaning up now. Someone had turned in the keys and they were lying at the edge of a table. I was still safe—safe for another day.

They were cleaning up the lobby, beginning to put things away. They took the table from the lobby to the back room. They were beginning to fold the collapsible chairs. I saw Edna, the woman who had organized it all. I wanted to say something. What did I want to say? "Thank you"? "Thank you for all the hard work"? "Thank you for putting this together"?

I approached Edna and stood about four feet from her. She turned her head slightly and saw me from the corner of her eye. But she looked vacantly.

Did she look through me? I had insulted her when I had come in. Perhaps I was not important. Perhaps she did not wish to have anything to do with me.

"We still have room in the back," she called out over her head to one of her helpers. "I think we can get some more chairs there. Seven or eight chairs. Maybe even ten."

"Yes yes," the other answered back. "Maybe even ten."

Edna was busy with the chairs. The others were busy with the chairs. It was time for me to get out of the way. To leave. To go home.

Home: what was this home? Where was this home? But they were big questions, why even think of them? The evening was over now. Done, *fini*. I had had a good time. I had learned so much about America. The world. It was time to go home.

Krishna

A short dark woman stood behind the grilled window. She wore a red sari, there was a black dot on her forehead. The people in line approached her window.

"Hey hey, where is my passport?"

"Five-year visa, how much?"

"Ten-year visa, how much?"

"My money, you did not give me my money back."

And then, again out loud so she could clearly hear them: "These people, they are so incompetent. Third World country. Just like a Third World country."

It was the Indian consulate in one of the major American cities. Some of the people there were Westerners, most of them were of Indian origin. They had come to get their Indian passports or their visas for their trips to India.

They clamored around the woman's window. It was a window with an iron grille, a small arc-shaped opening at the bottom.

The woman attended to them, tried to stay polite. They were not impressed. She tried to be professional, tried not to lose her temper. They were not impressed.

One man came, said that he wanted to see Mister Saxena.

"He is not available," she said.

"I talked to him on the phone. I have five passports—my wife and I, three children. We are leaving tomorrow. I need them today."

"Mister Saxena is a busy man."

"Busy man! I spoke to him on the phone. He will see me."

A second man came to the window.

"Mister Saxena is an important man," the Indian woman said.

"Important man! Only one man is important. And that man is Allah!"

A third man came. "Look," said the Indian woman. "Mister Saxena is a busy man, an officer. You cannot just go in, see him like that."

"You go and see Mister Saxena. You tell him I am here. I am waiting."

"Mister Saxena is an important man, an officer. He has assistants working for him. You want to see him—you talk to one of his assistants; they will help you."

The people in line heard her, thought that she was a funny woman. Or, worse, a silly woman. She had a silly, and small, view of the world.

"*Mister Saxena is an officer,*" they said, making a face and copying her singsong voice.

"*He has assistants working for him.*"

"*You have a problem—you see the assistants. You see the assistants first!*"

Perhaps she was a silly woman in some ways. Perhaps she did have a small view of the world. But must they mock her so openly?

She was a good woman. She was only doing her job. But did they care?

This was America, yes. But was it the America the woman had dreamed about? When she had received the news about her three-year posting to America, her parents had broken down and cried. They had told her how proud they were of her. Her friends had come to the house and said the same thing. And then they had said that they were envious of her as well. She was going to America—all the way to America. "America is a great country," they all said. "The best country in the world."

But this is the America she saw. She came to the Consulate and stood behind the iron-grilled window. (No one gave her a chair to sit on.) She gave people their visa and passport applications. She collected their money. And she listened to them talk. She listened to them make fun of the Consulate. She listened to them make fun of India, of her. Sometimes her dark face burned from the anger (or was it the shame?).

***

The morning work was over and the window was closed. The lunch break was one hour—from 12:00 p.m. to 1:00 p.m. Then she would spend the next three hours processing all the applications they had received. At four o'clock in the afternoon the window would be open again. And she would be back again attending to all the customers.

As she came to the back room for lunch, her friend Sheila greeted her.

"How was the morning?" she said.

"The same."

"The customers are rude?"

"Maybe they have a good reason."

She walked to the refrigerator and took out the blue lunch box. Two curried vegetables, some rice. On the side, half an orange, cut and wrapped in aluminum foil.

There was a mid-sized lunch table with six chairs cramped together. She went and sat in the chair at the corner.

Sheila, who had collected her own lunch, came and joined her.

"But heat the vegetables first," Sheila said, looking at Krishna already beginning to dig into the food. "Don't tell me you are going to eat them cold."

"I'm too tired to heat them."

"Here, let me heat them for you. The microwave, such a great invention. Two minutes …"

Krishna protested but Sheila was in no mood to listen.

"If a friend cannot heat for a friend …"

"But I'm fine, I tell you."

"Listen, Krishna, you do not take care of yourself. You are losing weight: five pounds, ten pounds …"

And thus they went, back and forth, back and forth. As others approached the lunch table, they lowered their voices.

"Oh ho, what is the argument?" said Mister Rastogi, a genial man of about fifty who worked in the Supply wing of the Consulate.

"Krishna," said Sheila simply, holding out her palm and pointing in her friend's direction.

The one gesture seemed to be enough. "I understand," said Mister Rastogi. "The girl works, she works. But she doesn't take care of herself. Ask her to take care of herself—do you think she listens?"

And then there was more conversation—this time between Mister Rastogi and Sheila—on Krishna's behavior.

Sheila brought the food, now heated, for her friend. Krishna sat there with a small stainless steel spoon, eating quietly. Between bites, she looked up, nodded.

They lectured to her and told her to take better care of herself.

"I will," she said.

"Look how thin she is." This was Sheila now (or perhaps Mister Rastogi)—after a while their voices were interchangeable to Krishna's ears.

"She has lost five pounds, ten."

"We need to find her a husband. When she is settled—when she has a purpose in life …"

And thus they went, on and on. Krishna nibbled at her food. She thought of India, far away. (Her mother, her father, her one younger brother.) She thought of all the applications that waited. (Review this, stamp that.) She thought of the grilled window—the one that reopened at four o'clock. And all the people—restless? angry? rude?—who would be waiting there.

***

Her name was Krishna Dayanand. She was from Chennai—or really from a small town some seventy miles from Chennai. In some ways it was not even a small town, but more like a village.

The place was near the Godavari River. Sometimes, as a child, she had walked to the river in her sandals. Sometimes she had walked in her bare feet, carrying the sandals in her hands. Sometimes she had walked all the way into the river till the water was knee-, or even thigh-deep.

But those were the old days, so far away. Why even think of them? This was America. A busy place, an official place. A place where you worked and worked.

There were palm and coconut trees near the Godavari River that swayed in the breeze. But that was all so far away as well. Why even think of such things?

At four o'clock in the afternoon, Krishna returned to her place behind the window. There was a line of ten or eleven people, the punctual people who showed up promptly at four when the office reopened. Then things would slow down a bit and would be steady for the rest of the hour. At five o'clock the window would be closed again. Then the last-minute cleaning: the filing away of the passports and applications that had not been picked up; the cleaning of the work area; the preparation for the next day's work.

It was demanding work—some would call it tedious work. But Krishna did it without complaint. This was America, the best posting in the world. Who was she to complain about the best posting in the world?

***

One day a man came with a lump on his neck, two children trailing behind him. One day a single man came—he said he was going to India for the Christmas holidays. One day a middle-aged woman came in a business suit, obviously a successful woman. She wore a Cambridge-grey jacket, the same color slacks. She was a little stout but attractive as well. Krishna looked at the woman for a long time. Krishna was especially fascinated by her hair—long, flowing, silky.

Krishna thought of her own hair: short and dry, sometimes with a barrette on top, sometimes in a bun. She thought of her dress: a simple lime-green cotton sari. Her mother had bought it for her as a present before she left for the U.S. She had been proud of the sari then—a new sari, a present—but in the face of this other woman, this *successful* woman, Krishna felt small. She took a quick peek at her sari and felt her shoulders droop.

One Saturday morning Krishna and Sheila went for a walk to the mall area. There were all these buildings there, all the museums. They went inside two or three museums but soon came out. Things, things, all these things. What exactly was one supposed to do with these things?

Outside at least the world made more sense. The sky was there—the nice blue October sky. Birds were there: pigeons, crows. Benches were there—they could sit on benches and look at the people. All these white people, pretty people. Some wore tennis shoes, some wore casual loafers. But how confidently they all walked.

Krishna sat silently, looking at the people.

"What are you thinking about?" said Sheila.

"Nothing."

"You must be thinking about something."

"Nothing." And then: "America is such a strange place. So big, so big. And yet …"

"And yet what?"

"Nothing."

"Nothing?"

"It is such a big place and yet so strange. I don't know *anyone* in this place."

"You know me."

Krishna smiled a small smile, from the corner of the lips. But the smile soon faded and she looked down at the ground.

"It is a big place: pretty, clean. All this grass, all this neatness. But to what does it all add up? What does it mean?"

Sheila was a perceptive woman. Perhaps she understood her friend. Perhaps she felt the same way herself.

"You are homesick?"

Krishna did not say anything.

"You miss India?"

Krishna did not say anything. And then: "Don't *you*? Don't you miss India as well?"

Sheila was silent for a long time. Perhaps it meant that she was thinking about it. Perhaps it meant that she agreed. Perhaps it meant that the answer was obvious. And when the answer is obvious—understood—what need is there to open your mouth and waste words?

Both women in the ill-fitting blue jeans sat on the bench in the October sun and looked at the America around them. They sat thus for a long time.

***

Krishna came to work, went home. She came to work, went home. Sheila was at work—and Krishna liked that. Mister Rastogi was at work—and she liked that as well. But then the customers were there as well—and was that so easy?

They could not give the visas and passports at once to the customers. There was a computerized database, and they had to check the names against the database. Terrorism was a big issue in India and they had to check for that as well.

"But I am an *Indian*," some of the customers said.

"But we still have to check."

"But it is not convenient for me to make two trips: one to leave the application, one to pick up."

"I am sorry."

"I tried to call before coming—the line is always engaged."

"A lot of people call. We have a very small staff."

"You should hire more people."

Krishna did not answer.

"A Third World country, nothing but Third World."

Krishna was silent for some seconds. And then: "We try to do the best, sir. We try to do the best."

But the other was hardly convinced. He complained, he complained some more.

Krishna listened to the other, controlled herself. What other choice was there? This was hardly a new scene. The scene was repeated day after day, day after day.

That night Krishna went home to her efficiency apartment some three miles away. It was not a great area but it was the only place she could afford. There were grilled iron bars on the windows. She lived on the second floor above a small alley filled with litter, broken glass all around. Sometimes she could hear the barking of a dog. Sometimes the loud music of some car or some teenagers going past.

Krishna went to the tiny kitchen. She was too tired to cook, so she heated the frozen bag of "Asian Vegetables" that she had bought at the Safeway. It was a mixture of vegetables: carrots, broccoli, "sugar snap" peas, water chestnuts. It took ten minutes for the vegetables to cook. Sometimes she boiled them, sometimes she steamed them.

While she waited for the vegetables to cook, she poured herself a glass of water with two cubes of ice. She opened the refrigerator, took out some salad dressing (she would use it on the vegetables). She took a piece of white bread, put it in the toaster. *Chapattis*, rice, who had time to cook them nowadays? The bread—with or without butter—would be enough.

The food was cooked, Krishna sat down at the dining table (round, with three chairs). It was a small table, but for her it was enough. After all, this was America and who ever came to the house? Who ever came to visit?

***

One day there was a small function at the Consulate. These functions were held every few months. Republic Day, Independence Day, Holi, Diwali—there was always some occasion. Krishna bathed, put on her blue silk sari with the gold border (it was one of two silk saris that she owned) and went.

The function was in the evening: there would be food, there would be drinks. The Ambassador himself would come. He would stay for half an hour, say a few words, shake a few hands. Then he would leave. After that, people would be relaxed and the fun would begin.

Krishna stood there waiting for the fun to begin. But what was the fun? Sheila was there (a good thing). Mister Rastogi was there (a good thing). But they were also the same people she saw every day. Doesn't one get tired of seeing the same people? Tonight most of the people had brought their families with them. Husbands, wives, children. Did Krishna have a husband? Did she have children?

She was thirty-one years old and not married. One day she would marry. When would it be?

Krishna went to the wall and leaned her back to it. There was a small glass of ginger ale in her hand (two ice cubes inside). People came, greeted her; she returned their greeting. They asked her to come and try out the food. She said that she would in a minute.

She heard conversation around her, laughter. Sometimes the screams of the little children who had gone outside to play in the small courtyard.

She liked the sounds, she let them sink in. It was not good to pity yourself. She moved from the wall and went to the long table with the food. All these dishes, all these smells. "Krishna," "Krishna," she heard her name a few times. She liked that. "Miss Dayanand, good to see you." She liked that as well. India was far away, home was far away. But now she was with friends, was she not? It was not perfect, but it was something. She was lucky—so much luckier than so many others. It was better not to complain.

***

But the days took their toll. Work, work, always the work. There were iron grilles at work; there were iron grilles in her apartment. Was this the America she had dreamed about? Krishna went to a movie. But she hated sitting in the dark and she left. On weekends she went for walks. Her neighborhood was not safe so she took the afternoon bus to a public place: some mall, some outdoor "festival." She liked the crowds there, the noise. But the others were in groups, she was alone; after an hour or two she grew tired, she left.

She did not want to return to her apartment—she seldom wanted to do that. So she tried to go to a church nearby. (She was a Hindu but what did that matter? A place of God is a place of God.) But it was Saturday and the church was closed. She went to a restaurant, asked for a seat near the window and ordered some tea. But how much tea can a person drink? They expect you to buy food, to spend money—something she did not have much of. She soon left.

She bought the newspaper on her way home, read it that night in her apartment. So much was happening in the city—or was it? So much was happening in the country. She tired of the newspaper, she put it away.

She turned on the small television in her room (thirteen inches). People talked, they talked. What did they talk about?

She felt alone, afraid. She dreamed of Monday—how far away it still was! The customers would come, the terrible customers. But at least people would be there. She would not be so afraid.

· ∗∗∗

The weeks and months passed. Slowly they passed. The posting was for three years and sometimes letters came from home. "Are you making friends?" they said. "Are you happy?" they said. "See if you can stay longer. Get an extension on your posting. A student visa of some kind. A green card. America is the place to be. The place to make money. To make your mark."

To make money. To make your mark. What did the words mean? Krishna wanted to run away and to go home. They would say that she was stupid to leave America. Let them say so. They would say that she was a failure. Let them say so. She was tired, you see. She wanted to run away.

Sheila was a perceptive woman and she saw many things. She brought her friend food from home. She talked to her, tried to cheer her up. Sometimes she even invited her to the house for lunch or dinner. Sheila was married and had a six-year-old daughter. Krishna could play with her daughter (how she liked it, too). In this way she could pass the time.

There were also one or two Indian men that Sheila knew. One had studied in the U.S., was now working as an accountant for a small company. Another was working as an Assistant Manager for the Holiday Inn. Sometimes she invited them as well.

They all sat in the small dining room, ate their meal. Then they moved to the small living room and drank tea. Sheila's daughter ran around in the background.

Krishna asked the man about the company for which he worked.

"It is a small company. But the work is good. A lot of responsibility."

"You like that?"

"Trial balance, general ledger. They let me work on that. Bank reconciliation. They let me work on that as well."

Krishna was impressed and told him so.

But the man was unfazed. Perhaps he was used to compliments. Perhaps he preferred compliments from more interesting—more *attractive*—women. Was Krishna one of these?

Another night the Assistant Manager for the Holiday Inn was there. He said that he had a girl-friend. White. American.

"And what do your parents say?" said Sheila.

"I am my own man," said the other calmly. "What others say, what concern is it to me?"

Krishna admired the man, admired his confidence. But he was busy, had a companion. Obviously he was not the right man for her.

Yes, there were these outings, these "adventures." All days were not bad. But where did these outings and adventures lead?

Sheila tried to reassure her friend. "Oh they are silly men, forget them," she said. "They have been in America for too long. They are too spoiled, too Westernized. But there are other men out there—of course, there are. Fish in the sea, fish in the sea—is that not what the Americans say?"

"I am vegetarian."

"We are all vegetarians, Krishna. But fish in the sea, it is a good expression. Do not give up hope. Be strong."

Krishna listened to her friend. She was grateful for her advice, grateful for her love. And did she heed the advice as well?

***

More days passed. Krishna went to work, she came home. The customers came—they were the same as before. Some were nice, many were not. The white people thought they were better, they said what they always said: "Third World country. Just like a Third World country." The Indians came, even they were rude. Perhaps even ruder than the white people.

Some of them had green cards now, some of them were American citizens. Perhaps they thought they were successful people now, people with money. They were better than the people at the Consulate and looked down on them. Did they not deserve to look down?

Krishna smiled at the customers—again she smiled. "Yes, sir," she said. "Indeed, sir," she said. She tried not to lose her temper.

She was learning about America—perhaps that was the moral in it. She was learning about the world: yes, that was the moral as well.

The weeks passed, the months. And now? More weeks passed and more months. One day there was a bomb threat at the Consulate. The fire department came, the building was evacuated. Later, men in suits came—even some from the FBI. They went from room to room, they looked, they looked. Then they let everyone return to the building. Two of the men sat in the lunch room, interviewed the employees one by one. Krishna's turn came and she went to the lunch room.

The men greeted her; she greeted them in return. The men said that perhaps the bomb threat was a prank, perhaps it was not.

"Do you have any enemies?" they said.

Krishna looked at them.

"Any people who do not like you? Who have said bad things about you?"

Krishna smiled, smiled again. It was a long list. Where did she begin?

Krishna told them about her work; the men took down a few things. Again she told them; again they took down some things.

At last the men rose and said that they had heard enough. "Thank you," they said.

Krishna rose, bowed to the men.

"We will call you if we need you."

Krishna bowed again. She left the room.

She felt happy—happy that she had told the truth. That she had unburdened her heart. But would anything change? Would anything really change?

One weekend Krishna was at Sheila's house and they were talking about the recent bomb threat. There had been no real developments, no real "leads." Perhaps it was a prank after all.

"These things happen," said Sheila.

"Yes," said Krishna.

"There are bad people in the world," said Sheila.

"Yes," said Krishna.

"They do bad things. Some people think that *we* are bad."

Krishna nodded.

There was a short silence. "Let us forget all this garbage," said Sheila at last. "Let us go outside, go for a walk."

It was a cold February day and the women collected their warm things. Sheila's daughter was nearby. Krishna got the girl's shoes from the corner, helped her put them on. Then she helped the girl put on the jacket, then the gloves.

"It is a little nippy out there," said Sheila. "Bring the scarf."

Nippy. Krishna liked the word. Whether the word was English or American, she did not know, but it was a good word. She went to the closet, took out the girl's pink and blue scarf (she knew exactly where it was).

"Yes, it is nippy today, very nippy," Krishna said.

The women and daughter opened the main door and stepped outside. It was indeed nippy. It was often nippy in America.

"But the sun is out," said Sheila. "I see it."

Krishna nodded.

"The sun—I like the sun."

Krishna did not say anything.

A few seconds passed. "But it is still cold," Krishna said suddenly. And here she scrunched her shoulders and blew out air through her slightly parted lips. "The scarf for the little girl—I will not forget the scarf."

My Father
Is Investigated
by the Authorities

I was ten years old then. My father was investigated by the authorities. One day some people came, they knocked down the door. They said that they were from the Income Tax Division. One day more people came: they said that they were from the Central Bureau of Investigation. They opened up suitcases, they opened up almirahs. They threw things all over the beds and the floor. They opened the few dressers we had. Again they took things, they threw them all over the beds and the floor.

"And what do you want?" we said.

They did not answer.

"What are you looking for?"

Silence.

The raids of the authorities were reported all over the newspapers. The reporters camped themselves outside our house—they were in the alley, they were in the veranda—they were there at all hours of the day and night. I would be on my way to school and the reporters would stop me: "And how much money did they find?"

"Money?"

"How much money did they find under the bed?"

I did not know what they were talking about, I had no idea. But I began to conclude that there had been a robbery. But then why were they looking—looking for this money in *our* house; looking for it under the bed?

At home all was hush-hush: no one would talk about it. Once or twice I asked the others and I was told only: "There are bad people in the world." And again: "They have no shame." And again: "They accuse others: they are bad people. This is just the way they are."

Old people came to the house, relatives came. There were raised voices, there were whispers. Doors were closed. There were (or so I assumed) secret meetings behind the doors.

What was it that my father had done? What was it that he had been accused of doing?

The reporters stopped me—again and again they stopped me on my way to, or from, school.

"And did they find money?" "How much money was there—how much money did they find under the bed?"

***

One day there was a hockey match at our school. It was a good match, we played for a long time. But after the match the sky turned grey and dark—a sudden rain began to fall. We all became wet (became drenched), we all hurried to find shelter. There were some hawks in the sky—even, I thought, one or two vultures. They circled overhead, circled ominously. What were they looking for?

"They are looking for your father," someone said.

"My father?"

"They are looking for anyone who has money under his bed."

In this way they spoke—what strange and cruel words they were.

"But did they find any money?" I suddenly burst out. "Did they find any money under the bed?"

But the others just looked at me—they looked.

I made my way—I tried to make my way home. There was water, water everywhere. In some places the water was up to my ankles; in one or two places it was even up to my knees.

When I arrived home I saw that the people had not left. Rain or no rain, the people would not leave. Some of them were outside, the black (and often large) umbrellas over their heads. Some of them had found shelter in the veranda. But there they were still—as if attached to the place, refusing to leave.

"And did they find money," they called out, "did they find money? How much money did they find under the bed?"

***

Yes, this is the way it was. My father was a good man, he was a decent man. And he had been accused.

How much money he had taken, no one would say. Why he had done it, no one would say. But *that* he had done it—done it, in fact—of that they were convinced. Of that they had already made up their minds.

One day a man came, he opened a tin box: there were a few coins. He opened a tin box: there were no coins. He opened a tin box: there were coins, all the coins in the world.

The coins, the coins: were they a symbol of some kind? A symbol of *what*?

***

One day an old man came to the house. His back was bent, there was a red mark on his forehead. The others went out to greet him. They said that there was a bad omen—a *graha*—over the house. And if they listened to the old man, if they followed his advice, would it not help? The omen—the *graha*—would it not go away?

He was an old man, he walked with a stick. They said that he was from the Red Fort (in old Delhi), or perhaps from Greater Kailash (just across from the market and near the chemist store). They said that during the day he brought a gunny sack, he sat under the tree there—sat there for hours. He took out his books—they were small leaflets, not even books—he read from them.

Sometimes it grew hot, the heat was unbearable. Then he closed the leaflets, he swung them back and forth gently—he used them as a fan.

He read from the books, often he read out loud. He read about love, he read about hate. He read about the things—all the things of the world.

"And these things," we said, "what are they?"

"One must be good," he said, "one must be kind. One must bring food to the father. When he is sick, one must bring him medicine. When he is sad, one must sit by his side, one must tell him stories."

"Stories, what kind of stories?"

"One must tell him about the past. The old days. Tell him a joke. A riddle. Make him laugh. Tell him anything (anything, I say)—anything to take the sadness away."

In this way the old man spoke.

We listened to the old man (how could we not?), we followed his advice. We brought food to my father, we brought him medicine. We sat by his side, we told him stories.

But the bad omen, the *graha*, did it really go away?

We went to the temple, we gave money at the altar. We lit the incense—all night we lit it.

But the bad omen, the *graha*, did it really go away?

I came home from school, the reporters were there (still there).

"And how much money did they find?"

"Money?"

"How much money did they find under the bed?"

I came home from school, they were there—still there. Some of them were young, some of them were old. Some of them wore white shirts (and white pants), some of them even wore suits.

They tittered, they laughed. They wrote things in their diaries, they wrote things in their notebooks. One of them had a typewriter. He sat on a chair, he laid the machine on a stool in front of him. And he banged away at the keys—how proudly he banged away.

***

One day I went up to my father. He was in his chair, his face was to the wall.

"Papa," I said.

He did not answer me.

"Papa," I said.

He did not answer me.

He was in his world, you see, he was in his own world.

I asked him to tell me what had happened, what had really happened.

He looked away.

I was his son, his only son. And if he would not tell me, if he would not confide in me …

But he was in his world, you see, he was in his own world.

***

One day a man came to the house, he opened a tin box: there were a few coins. He opened a tin box: there were no coins. He opened a tin box: there were coins, all the coins in the world.

The coins, the coins: were they a symbol of some kind? Were they a good symbol, a bad? A symbol of what, of *what*?

***

There was a man (a distant uncle)—he lived at the edge of town. He was a smart man, he was well-renowned. There was an alley downstairs. He kept his horse carriage there, in a garage.

One day we changed our clothes, we packed our tiffin. And we went to see him—to see this man.

We went past the cemetery and we went past the bank. We went past the taxi stand and we went past the public latrines. There was a small stall there (a store of some kind). We turned—we made our way to the right.

He was a tall man, he was handsome. He wore a silk shirt, he wore a scarf around his neck.

63

We explained to him the case, the specifics of the case.

He looked at us.

Again we explained.

"And how much money does he make?" he said (he was referring to my father).

We told him.

"My bookkeeper makes more," he said.

"And how much money does he make?"

We told him.

"I pay more than that in taxes," he said.

They were strange words, what strange words they were. But in this way he spoke.

Perhaps he was trying to insult us; perhaps he was trying to insult my father. Perhaps he was trying to show that his fee was high, that we could not afford it.

We explained to him the case, again we explained.

He seemed indifferent, he seemed bored. Once or twice—or so I thought—he covered his mouth with the back of his hand. Once or twice—or so I thought—he tried to suppress a yawn.

It was a cold night, there were stars in the sky. "The world is a big place," he said. "This is the way it is."

It was a cold night, there was the moon there as well. "The world is a cold place," he said. "This is the way it is. This is just the way it is."

That night we came home, the people were there, still there. They had put out the string cots—they had put the bedding on top—the pillows, the blankets.

We sat inside (we sat on the floor), we pulled on our ears. We sat inside, we said our prayers.

But the people were there, still there. They would not leave.

I got up in the night (in the middle of the night I did it)—I got up and I looked through the curtains.

But the people were there, still there. *They would not leave.*

***

They say that the world is a good place—is it really? They say that the world is a bad place—is it really? They say that the world is what it is—it is just the way it is.

Some time passed. We learned that the case had been forwarded to Delhi now. It was under the jurisdiction of a new man—the Additional Commissioner of Police.

There was a police office in Saket—a nice (and even posh) area of Delhi. Sometimes he went there. There was an office in Paharganj—a simple (and much-maligned) place. Sometimes he went there as well.

I was the son in the house, the only son. And was it not my duty? I was the son, the only son. And was there any other way?

One day I rose, I brushed my teeth, and I made my way.

It was cold outside, it was dark. There were trees on the street, there were shadows. But I was who I was—I made my way.

"Who goes there?" they said.

"It is I."

"Who goes there?"

"It is I."

I walked, I walked—I walked for some time. At last I came to a building (it was a simple place, nondescript). There were some horse carriages outside, there was an open drain.

There was a courtyard outside. People walked in the courtyard. Some of them were well-dressed and young: they were no doubt the students, the future leaders of the world. Some of them were poor, the laborers. They carried baskets on their heads (with bricks); they squatted before some bushes or some grass, they watered the same.

I arrived at the door, there were two sentries outside. I went past them, a clerk was there. I was allowed at last—I was allowed to enter the demesne.

There was a low table, a fan on the table. There was a window behind the fan; the glass was broken—part of it was covered with some black tape.

There was a ceiling fan overhead. I took a peek at the fan: the fan was not running, a bird had come and made a nest in the fan.

The Commissioner greeted me, he asked me to sit on one of the chairs.

I sat down.

"The son has come," he said.

I looked at him.

"The son of the corrupt."

"The *accused*," I said.

The Commissioner smiled (he allowed himself a smile). The window was open, and screenless—a bird came through the window, it sat on the ledge.

"The son loves his father. And he has come to plead—to plead on his behalf."

"To speak," I said.

"There will be an inquiry, there will be proceedings."

"But what is the charge?"

"It will be made clear."

"*When*?"

"It will be made clear."

But the Commissioner (it seemed) had said enough. He would say no more.

He was a polite man, he was incapable of being otherwise. But he was also shrewd. He was an important man, he had not risen to his position by being otherwise.

I could stay there—stay as long as I wanted. I could speak—speak as long as I wished. But no more information—no more information would be forthcoming.

"Is the world a good place?"

"It is."

"Is the world a bad place?"

"It is."

"It is the way it is—it is just the way it is."

***

At last it came—the day of the trial came. The courtroom was packed—there were men there, women, children. There was the Additional Commissioner (an important man). There were the reporters, the spectators: they were there as well.

My father sat in a corner (on a raised platform), his head was bowed and shaved. How timid he looked!

I wanted to go up to my father, to comfort him. I wanted to tell him that I loved him, that I would fight for him—fight until the end.

But was it so easy—as easy as that?

The man from the other side rose (he was dressed in black robes). He began to speak.

There was silence in the room.

Again he spoke.

There was silence in the room.

"The father is an evil man," he said.

"An evil man?"

"He is a villain—he is a villain as well."

There were gasps from the crowd. There were murmurs as well.

The man took a bed, he dragged it into the room. (It was a big bed, it took some time.) They looked under the bed: there was *money underneath*.

"The money is real, the money is imagined. The money is real, the money is a symbol. But it is there, it is there: *it is just the way it is*."

There were gasps from the crowd. There were murmurs as well.

I looked at my father: how timid he looked. I looked at my father: his eyes were lowered. I looked at my father: he did not look at me, *he looked away*.

"The father took the money, he took it for his family. He took the money, he took it *from* his family. The money is a symbol: he took something else, something else as well."

"This something, what is it?"

But the man would not say.

"This something, what is it?"

Silence.

The man, it seemed, had said enough. He smiled, he laughed. He told a joke (and then a second). He told a joke (and then a third).

And then he sat down.

They were strange words—what strange words they were. But in this way he spoke.

At last he rose—the lawyer for my father rose. He said that all men are not the same—this is just the way it is. He said that God made the world, not man—this is just the way it is. He said that the words by the other were rambling, were confused. One must stick to the facts, *only to the facts*.

But was anyone even listening to the man—listening to a word that he had said?

He said that the charges had to be made clear, made clear. He said that symbols are nice and good, but one must stick with the facts, only the facts. He said that a bed is a private matter. *There is no need to look under it.* He said that a bed is a private matter. There is no need to look under it: *no need to look under the bed.*

He spoke, he spoke—he spoke for a long time.

At last he finished, he sat down.

But was anyone even listening to him—listening to a word that he had said?

I looked at my father: how sad he looked. I looked at my father: how small he looked. I looked at my father: and I grieved for him (dear Father). How deeply I grieved!

***

The trial went on, it went on for days. They spoke about God, they spoke about man. They spoke about the symbols—the symbols all around.

There was money under the bed, there wasn't. There were symbols under the bed, there weren't. But did it even matter? Something was there, something. And was that not enough? Something was there, something. And was that not the important thing?

I came home that night, the reporters were there, still there.

"And how much money did they find?"

"Money?"

"How much money did they find under the bed?"

The people seemed gleeful that day, especially gleeful. But perhaps this is the way of the world. This is just the way it is.

There was money under the bed—there wasn't. The money was a symbol—it wasn't. But so gleeful they were, so gleeful. This is just the way it is.

***

The trial went on for days, it went on for weeks.

One day my father came to my room, he sat beside me. He spoke to me in whispers, he spoke in hushed tones.

"Son," he said.

He rose, he left the room.

One day my father came, he went to my mother's room. He sat by her side.

"Wife," he said.

My mother was good, my mother was kind. She ran her fingers—she ran them through his hair.

And then she did it—she did it again.

The trial went on for weeks, it went on for months.

One day some men came, they put a rope around my father's wrists. (They spoke in whispers, they spoke in hushed tones.) And then they took him— they took him away.

My mother was weeping; my sister clung to his legs. But do you think they cared? They just took my father (my sister still clinging to his legs)—they took him away.

We followed my father—we tried to follow him. But do you think it helped?

Again we followed him—do you think it helped?

They just took my father (like that, *like that*)—they just took him away.

***

My father was kept in the prison (the building): he was kept there for three years.

One day we went to see him: we were not allowed. One day we went to see him: we were not allowed. A third day we went: we were taken to a room in the back. It was a small room—the windows were closed, the curtains drawn.

He sat in the corner—how quietly he sat.

"Papa," I said.

He did not answer me.

"Papa," I said.

He did not answer me.

He was in his world, you see. He was in his own world.

One day we went to see him: we were not allowed. One day we went to see him: we were not allowed. A third day we went: we were taken to a room in the back. It was a small room—the windows were closed, the curtains drawn. There was a ceiling fan there (I saw it). And there he was (my father): he was hanging from the blades of the fan!

His chest was bare, his genitals were exposed. And there he was (dear father): he was hanging from the blades of the fan.

My father had tired of life (or so they said). The fan was turned off. There was a bird there (it had come, it had made a nest). It was a pretty bird: it was small, it was light brown. And perhaps it had given my father company—given him company at the end.

We went to my father: we kissed his legs. We went to my father: we kissed his feet. We went to my father: we looked at him, we looked at him—and then we *looked away*.

That night we came home. And the reporters were there—they were still there.

"And how much money did they find?"

"Money?"

"How much money did they find under the bed?"

The people were gleeful (how gleeful they looked).

"And how much money did they find?"

"Money?"

"How much money did they find (*how much, how much*)—how much money did they find under the bed?"

A Small Market

The woman with the baby carriage came to the register. She used the carriage in different ways: to carry the baby, to carry the baby and the groceries, to carry only the groceries. Today, since the baby wasn't there, it was used—probably—only for the last purpose.

"So what do you think?" said the woman. "Are you scared?"

"Of what?" said Kim.

"You know," said the woman.

"No, I don't," said Kim.

"The other day. Wednesday night. You mean, you really don't know?"

"No, I don't," said Kim. His heart sank.

"The holdup, the robbery. Everybody knows."

"Oh," said Kim. He was barely audible.

The woman paid for her goods. "I don't know how you can put up with it," she said. "You should go back to school, get another job."

The man from the liquor store came. He was muttering. Kim rang up his Coke and cupcakes. "Thank you," Kim said. The man said nothing and left.

It was always busy at this time: three-thirty in the afternoon, four. The children were coming home from their schools. Also, it was the change of the shift.

Dale, the manager, was in the back room. He was making the deposit, filling out the vendor sheets. Kim wanted to talk to him, to ask him. He had said nothing when Kim had come in an hour earlier.

Mike, who also worked there, came in through the store doors. He winked at Kim; Kim smiled. The line was long and, instead of walking past the customers, Mike made an immediate left turn. He went past the sodas and past the ice cream, making a right and going along the detergents and the eggs and the cheeses. In this way he walked to the store room—and to the small office there—in the back.

***

Kim had begun at the store eighteen months before. He had learned a lot. But the customers? They were not nice.

"Are you married?" they said. "Do you work here?" they said. "I would never work here," they said.

They were proud people. "Are you Chinese?" they said. "Are you Japanese?" they said. "You did not finish high school—why don't you go back and finish high school?"

In fact, Kim was in college completing his second year. But they were busy and important people. What did they care?

But yes, Kim had learned a lot at the store. He ran the cash register and he stocked the shelves. He stamped the prices. He swept the floors and he mopped them. He checked the vendors when they came in with their deliveries and made sure that the store was not cheated. He reconciled the receipts at the end of the day.

He had learned a lot about food. He had learned about tuna fish and sardines and kidney beans. He ate kidney beans at home but, before, he could not tell the beans apart. Now he could even tell a kidney bean from a lima bean. He had learned to tell apart the vegetables as well. The fruits. The different sizes of milk.

So much.

But the customers—.

Mike came up to the cash register. He had put on his green smock, tied in the back with a string. "You want me to relieve you?" he said.

"Sure," said Kim. "Only ten minutes."

Kim slid up the narrow aisle between the two cash registers. He made a left, and walked towards the store room in the back. There was a lock there— newly installed about two weeks before. Kim used his key to get in.

Dale was in the small office next to the room. He was a man of medium height with short black hair— almost a crew cut. He was licking the seal around the afternoon deposit. Kim wanted to ask him, but he did not want to seem too obvious. It was a sensitive and unpleasant topic.

Kim took a shopping cart and began emptying some cans into it: peaches, peas, dried milk. He was pretending that he was filling the cart to take up front and stock the shelves. He made only enough noise to let Dale know that he was there, being careful not to seem too obvious.

"So what's new?" said Dale, glancing over his shoulder in Kim's direction.

"Not much," said Kim.

"How's school coming?"

"It's all right," said Kim. "Not good, not bad."

"You passing everything?" Dale swiveled in his chair to face Kim.

"Too early to tell," said Kim. "We haven't had exams yet. First exams are next week."

Kim stood on his toes and peered at the higher shelves, as if to make sure that he had not missed anything.

"You'll do all right," said Dale. "Just study hard."

"I'll try," said Kim.

Kim turned the cart to face the door. He slowly pushed the cart as if to go back out.

"I guess you've heard," said Dale, when Kim was almost to the door.

Kim stopped.

"When it rains, it pours, I guess."

He knew what Dale was talking about. Of course, he knew.

He pulled back the cart and retraced his steps. He stopped at the office archway, next to Dale. "What happened?" he said. "Was it very bad?"

"At least a little funny," said Dale. He laughed softly. "There were these two black guys—niggers, I say, they're always the same. They pulled out a gun and said: 'This is a stick-up.' So Mike—he was behind the counter—he says: 'Hell no.' They slapped him and asked him a second time. 'Before I give it to you,' says Mike, 'I'll put it in my own pocket.' So they grabbed him by the throat, pushed him down. Then they took the money. All of it."

"Was anybody else in the store?" said Kim. His heart was pounding.

"A young couple—I'm sure you've seen them before—but they were by the egg section. Didn't see a thing. An old man was by the frozen foods but he didn't see a thing either. He's too blind anyway. The old man walks up with his purchase and gives Mike a ten-dollar bill. When Mike couldn't change it, 'What kind of place is this?' says the old man. 'You can't even change a measly ten.'"

As he spoke, Dale imitated the speech of the old man. He laughed.

"Is Mike all right?" said Kim.

"Oh he's all right," said Dale. "Only next time, I told him, don't be such a hero. Give the guy the money."

Dale laughed again but it was not a funny laugh. It was short and choppy and unnatural.

There was a long pause. Dale had spoken. What was there to add?

"Well, I better go up front," said Kim at last. "Mike is waiting for me."

"I'll walk out with you," said Dale. "I've got to make this deposit."

The safe was in the front, to the right of the second register and near the beginning of the produce section. It was a funny place to have a safe, in the open like that.

***

Kim walked up to the front, stocking along the way the few cans he had brought. Then he went back to the register.

The lines at the register were getting long now. Mike was fast but not as fast as Kim. Kim could, if he wanted, add the totals in his head even before the register. In the early days, to impress the customers, he had sometimes done just this: tax and everything. But that was so long ago. The customers were not so important now—he had given up the habit.

Kim took over at the register. Mike helped with the bagging for a while. Kim rang, Mike bagged. Kim rang, Mike bagged.

At last the lines got smaller. Mike left and went to restock the drinks cooler. It had been a busy hour. A lot of people had bought cold things.

The cooler was in the middle third of the store. As you came in you had to walk up about fifteen feet and go left about five. It was a fairly big cooler: five sections, each separated from the outside by a glass door, and each with three shelves. On the left two sections were the milk cartons; in the middle two sections were the fruit juices and fruit drinks; and in the extreme right section were the miscellaneous milk products.

Kim liked the cooler. It was here that he had learned to visualize, for the first time, the different sizes: pints, quarts, half-gallons, gallons. He had learned also about half-and-half milk and—during the Christmas season—about eggnog.

Seeing that Kim was watching him, Mike began to make faces from inside the cooler. Kim smiled. Mike was a middle-aged man, about forty, with short greying hair. He was a little chubby, but not fat, and Kim liked him. Mike did not think that Kim was handsome, but he was nice to him as well. He told him jokes. Sometimes he played pranks.

Two girls from the Catholic school came into the store. They were dressed in light blue uniforms. They walked towards the cooler. When they saw Mike making faces, one pointed to him: "He was the one who was slapped," she said. "A real case study," said the other.

Seeing the girls, Kim's heart began to pound again. He cleared his throat so as not to get a lump there.

"Hello," he said to the girls as they came to the counter. They smiled but did not say anything. Kim began to blush. He put their milk and bread in a bag.

"Thank you," he said, but the words stuck in his throat. The girls took their bag and left. Outside, as they closed the door, they began to laugh.

"Proud girls," said Kim.

As Kim's eyes turned towards the cooler, he saw Mike again. Mike smiled, making a face. Kim smiled and, this time, made a face in return. Mike laughed.

Two more girls came in from the Catholic school. They were not in their uniforms. They were with their male friends and they were talking loudly.

Again Kim's heart began to pound.

"Hello amigo," said one of the girls when they finally came to the counter.

Kim smiled and nodded.

"Bonjour amigo," said one of the friends. "You no speak?"

"I speak," said Kim.

The friends and the girls all laughed.

"Are you Chinese?" said one of the girls.

"Japanese? Korean?" said the other girl.

Kim was ashamed, not so much of being Korean but of looking like one. "Korean," he said quietly.

"Are you married?" said the girls. "Do you have a girlfriend?" they said.

Kim was ashamed of his looks and the questions made him blush. He did not answer.

"*Rouge*," said one of the friends, and they all laughed.

When they left, Kim's face felt warm. His heart was pounding even more.

"Proud people," said Kim. "They do not know that I also speak French. That I go to college. And how do they think that I am married? I lied about my age even to get this job."

"Proud people," said Kim again. "I do not like them."

***

The time passed. At a few minutes after six, Dale came to the front. He had taken off his smock but he was still wearing a tie. He always wore a narrow tie, usually black, sometimes blue. It was a clip-on tie, not the type you knot yourself. "Those knots are a nuisance," Dale said.

Dale limped as he walked. The limp seemed to be getting worse. It was an old—a disk—problem, but the company would not pay for it. "It is a chronic disease," they said, "you had it before you joined us."

Dale had been with the company for some time now, almost eleven years. When Kim began he thought—because the person who got him the job had told him—that managers made a lot of money. But Kim did not think that Dale made a lot of money. And he thought that Dale was always working: six days a week, seven days. Ten hours a day, eleven.

One day Dale had explained it to him. "It is the budget," he said. "They give you so much money—so many dollars—for the employees. After that, it comes out of your own pocket."

"But it is not fair," said Kim.

"I guess not," said Dale. "In the smaller stores it is all right. But this is not a small store—there is so much more work. It is like a small market."

Kim had gotten so upset that he had sent a letter to the District Supervisor. Six handwritten pages, maybe seven. "It is not fair," he had said, "making a man work like a slave." He had sent the letter through the company mail.

The District Supervisor had made a special trip and come to see Kim. "I appreciate your comments," he said, "I really do. But it is not like slave labor. Just a budget, a management tool. Even *I* am under a budget."

Dale had appreciated the letter—or so he had said to Kim. But nothing had happened, nothing had changed.

"Everything okay?" said Dale, coming up to Kim and standing in the aisle between him and the second register.

"Sure," said Kim. "Everything okay."

Mike also came over. "Everything's fine, boss," he said. He saluted.

Dale made a mock fist at Mike, as if to hit him.

Mike covered his face and ducked.

"Carry on troops," said Dale.

Kim smiled.

"*Ciao*," said Dale, and walked out of the door.

***

Friday nights were always busy—always people going in and out. Kim remained at the register. The people came, they came.

Mike restocked the drinks cooler. Then he unpacked boxes, stocked the shelves. Then he emptied the register for the eight o'clock deposit.

When Mike left to go to the back and make the deposit, Kim became nervous. It was dark outside now. "But it is all right," he said to himself. "Nothing will happen: too many people."

By nine o'clock things had begun to settle down. Mike came up to the register. "You want to take a little break?" he said.

"Sure," said Kim.

Kim walked around the store and collected himself a sandwich, a bag of potato chips, and an orange drink. He went to the register, paid for these. Then he walked to the back room.

The employees seldom paid for their goods. Kim was different. Sometimes the employees even took things home at night.

Kim went to the office in the back. He sat in the simple wooden chair, he ate his food. In ten minutes he was back.

It was 9:15 now and the store was almost empty. It had begun to rain outside.

Mike was leaning back against the second counter, smoking a cigarette. He was a chain-smoker—up to two packs a day.

"Feel better?" said Mike.

"Yes," said Kim. "How do *you* feel?"

Mike took a deep puff and blew out the smoke. "I'm okay," he said after a pause.

Kim also paused. "Were you scared?" he said finally. He spoke carefully, timidly. "Wednesday night?"

"So you want to know, just like the rest," said Mike. He laughed.

"No, *not* like them," said Kim.

Kim took his right hand and rubbed the back of it across his face. At the same time he cleared his throat: he did not want Mike to see the lump that had gathered there.

"I wasn't scared *then*," said Mike. "But a few minutes later I was shaking."

"And where was Gustavo?" said Kim. Gustavo also worked at the store.

"He was in the back, resting. Sleeping probably." Again Mike laughed.

A customer came and Mike rang up his goods. "Thank you," he said. The customer said nothing. He opened his umbrella and hurried out of the store.

The rain had become much harder now. Every few seconds, thunder could be heard. Mike exhaled from his cigarette, looked at Kim. He smiled.

"The people," said Kim, looking more at the floor than at his companion, "are they cruel to you? Do they ask you questions—about the holdup? Laugh at you?"

"You think that they are cruel?" said Mike.

"I think so," said Kim. Again he spoke carefully, timidly. "They—like the man who just left—they do not even say thank you."

"They're all right," said Mike.

"No, they are not," said Kim. "Not even the neighbors are nice."

"You mean the man from the liquor store?" said Mike. "I wouldn't worry about him."

"But I mean the others, too," said Kim. "The dry clean man, the drug store man. The barber. Two weeks ago I went to the barbershop and he asked me if I liked getting robbed. I asked him for a haircut—he looked offended. I got the haircut, I even gave him a nice tip. He got even more angry—he did not even look at me."

"He's all right," said Mike.

"They own their stores, we don't. We just work here. We are low-class people. Is that it?"

"Oh, they're all right," said Mike. "Here comes a customer."

Mike rang up the goods. The customer said thank you, commented about the weather. Then, covering his head with a newspaper, he hurried out.

"See," said Mike, "now *he* said thank you."

"He does not live here," said Kim. "He is the exception."

Kim tried to laugh but he was getting emotional now; his voice started to crack. The thunder had increased and streaks of lightning could be seen across the sky. The store was empty.

"This is our home now," said Mike. "Noisy out there, quiet in here." He look a long puff from his cigarette. He smiled.

"Yes," said Kim. His voice fell. And then, slowly, quietly: "Tell me, Mike, why do the people not like us? Why are they always rude?"

"I don't know," said Mike. "Not rude, maybe just negligent."

"What does that mean?" said Kim.

"That means that they don't mean to be rude, they just don't know better. They're too busy with their own lives."

"But that is no excuse," said Kim.

"Maybe not," said Mike. "But they're not all bad."

He dropped the cigarette butt and crushed it under his foot. He looked at the rain—a few drops had sprinkled inside from the door opening when the customers went in and out.

"I don't know about the neighbors either," he said. "Maybe it is because, as you say, they *own* their stores. They are a part of the community. We—we are just employees. We just work here, we're open late. And we get robbed."

"People enjoy that—us getting robbed?"

"Maybe," said Mike. "It's human nature. It's exciting. You might enjoy it, too, if it happened to someone else."

"I don't think so, Mike."

"I don't know, Kim. You say people are rude but how much attention do *you* pay to the employees when you go to another store? When you get on a bus? When you go past a toll booth? It takes time and effort to be kind. It is easier to be—well, negligent."

Kim did not say anything. He looked at the floor.

"Forget about it," said Mike. "You go to college and get your degree. I'm the old man—grey hair, forty years."

Mike lit a second cigarette and took a deep puff. He looked at the rain outside. It showed no signs of letting up.

***

The days passed. Kim went to school, he came to the store. He went to school, he came to the store. He worked four days a week—sometimes in the daytime, sometimes at night. He minded the day shift less: he would work with Dale, and it was broad daylight. He felt less nervous.

Dale was a nice man. Sometimes he got angry at the employees and he lost his temper. "You work for me or I work for you?" he would say. He never lost his temper at Kim, though. He let him work any hours he chose: full-time in the summer and whatever hours suited him during the school year. Dale said that Kim was a good worker and that he never complained.

One time Dale asked Kim about taking computer classes. "You think that *I* could take them?" he said. Another time he said that he might leave this small place and go work for a supermarket. "The aggravation here," he said, and his voice trailed off. Kim encouraged him to quit.

"But I won't be manager," said Dale.

"Not at first," said Kim, "but you can work your way up."

"I don't know," said Dale. "I don't know."

Kim wanted to help Dale, but he did not know what to do. He did not know what to say.

Dale was the manager, but most of the time Kim worked not with him, but with Mike. Kim liked working with Mike as well. Mike was a funny man. Sometimes Kim would say the Buddhist chants and Mike would try to copy him. They would both laugh. Kim especially liked Mike when he counted the money for a deposit or at the end of the day. He made sure that the bills all faced the same way. He licked his right index finger with his tongue to prevent the bills from sticking. And he counted the bills—again and again, again and again. Sometimes, as he counted, beads of perspiration gathered on his forehead. Even his lips moved silently.

"I get goose bumps watching him," said Kim one time.

One day as they were working two customers came in. They were well dressed, middle-aged. They were arguing with each other. They argued and they argued. Kim looked at them for a long time.

Other customers came. One was an old woman, she walked with a cane. One was a boy—about ten years old, perhaps eleven. He had come to get ice cream. Customers and customers—from where did they come?

One of the customers dropped a carton of milk. The carton broke and the milk splattered all over the floor. Kim hurried to the back and got some paper towels. He also got a bucket and a mop.

First he got on his knees and tried to clean as much as he could with the paper towels. The paper towels he had brought were all soaked. He hurried to the back and got more towels.

There was so much milk, people were walking in it, stepping all around it. Then he used the bucket and the mop. It took a long time—twenty minutes, almost twenty-five. But at last it was all done. He was pleased that it was done.

"Success?" said Mike.

"Success," said Kim. And they both laughed.

***

The days passed. There were small successes, and Kim was grateful. One day passed, nothing bad happened. One day passed, nothing bad happened. If nothing bad happened, was it not for the best?

Kim worked at the cash register, Mike bagged. He worked at the cash register, Mike bagged. When it slowed down, Mike went and re-stocked the drinks cooler.

Sometimes, for a change, they switched around. Now Kim did what the other had done.

One day it was the day shift and Dale and Kim were working together. Dale was not feeling well. "You go home," said Kim. "I'll take care."

Dale protested, but Kim would not hear of it. "You need your rest," he said. "You need to get better."

"But the others won't be in for another few hours."

"That's all right," said Kim. "I'll manage."

At last Dale agreed. It was drizzling and business was slow. Perhaps it wouldn't be so bad.

Dale left, and things were indeed not so bad. Customers came, they left. They came, they left. Kim was a good worker. He could take care of them.

It was two o'clock in the afternoon. A group of teenagers—all black—came into the store. Maybe five of them, maybe six. They roamed and roamed around the store. Kim locked the register and kept his eyes on them. They asked him prices and then put back the goods. They asked him prices and then put back the goods.

They roamed around the store for almost ten minutes. Then they came to the register and formed a semi-circle around Kim. One of them was wearing a blue jacket. He had his hand in the jacket pocket.

"This is a stickup," he said.

"You're kidding?" said Kim.

"No kidding," he said. He pointed to the register: "*All* of it, chinko."

Kim opened the register and gave him all the money. His hands were shaking but, for some reason, his heart was not pounding—not at all. He remembered that detail later—he remembered it many times.

The teenager removed his hand from his pocket, showed a gun. He waved the gun around, and then threw it up in the air. The gun bounced on the edge of the counter and then it fell to the floor.

The gun was plastic.

The teenagers laughed. They took the money and they ran out. Kim called the police. When he spoke, they had difficulty understanding him.

***

Two days later Kim was given a lie detector test. Dale objected but the company insisted on it. It was "company policy."

It was Kim's eighteenth birthday. He told Ahmed, one of the other people who sometimes worked there. He told him the occasion—not the age.

"Happy birthday," said Ahmed. Was there irony in his words?

A few days later, Kim went up to Dale. Dale was in the back room, preparing to take the trash to the dumpster. He had put on his leather gloves, he was standing next to the canvas trash cart with wheels. The cart was overflowing and it had begun to smell a little.

"I have to leave," said Kim.

"Leave?"

"I have to leave."

There was a pause. Dale understood. Of course, he understood. Kim did not like the place. And he was afraid—he was always afraid.

"I might leave, too," said Dale after a while. But there was no conviction in his voice. There was only sadness. Only resignation.

Only that.

Many months passed—six months, maybe seven. One day Kim got a call at home. It was Ahmed. "Dale got his operation," he said. "The company paid for it."

Kim was happy and he sent Dale a get-well card. He thanked him for everything. He said that he had, after much looking, finally found another job. He also said other things.

But he did not want to sound too sentimental. So he signed his name backwards.

A few days later Kim picked up the phone. It was Dale. "Is *Mik* there?" he said. He put a special emphasis on the word. They both laughed. They talked for quite a while—for over half an hour. They promised to keep in touch.

The Servant

We sat in the veranda in the back of our simple quarters. An open drain ran nearby. A bridge was above us. The bridge was really no more than three long wooden boards. But they had put them there, nailed them with diligence and care.

The bridge connected two buildings, with small flats made of stucco. When people walked on the bridge, it swayed and the boards creaked. Mister Sharma, the businessman who lived next door, told us that we should be careful, that we should stop eating in the veranda. "What if the bridge collapses?" he said. "What if the people fall? They will fall on you. Where will you turn, where will you go?"

Mister Sharma was right, or almost so. One day a servant was crossing the bridge and the boards broke. The servant fell, not on the veranda but on the ground next to the veranda. He fell about twenty feet. There was a pool of blood, a crowd of people gathered.

The servant did not fall on us, thank God. But he did lie there. And what now? What next?

No one intervened, no one lifted a hand. At last Sandeep Ravindran did. He was from the south—from the state of Tamil Nadu. It was by accident that he had ended up in Delhi. He had no respect for northerners, and certainly no respect for the low-class Punjabis who filled the city.

"I am a Hindu," he said often, "a devout Hindu. I pray to the Lord Shiva, I pray to the Lord Vishnu. These Delhi-wallas, they pray to money. They pray to the bank, to the corrupt officials who can help them steal money from the bank." He seemed to have made a joke, was pleased with the joke that he had made.

When the servant fell, no one but Mister Ravindran intervened. He did it with hesitation, but he did it. He went to the neighbor's house, the one with the telephone. He called an ambulance. When the ambulance came, he accompanied the servant to the clinic.

But did Mister Ravindran realize what he was in for? The clinic was a private, not a public, place. The servant was there for twenty hours, and then he was transferred to a public hospital. But there was a bill. The bill came to an astounding eight hundred and fourteen rupees—and someone had to pay the bill.

"What is this?" said Mister Ravindran. "I went to the neighbor's house; I used the phone and made the call to the ambulance. Is that not enough?

"I accompanied the low-class one to the clinic—the ambulance people insisted that someone must. Is that not enough? I stayed at the clinic for four hours—*four*. I had not read the newspaper for the day; I had not even done my morning ablutions. Imagine!"

But the rules are the rules. The servant was admitted; the servant was taken care of. Charges had been "incurred"—just the word the lady at the clinic repeatedly used. Must someone not pay for these?

"It is the sign of the times," said the cheerful lady at the clinic. She sat behind the desk, all the papers in front of her. "Everything is so expensive nowadays. But he must be a good servant, Mister Ravindran. Take it in good spirits—you did the right thing. It is so hard to get good help nowadays."

Good spirits! Good help! "But he is not even my servant!"

The lady was at a loss. "What is this?"

"He is not even my servant."

"But you brought him here."

Mister Ravindran shook his head. "A mistake, you see, an oversight. Chance, just chance. These other idiots—these Delhi-wallas—they just stood around. They babbled, they gawked. The boy was bleeding, bleeding. Perhaps he was dead." Here, Mister Ravindran wished that the servant *had* been dead. "No one lifted a hand. They talked, they talked. Someone had to do something."

The lady was bewildered. A servant, just a servant. Where was the obligation? What would she have done? The lady was lost in thought for some time. Would she not have talked and talked as well?

"But you did the right thing, Mister Ravindran," she said again cheerily. "You did a good thing. God will reward you."

"But eight hundred and fourteen rupees …," began Mister Ravindran, but he did not finish. He was a stupid man. He had always considered himself superior to the Delhi-wallas, but was he really so superior? He had done it all for a stranger—a stranger. For a *servant*, no less. Who was the superior one now?

***

The days passed. Mister Ravindran fretted; he fumed. Eight hundred and fourteen rupees—what had made him do it?

He brushed, he shaved, he castigated himself. He walked to the bus stop, he cursed himself. He sat at the office, busy with the ledgers in front of him, his mind wandering.

Eight hundred and fourteen rupees. How long does it take for a man to save so much? He was not a big industrialist—a Birla, a Tata; he was a simple man who worked in an office. He made eleven hundred rupees a month. Not a paltry sum, but hardly anything of consequence.

Mister Ravindran was ashamed of his action, he mostly kept the secret to himself. But once in a while, he shared his secret with others. And to his surprise, the others seemed intrigued.

"Eight hundred and fourteen rupees," they said. "Quite a sum!"

"For a servant no less!"

"And he is not even *my* servant!" said Mister Ravindran.

The others expressed wonder. Some chuckled. Some guffawed. But most were in awe—actually in awe. "Wah, wah!" "Indeed!" "A tale for the ages, Mister Ravindran, quite a tale!"

Mister Ravindran was surprised, and intrigued, by the reaction. He thought they would laugh at him—but they did not laugh, at least not often. Eight hundred and fourteen rupees—it was a waste, of course it was. But there was a tale that the others liked. Perhaps it was not a complete waste—no no, not a complete waste after all.

***

The days passed. Mister Ravindran went to work, he came home. He crossed the veranda where the servant had fallen. The blood.

He went to work, he came home. He reproved himself. He told the tale. One day he paid the money to the clinic—half the amount. Another day he paid the rest of the money.

But there was a tale in it—was that not something?

"No one else lifted a hand—I did!"

"What a villain I am—an idiot!"

"A servant he was, yes, but is a servant not a man?"

The others would purse their lips. They would nod their heads—nod in appreciation, nod wisely.

"A tale, Mister Ravindran, quite a tale!"

"You will be rewarded, Mister Ravindran, rewarded for years to come!"

"Not just years but lives—for lives and lives to come!"

Mister Ravindran liked the words—he liked lingering on them. He would be rewarded—what would be the reward? A promotion, of course. A promotion to Supervisor I. Or, forget Supervisor I, why not Supervisor II? His mind would begin to wander; his imagination would take over. "Why not Manager—am I not qualified? Of course I am. Why not Manager as well?"

Yes, in this way Mister Ravindran would indulge, in this way his mind would wander. He allowed his mind to wander.

Mister Ravindran would come in to work, he expected the reward to be there. A cake on his desk. A letter from the Manager about his promotion. Not a letter but a personal visit. No no, a visit from the General Manager himself!

But no, no visit came. There was no cake and no letter either. Just the ledger on his desk. The work, the work.

"Is the job finished, Ravindran?"

"The job, sir?"

"Is the ledger done?"

"The ledger, sir?"

"We have deadlines, you know. This is a private company, not a government office. Deadlines mean something."

Deadlines, deadlines. Who could ignore them? Work, work—always the work.

***

The servant had been taken from the clinic to a public hospital. He was there for eight days. There, he was paid for by the government—by society. A fractured arm, a fractured ankle. "But it all depended on the way he fell," they said. "It could have been worse—so much worse."

The servant was released, and one day, he came to thank his benefactor.

"You are a god, sir."

Mister Ravindran looked at him imperially.

"My life, sir …" And he fell at Mister Ravindran's feet.

There was a cast on his arm, a cast on his ankle. Mister Ravindran was quite pleased at the scene at his feet, but he tried to hide his feelings. "Oh ho, what is this?" he said with some severity. "A deed is done, a man does it. He does what is best …"

He was moved by his own words—how could he not be? But he found no reason to continue.

The servant lay there weeping, kissing his benefactor's feet. The servant's brother was nearby. He had come from the village to take care of the servant. He fell at Mister Ravindran's feet as well.

The two simple ones wept, they praised their savior. And then they rose. They left.

They left.

The servant was in no condition to stay in Delhi. The brother would take him back to the village—give him care, affection. The other relatives would be there—they would give him the proper time to recover.

Mister Ravindran was left to himself. He had observed the scene, enjoyed it. But what now? What next?

Mister Ravindran had spent eight hundred and fourteen rupees. Did he not deserve a *better* reward? He had spent all this money for a stranger. Should he not come to thank him daily—day after day, day after day?

But no, life is not like that. The servant was gone and Mister Ravindran was left by himself. Left to ponder life, left to ponder the world. What a strange world it was indeed.

***

More days passed. Mister Ravindran went to the office, he came home. And did it help? He wandered the streets, he tried to lose himself in them. But did it help?

He saw poor people on the street—laborers, servants. He imagined that they fell off buildings, off ladders. He rushed to help them—or perhaps he did not. They garlanded him with marigold flowers, they asked him to make speeches. He complied—or perhaps he did not. Should he get involved? Was it really his business? Had he not learned his lesson already?

It was a big world, yes. It was a complicated world. He had done his great deed. It should accumulate him merit for years and years to come.

"But the reward," he said. "Where is the reward?"

He tried to comfort himself. Was the good deed not reward in itself? The servant had come to thank him, he had fallen at his feet. Was that not reward? He had played cards four nights ago, won forty-two rupees. Forty-two rupees, was that not reward?

One day he was running to the bus stop and stumbled and fell on some thorns. He cut himself, his right arm and elbow bled for some time.

"But who knows?" said a colleague at work. "You may have been destined to fall not on thorns, but on a snake. Your good deed—did it not help you? Help you even there?"

Mister Ravindran paused, listened to the other. There was truth to what the other said. Or was there? And was Mister Ravindran convinced—was he really convinced?

Mister Ravindran tried to forget the deed—why indulge in unpleasant things? He tried to lose himself in his work. And work, there was always that. The files, the ledgers. The files, the ledgers.

There was the file on the Gupta case—he worked on that. The file on the Mahajan case—he worked on that. These low-class people, these merchants, and how much money they had! It was all in the files, it was all there in front of him. He won forty-two rupees in cards, he lost eight hundred and fourteen rupees for a servant. And these northerners, these merchants, they dealt in thousands—in hundreds of thousands! My Lord, were there really people like this in the world? They went to lunch, they had food, they had drinks, the bill came to sixteen hundred rupees. Five hundred more than his salary for the whole month. It was all right there—all there in the memos and vouchers in front of him.

Mister Ravindran sat there, he brooded. What an unfair world it was! Some wore suits and Rolex watches, they went to the Taj Hotel. Others wore simple shirts and pants, they sat with the ledgers—always the ledgers—in front of them.

Mister Ravindran's mind wandered. He married a rich woman—the daughter of an industrialist; he became a rich man. He wrote a famous book, he came up with a big invention—the telescope, the rocket; he became a rich man. He defeated the enemies of the country—China, Pakistan, some enemy not yet known. He was garlanded and given a rest house (he liked the term) and pension for life.

But ah cruel life, cruel fate. Were these things really happening—were they coming to pass? Did they have any *chance* of coming to pass?

Mister Ravindran admonished himself, he admonished the world. He castigated God's creation—"A joke," he said, "all a joke." And he sat at his desk, and he brooded.

***

One day Mister Ravindran rose from his desk and he made his way home. Usually he took the bus, but today he decided to walk. It was a long distance—almost three miles—but why not? A man needs to indulge. He repeats the same thing day after day, day after day. He gets into a routine, a rut. Does he not deserve a change?

There was the bank on the way—he passed that. There was the taxi stand—he passed that. There was a market—so many restaurants there, so many confectioners' stores. Ah, these Delhi-wallas, how they liked to eat! Low-class people, nothing but low-class. The people of the South, of Tamil Nadu, they had breeding. They studied mathematics, they studied science. Why had he not studied science himself? He had studied commerce—a low-class thing. Perhaps he should start again. Too late now. But in his next life he would do it differently. The next life, yes …

A small boy walked by, begging for money. He was in his bare feet, his legs were caked with dust. "Four annas, sir, two annas." He rubbed his stomach; he raised his fingers to his mouth, indicating that he needed food, that he would use the money for food.

"Not for drinks, boy?" said Mister Ravindran. "Are you sure that you will not use the money for drinks?"

The boy was startled by the words. They were strange words, what did they mean?

"Go, go," said Mister Ravindran. "I already gave eight hundred and fourteen rupees. *Eight hundred and fourteen.*"

The boy looked at this strange man with wonder. Was the man drunk? Was he ill?

But Mister Ravindran had no patience for the boy. He moved on.

There was a cinema hall with a long line outside. He passed that. There were white pillars outside the cinema, posters all over the pillars for upcoming films. There were walls nearby—more posters pasted on these.

He passed an alley to the right of the cinema. The smell of refuse and urine was strong. He covered his nose with his handkerchief, hurried on. "These Delhi-wallas," he said again. "What low-class people they are."

He walked, he walked, he continued to walk. He had walked to change his routine, to lift his spirits.

Mister Ravindran arrived home. He was tired, just that. He boiled the water, he made the tea. There were some old curried vegetables in the icebox. He took out the vegetables, he heated them.

"A dog's life!" he said. "Stuck in the north, stuck in a pointless job. Does a man not deserve better? Does he not deserve more?"

***

Many months passed. Mister Ravindran went to work, he came home. He went to work, he came home. One day, Mister Ravindran was sitting in the front room, facing the window with the crisscrossing wooden shutters and cursing his fate. There was no decent veranda in his humble quarters—he could not sit there.

He sat in his front room reading his newspaper. His mind wandered. He turned the page. He heard some scraping at the front steps. Who was it? Someone was climbing the cement steps, scraping his feet there.

"Sir?"

Mister Ravindran lowered his newspaper. It made a loud crinkling sound.

"Sir?"

There was a dark man at the open front door. Five feet, three inches or so—perhaps an inch more.

He had seen the man before. Where had he seen him?

"I am Ratna, sir. Do you not recognize me?"

Ratna, Ratna. Who was this Ratna? "My boy!" he called out. "My boy!"

It was the servant, of course, the servant whose life he had saved. The great deed he had done. The large sum, the rupees—the eight hundred and fourteen rupees.

"Ratna, Ratna," he said warmly, rising briefly from his chair but then sitting down again. (Was it not the respectful thing to do?) "Are you better?"

107

The hair on the visitor's head was shaved. The cast on his leg was gone. The cast on his arm was gone as well.

"I am better, sir, much better. It is God's will, sir. It is God's blessing."

"And *my* blessing?" Mister Ravindran wanted to add. But he checked himself.

The servant stood at the entrance—it would have been presumptuous for him to proceed further. He did indeed look better. A little weak, perhaps, but better. What a cry—a far cry—from the man he had taken to the hospital. From the man who, accompanied by his brother, had fallen at his feet.

Did he not want to fall at Mister Ravindran's feet again? Was it not the right and proper thing to do?

"I am back from the village, sir."

"Yes yes, so I see."

"I am now a messenger, sir."

"What is this?"

"The servant work, sir, it is too hard. My condition …" He pointed to himself and did not finish the sentence. "But the company, sir—the bank nearby— they have been kind to me. I get them water, I make them tea. I do small errands. But in the evenings, sir, I go home. On Sundays, sir, they are closed. I get to stay home as well. To rest. "

"That is great," said Mister Ravindran. "That is great."

And did he mean his words? Or was he jealous of the servant—actually jealous? The servant was moving up in the world. Off in the evenings. Off on Sundays. Was he becoming like him?

"That is great," he said again.

The servant bowed. "I just wanted to come, sir. To thank you. You are a kind man, sir. God will bless you, sir. Bless you with all the rewards of the world."

All the rewards—ha! How little the low-class one knew. Mister Ravindran lived a donkey's life. He worked, he worked. He waited, he waited. Did the rewards ever come?

The servant bowed—bowed again. And he began to leave. As he did, he hesitated about turning his back. It might be seen as a sign of disrespect, and he did not want to be disrespectful. But did he have a choice? The steps were there, all the steps leading to the dirt ground in the front. He did not want to stumble down the steps and fall—to fall all over again.

The servant left, his back turned, and Mister Ravindran was left by himself. He returned to his chair. To the newspaper. The servant was better. Was that a good thing? The servant was back. Was that a good thing? Mister Ravindran was reminded freshly of his great deed. "And the reward," he said. "Where is the reward?"

Mister Ravindran sat there, the newspaper in front of him.

He sat there for a long time. The light in the room began to fade, the shadows in the room grew long.

And then, softly, very softly (perhaps he did not want the world to hear): "I will see him, yes. I will see him more often. And perhaps he will come and thank me—he has to, it is his duty. He will come and thank me again and again for my great deed. "

Gurmeet Singh

Gurmeet Singh was a short man with two long beards, one on each side of the face. He gave one the impression of deformity. He talked, not surprisingly, of tropes. But was he satisfied?

He looked at the subject—"*la nature du sujet*"—but also at a movement leading towards something—"*qui conduit*." Something, what something? In a letter to his brother-in-law (his sister's husband), he spoke at length of the crisis that he was going through. Was he a Sikh or wasn't he? Should he tie his turban, should he not? If the turban was tied, was it, perhaps, tied too tightly? Should he loosen it?

America was a big place. He wanted to fit in, yes. But would he then lose himself? Or would he then be free? Be for once the *real* Singh?

These questions he faced, and more. Oh, the self-doubts that he must have gone through. The vagaries, the horrors!

We met at the Denny's in Las Vegas, and then at the Howard Johnson's in Cincinnati. He ordered two eggs, bacon, ham; I ordered pancakes with a side order of fries. We both had coffee, ordered refills.

"I like life," he boasted. "I like living. Am I therefore a fraud?"

I told him that he was no fraud. He was the last person I would consider so.

He seemed pleased by my words.

He spoke of "luminous profiling," a "terrible afflatus." But he would give no details. What it all meant—or how it all tied together—was beyond me. But so it was.

He had studied the works of the literary critic Frank Kermode—*Puzzles and Epiphanies*. He had studied the works of the French man of letters Otto Hahn—*Les Temps Modernes*. He tried to put his studies to use. Was he able?

He attended many lectures, liked going to them. They gave him a chance—or was it an excuse?—to see people. To see the world.

He wandered the streets. He lived with his cousin in Cheverly, Maryland. He lived with his aunt in Seattle, Washington. But most of his time was spent in motels, small and nameless motels throughout the country.

He studied with the experts, he read books, he read books. But was he satisfied? Was he happy? That above all else. Was he that?

***

Gurmeet Singh was born in Punjab, India, in 1963. He came to America in the early 1980s. He worked at odds and ends. Then he went to college, got his degree. He went back again, studied the esteemed critics. The real question was: was he satisfied? Was he pleased?

He went for long walks—liked to do so. He often carried a small plastic bag with him. A bag from Safeway, from CVS, from Walgreens—it mattered not. There was something small—his scarf, his gloves—inside the bag.

"Why do you carry the bag?" I said.

"I walk, I walk. People look at me."

"And so?"

"They should not think that I am walking, just walking. Walking *idly*."

I was surprised at his words. He seemed a sure and confident man. Why then this concern for what others might think?

But I did not want to pursue the matter, not now. I let the matter go.

Seminars were being held at the time—seminars on fashion, on semiology, on the semiology of fashion. He studied all of these. New designs were being offered. Custom-made or *prêt-à-porter*, he did not care. He studied all of these.

He wore a colored turban. Was it a fashion as well? Was it something more? A matter of religion? A matter of the *soul*?

At one of the seminars, some woman rose, a professor from a southwestern college. She spoke on mesas, on canyons, on the origins of canyons. He listened—with what interest he listened. The beginning of things—how they were, *why* they were—this intrigued him. But his own questions—the "rumblings" he called them—were they now calmed?

In Cheverly there was a cinema with a parking lot behind it. Sometimes young girls gathered there. They were newly graduated from high school; they had studied typing there, bookkeeping. The job market was tight, the money too little or too unsatisfying. They painted their nails, they walked around the parking lot.

The men came. Were they pleased? One day Gurmeet Singh put on a purple turban—how dapper he looked (or so he thought). He combed his beard, put a net around the beard. And he went to the parking lot.

He went there—why did he go? Did he go to meet the girls, to spend time with them? Did he go to speak his ideas on the world, his great ideas?

He spoke about the villages in Punjab, the games that he had played there.

"Were there dust storms in Punjab?" they said.

"Yes," he said. "They came all the time."

"You played *pithoo*, you played *gulli-danda*?"

"Yes," he said.

"You understand the world—how it is, why it is?"

Gurmeet Singh smiled. He smiled again. There was a gap between his middle two teeth. "I am a small man," he said. "The esteemed critics are big. I am small. There is so much that I still have to learn."

The girls looked at him and smiled in return. Perhaps they were impressed by him—impressed by his sincerity, his modesty. But they had work to do, money to make. Must they not return to this work?

***

The days passed. Gurmeet Singh went to his lectures and he took notes. He made entries in his journal and then more entries still.

There was a small grocery store on Ager Road (near Hamilton Street). A tall man—he had played baseball for a professional team once—owned the store. There were four aisles in the store but hardly any people there. There were bigger stores nearby— Safeway, Giant—people preferred to go there. But Gurmeet Singh often went to the store. He liked going there. He walked up and down the aisles. There was canned food, there were detergents. There were frozen foods and even a few fruits and vegetables.

Near the fruits and vegetables, a small mirror hung from the facing of the display. If you stepped back a little, and bent down, you could see your face. Sometimes Gurmeet Singh stepped back and bent down—he looked at his face.

Gurmeet Singh liked looking at his face. The brown skin, the small mole near the ear. The purple turban, the hair that stuck out from under the edges. The gap—the famous gap between the middle two teeth.

A man looks at his face, why does he do it? Is it from insecurity? Is it from shame? Is it because he wants to see things, understand them? See things—what things?

Gurmeet Singh wandered the streets of America—he continued to wander them. There were big men trying to answer the big questions of the world. And Gurmeet Singh, what of him? Was he a big man? Was he even close? In the eyes of Americans, was he even a man at all?

"He has studied science!"

"He has studied fashion!"

"He knows it, the Sikh man, he knows it all!"

In this way the others spoke. Did they speak seriously? Did they mock Gurmeet Singh? And Gurmeet Singh, dear Gurmeet Singh, was he impressed? Did he agree?

One day I met him at the Howard Johnson's—the one on Riverdale Road. We spoke of life, we spoke of death. We spoke of the calm, the calm that comes at last. He spoke for some time. There was so much that he wanted to say. And sometimes how it came pouring out!

"I am alone in America."

"Yes."

"It is not easy to be a Sikh."

"No."

"I wash my turbans, you know. I iron them as well."

They were intriguing words, I did not know what to say. And then: "It is important to be clean. A man's turban is clean. But what of his heart? His *soul*?"

His heart, his soul. They were serious words, I tried to take them seriously. We ate our chicken

sandwich and fries, we drank our Coke and our va-
nilla milk shake. And we spoke, yes, of the important
things of the world.

***

Gurmeet Singh read, he read. He read vora-
ciously. He read Kant, he read Hegel. He read the
Romantic poets, he read the classicists. He read J.D.
Salinger (*Franny and Zooey*) but also J.C. Scaliger
(*Poetices Libri Septem*, Lyons, 1561). He said that
both knew something about poetry and prosody,
Scaliger perhaps a bit more. The latter spoke of *mel*
and *fel*—sweet and sour, sugar and salt—and made
other contrasts as well.

One day I saw Gurmeet Singh. How heatedly he
spoke on the subject—with what passion. "Poetry,
poetry, how important it is. It stirs the soul, it calms
it. It stirs and calms at the same time. But do I understand poetry, really understand?"

I agreed on poetry—the value of poetry—how
could I not? But I also told him that he was being
too hard on himself. Poetry was difficult, very difficult. For some it took years to understand, for some
a lifetime!

He seemed reassured by my words. Or was he?

He spoke again of his texts—with what passion
he spoke. He spoke of the texts that he admired—
Baudelaire's *Les Fleurs du Mal* and Paulhan's *Les
Fleurs de Tarbes* (1941). He spoke of the texts that
troubled him—Blanchot's *Faux pas* (1943).

It was late twilight. He came out of the house, sat on the low stoop. The sky was orange and grey and blue; the children were playing in the distance. Some were skipping rope, some were playing with a pink rubber ball. The light was fading, it was harder and harder to see the ball.

"Be careful, children," he called out. But children are children. They are self-absorbed, they are immortal. Do they have time for such things?

He called out to the children—why did he call out? Because he cared for them? Because he was timid and wanted the children to be the same—to not take risks?

The hours passed. He sat on the stoop, he continued to look at the children. India was far away, the Punjab was far away. Was happiness far away as well?

Gurmeet Singh rose the next morning. He came out and stood in the veranda. He was living in a cheap motel. He stood under the blue awning. Cars were around him—old cars, cheap cars. The metal trash cans were around him as well. Some were filled to the top, brimming with refuse. They had not been emptied in days.

Was this what America was? Was this what life was—*his* life?

***

Gurmeet Singh walked the streets—he continued to walk them. He lived in America—was he happy there? He lived in America—did he fit in? He lived in America—did he understand things?

Things, what things?

One day, at a conference, he met the famous jurist Mo Tan. The judge had been born in Tibet, he had fled, with a few others, to America in the late 1950s.

Gurmeet Singh spoke of his days in Punjab. Was the other impressed? Gurmeet Singh spoke of his walks, of the plastic bags that he carried with him. Was the other impressed? Gurmeet Singh quoted from the esteemed Hegel in his *Phenomenology*. He spoke of family, of intimacy, of a man's search for the same. He spoke of the various paths he had taken. He noted—quoting Hegel—that a path, though necessary, is *not* the only possible path.

The jurist listened—listened with some attention.

Gurmeet Singh spoke at length of his turban—the colors he wore, the hair inside.

"The hair is long?"

"It is."

"You cut it?"

"I do not."

"And of that you are ashamed? You are proud?"

Gurmeet Singh paused, smiled. Shame, pride, what idle words they were. A man does what he does. Is that not enough?

But the judge was not convinced. He spoke—citing Gurmeet Singh's own words on Hegel—of analysis and motivation, of the *need* for analysis and motivation. "We are not animals," he said. "We do because we *choose* to."

Gurmeet Singh was struck by the word. What an interesting word it was. One did, one did not—that he understood. But to choose to do, to choose not to do?

"My sister is getting married," said the jurist simply. "I want you to come to the wedding."

Wedding, wedding, what was this strange talk? But the judge was an important and influential man. Who was Gurmeet Singh to refuse?

The wedding was held in a small hall at the edge of town. Chinese lanterns had been set up; here and there were pictures of Jesus Christ. The bride was Tibetan, the groom was American—*white*. Gurmeet Singh stared at the scene, marveled at it.

During the ceremony the jurist came up to Gurmeet Singh, greeted him.

"Do you see now?" he said.

"See?"

"The girl likes the boy, she *loves* him. It is a matter of choice, Mister Singh. Not parents, not God. But choice. An individual's choice."

Again Gurmeet Singh marveled at the jurist's words. What an amazing world it was. Choice, choice, still that emphasis on that word. There was so much in the world—so much perhaps that he still did not know.

***

The days passed. A major conference was held at the university. Gurmeet Singh washed and ironed his purple turban (how resplendent he looked!) and he went. Some of the biggest scholars were there—Derrida, Poulet, Todorov, Girard. They spoke of signs, they spoke of signifiers. They spoke, longingly, of a center; they spoke, not so longingly, of the "burden of our Hegelian metaphysical heritage." Gurmeet Singh listened—with what rapt attention he listened.

Someone asked a question on the meaning of life.

The scholars spoke of "systematic reference points," of "successive conceptual webs."

Another person asked a question on the possibility of truth.

The scholars laughed—with irony perhaps, but not venom. They spoke of "indirections," of "interstices." They spoke of the "vacant spaces between things, words, ideas."

I looked at my friend: I had never seen him so happy, so alive. People speak of the power of religion to uplift, the power of yoga to transport you to another dimension. My friend did not need religion or yoga. He was there, good man. He was already there!

That evening we met at the Howard Johnson's. My friend spoke—how rapidly he spoke.

"I am happy," he said.

"Happy?"

"God exists," he said.

"He does?"

"These men are his disciples. His messengers as well!"

I was not sure that the men he referred to even believed in God. I doubted strongly that they would accept such an analysis. But my friend was happy—was that not the main thing? Happiness comes so rarely, to so few. Why quibble with it when it is there—why quibble at all?

***

The days passed. The euphoria of the last few days did not last. How could it? The conference was over and the men had come and gone. Their books remained, but was that enough? Their ideas remained, but was that enough? Could it be?

Gurmeet Singh walked the streets—he continued to walk them. He read books—he continued to read them. And did he fit into America now—did he fit in better? Did he understand America—did he understand the *world*?

"I am someone," he said.

"Someone?"

"I am no one," he said.

"No one?"

"I try," he said. "How hard I try!"

He spoke his words seriously. But was there pity in the words, self-pity? Was there cheap sentiment there as well?

A man wants to learn—then he must *really* learn. A man wants to understand—then sentiment must have no place in that understanding. A man must look at the truth, face it. He must look the truth straight in the eye.

One day Gurmeet Singh went to the market. What did he see there? He went to the mall—what did he see there? He walked in his neighborhood with his hands crossed behind his back. There was an oak tree, he stood under the tree. There was an apple tree, he sat at the base of the tree. There was a squirrel in the tree that made loud and screeching noises. This was its home, perhaps it did not want any strangers—any intruders—in its world.

Gurmeet Singh was in the strange world of America. People did not want him there. But he had his own world as well. Did he want people *there*?

Choice, choice—the words of the jurist rang in his head. How much of the world was determined (*a priori*)? How much of the world did we make ourselves?

***

One day I saw Gurmeet Singh again. It was in Austin, Texas—at the Denny's on Ben White Boulevard. It was in the early hours of the morning, there were hardly any people there.

We found a booth in a corner and we huddled with our thoughts. There was a glass salt shaker— Gurmeet Singh played with that. There was a packet of sugar—Gurmeet Singh played with that. It was raining outside, a light drizzle. My friend sat there, he shook his head.

"I am tired," he said.

"Tired?"

"I have studied, I have studied—for what? The books have taught me—what have they taught me?"

I tried to encourage my friend. I told him that he was being too hard on himself. He was going through a temporary period of self-doubt, no more. Humans are humans—we all go through that.

But he would not be appeased.

The waitress came, asked us if we were ready to order. She was an older woman—in her late fifties, perhaps even her early sixties. She had curly white hair, a pencil tucked behind her ear. But what struck me were the nails on her fingers. For all the work, the hard work, they were delicate and long. And they were painted pink, perhaps an orange-pink.

I noticed the nails. Did my friend notice them as well?

I thought of the parking lot in Cheverly, of the girls who came there. They studied typing in school, they studied bookkeeping. Had this woman done the same? The girls grew up, married—or did they? They had children—or did they? They painted their nails in their youth; they grew up, tucked pencils behind their ears and worked at Denny's. Was this the way?

I looked at the woman with interest. Did my friend do the same?

"What would you like?" The woman spoke at last, the small green pad in front of her—the pencil in her hand now, no longer behind her ear.

My friend pointed to the item in the menu. (Is this what he wanted to say?)

"Any coffee? Tea?"

My friend answered. (Is this what he wanted to say?)

She asked me questions as well. Food, drink; food, drink. I answered as well. Simply, directly—I answered as well.

The years pass, we grow old. The years pass, we grow tired. We paint our nails, we do not paint them. We go to Denny's, we do not go. We find the truth, we do not find it. Does anyone remember? Does anyone care?

But people ask you questions, it is best to answer. Simply, directly. The best you can. It is the best thing to do.

The time passed. The food came, we nibbled on the food. The drinks came, we sipped on the drinks. My friend was in a bad mood—it was not easy to shake him from that mood.

The rain was falling harder now. The wind had picked up as well. We nibbled on the food—my dear friend and I—we nibbled for a long time.

"The toast," said my friend at last.

"The toast?"

"It is nice and crisp today."

My friend smiled. I was glad that he smiled.

"It is nice and crisp today. I *like* that."

Again my friend smiled. It was a fleeting smile. It lasted a second, perhaps a fraction of a second. But a smile, any smile—for a second, even for a fraction of a second—is that so bad? Is that really so bad?

It is a big world. We are small men. Sometimes we take what we can—is that not the best way? We take what we can. Is that really so bad?

Mother of Gulu

I t was 1947, Bipan, a long time ago. The Muslims came, they killed him. Seven there were: three with knives, two with sticks, and the other two (did I tell you)—they kept watch at the door. Muslims they were, yes, and they killed him—they killed my husband.

"Rapidly I blinked my eyes. But no, that was not a new habit; since I was a child, I would blink them so. And now before my eyes they were killing him. I screamed, yes, but no one came; my husband screamed as well—but no one came. Rama was not there and Krishna was not there; Lakshmi was not there and Durga was not there. For thirty-two years I had prayed to the gods. But when the Muslims came—seven there were—the gods did not show.

"It was 1947, Bipan, it was the partition. Nehru said this and Jinnah said that. Gandhi said this and Patel said that. Lahore it was and we all listened. The city was in flames and we listened. July 1947—he was there. August—he was not. The Muslims had come— seven there were—three with knives, two with sticks, and the other two (oh yes) they kept watch at the door.

"So the Muslims came, so they killed him—so they killed my husband. A sad story, Bipan, is it not? Will you listen, will you turn away?"

The mother of Gulu spoke, rapidly she blinked her eyes. Sometimes she tried to control herself but she could not: she blinked.

Many things about the story we liked, but the blinking of the eyes—that we liked the best. At times we would go around the kothi and try to copy her. But we could never be as good. A few times we would blink but, no no, it was nothing like hers.

At the copying, Kailash was maybe the best. Eighty-seven times he blinked once in a minute—but the two hundred times of the mother of Gulu, the two hundred and three, no no, it was nothing like that.

"The Muslims came, I saw it. But Shammi, I wonder, did she see it? Gulu, I wonder, did he? Shammi was then three, she was in the other room; curious, when I went to her room, she was still asleep. The screams, they did not wake her. Gulu—a baby he was, four months and then a few days—but no, the screams did not wake him either. Often I think about that—seven Muslims in the room, three with knives, two with sticks—and the other two—and yet with all the noise, the children did not wake.

"God's will—perhaps it was God's will that the children be spared. Oh now they know like the rest. In

July he was there, in August he was not. The Muslims had come—three with knives, two with sticks, and the other two (oh yes)—they kept watch at the door."

The winter afternoon it was, in the back of the kothi we sat. The mother of Gulu sat on the string cot (or on the ground). She rocked back and forth. We sat on the ground (we sat at her feet). We listened: we did not turn away.

"Seven there were, yes. 'Your son,' they said, 'is it Gulu?' 'Your husband,' they said, 'is it Ram Das?' 'We have come,' they said, 'with knives we have come, with sticks. Look!'

"The knives were long, they glinted in the dark. The sticks were long, they held them to my neck.

"I screamed in the night, I pulled out my hair. I clasped my palms, I fell at their feet. (Do you think it helped?)

"'The henna,' they said, 'o mai, is it not a good thing?' 'The henna,' they said, 'oh look: see how it dyes the world red!'

("The henna was there, it was all over. And yes, it did it: it *dyed the world red*.")

"The neighbors came, they hid in the corner. The neighbors came, they stood at the door.

"'But my husband,' I said.

"'Yes,' they said.

"'But my husband,' I said.

"'Yes,' they said.

"The relatives came, they hurried me away.

"'But my husband,' I said.

"'Yes,' they said.

"I hit my breast, I pulled out my hair. I broke my bangles, I removed the sindoor from my forehead. (Do you think it helped?)

"'Have some tea,' they said. 'Eat,' they said. 'You must eat,' they said.

"A horse carriage was there, it stood outside. 'Have some tea,' they said. 'Eat,' they said. 'You *must* eat,' they said."

Sometimes it was the winter but sometimes it was the summer as well. We sat in the veranda (we sat in the shade). The mother of Gulu sat on the string cot, she rocked back and forth. The women sat on the cots, they knitted their sweaters. Some of them ate peanuts, they threw the shells on the ground. Some of them removed the lice—they removed the lice from the children's hair.

"From death I tried to bring him back. Do you think I was able?

"Savitri I was not, Behula I was not. I could not— I could not bring him back.

"At the funeral I cried. 'Cry,' they said, 'why do you cry?' They pointed to a ledge, on the ledge was a crow.

"But a crow was a crow, not my husband. I could not bring him back.

"I followed the body to the pyre—'Go back,' they said. I wept, I shrieked—'Go back,' they said. 'But my husband,' I said, 'I weep for my husband.'

"An old man, a sadhu, was there (his hair was white, his back was bent in half). 'Look, o mai,' he said, 'there is your husband.'

"I looked: and there on the ledge was the same crow.

"But a crow was a crow, not my husband. I could not bring my husband back.

"For years I worked at the funeral grounds, for years I lay my face to the wall. For years I went from kothi to kothi talking about death. But do you think it helped?

"They told me the story of Buddha. 'Go from house to house,' they said, 'find lentils in a house that has not known death.'

"They were right, death was everywhere. But my husband was dead, I could not—I could not bring him back."

("And so it was, Bipan, so it was. Are you there, are you listening? Will you turn away?")

"Sometimes the people tried to comfort me. 'We will get the moon for you,' they said, 'we will get the sun. In a tonga we will go, we will bring it to your door.'

"'The moon,' I said, 'can it take the place of my husband?' 'The sun,' I said, 'can even the sun?'

"I cried, the tears came. 'The hair of Shiva,' they said, 'the hair of Shiva we need.'

"The hair of Shiva had once stopped a flood. But the flood of my tears, could it stop that?

"My husband was dead—I could not bring him back.

"My husband was dead—I could not bring him back.

"My husband was dead—Bipan, are you there (are you listening?)—I could not—*I could not bring him back.*"

***

The women sat in the back of the kothi. They sat on the string cots (and sometimes on the ground), they knitted their sweaters. The mother of Gulu told her story—she would begin to tell it.

"1947 it was."

"Yes."

"Partition it was."

"Yes."

"And the seven, did I tell you ..."

Sometimes the women would nod. Sometimes they would purse their lips sympathetically. Sometimes, pausing an instant from their knitting, they would shake their heads.

"It happens," they said.

"It comes to pass," they said.

"O mother of Gulu, do not be sad—do not be sad," they said.

But sometimes (I will say it), the women grew tired of the tale. They liked the mother of Gulu, but the story, how many times had they heard it?

They were old, they were weak. Did they not have problems of their own?

The mother of Gulu would leave the old people, she would come to us.

"The others are busy," she would say, "they do not care. But you are children, you will listen. Is it not so?"

"Yes," we said.

"You will listen. Is it not so?"

"Yes," we said.

Not only did we listen, but we listened with care. And the mother of Gulu, as she spoke, her enthusiasm seemed to grow as well.

Tingoo was there and Binoo. Kailash was there and Raman. And the others—they were there as well.

The mother of Gulu—she would tell her story. We would sit at her feet (we would sit on the ground). And we would ask questions—ask questions as well.

"The three with knives," we said, "what did they look like?"

("Yes yes," we said, "the three with knives.")

"The two with sticks," we said, "what kind of sticks were they?"

("Yes yes," we said, "the two with sticks.")

"Of the neelam tree they were not made, that we know. But of what *were* they made, can you tell us, did you have a chance to look?"

"And the two who kept watch at the door, did they have any weapons? Knives they may not have been, sticks they may not, but was there something else perhaps—something *hidden*?"

At first we had feared that the mother of Gulu might be offended by the questions. But no, she did not seem upset; or if upset, she did not show it.

Politely she answered our questions: one by one she answered them.

Sometimes it was even like a game. She would laugh. And we would laugh as well.

She would wink. And we would wink as well.

"The knives," she would say, "ha ha!" "The sticks," she would say, "ha ha!"

Rapidly she would blink her eyes. Again she would blink them, and again!

Many things about the story we liked, but the blinking of the eyes—oh yes, that was always the best. At times we would go around the kothi and try to copy her. But we could never be as good. A few times we would blink but, no no, it was nothing like hers.

At the copying, Kailash was maybe the best. Eighty-seven times he blinked once in a minute—but the two hundred times of the mother of Gulu, the two hundred and three—no no, it was *nothing like that*.

(The two hundred times—the two hundred and three—no no, *it was nothing like that.*)

***

The mother of Gulu was sad, she walked around the grounds of the kothi. She heard a voice: "What is *that*?" she said. She heard the noise of the crow: her whole body shuddered. The noise of someone hitting the clothes with the paddle: she covered her ears with her hands. "Hey Ram," she cried, "Hey Ram—is there no peace in the kothi?"

We saw the mother of Gulu, we tried to stop her.

"O mother of Gulu," we said, "where are you going?"

"I am going to Lahore."

"Lahore?"

"My husband calls me. Is it not time that I went back?"

"A place there is," she said.

"A place?"

"There is a small house. The boards of the door, they crisscross.

"The rooms of the house, oh I can still smell them. (The floors of the rooms, how cool they were.) The mai would come in the morning, she would clean them. The smell of phenol was there. In the summer afternoon, how nice it was to take a pillow, to lie on them!

"Shammi would lie on one side of me. And Gulu (did I tell you)—I put some bedding under him—he would lie on the other."

The mother of Gulu would speak, she would rock back and forth. Like this (like this!) she would rock back and forth.

Like this (like this!) she would rock back and forth!

***

We were afraid for the mother of Gulu, we tried to comfort her.

(But do you think it helped?)

We gave her toffee, we gave her peppermints.

(But do you think it helped?)

We rubbed her legs—and then we did it again.

(But was it enough. Could it ever be?)

"My husband," she said, "he was a nice man."

"Yes," we said.

"He gave me saris, he gave me gifts."

"Yes," we said.

"The old people in the kothi, they laugh at me, they do not care. But he loved me, he loved!"

"Yes," we said.

One day an old man came to the kothi. His back was bent, he had a prayer mat in his left hand, a neem twig (what, did he wish to brush his teeth?)—a neem twig in the right.

He scraped his feet on the steps, he left the sandals at the door.

Who was this man, we did not know. Why he had come, we did not know. But we were near the door: we stood, we watched.

"O mai," he said, "I am not Mahmud of Ghazni, I am not Tamerlane. I am not Genghis Khan, I am not Aurangzeb. The fighting, the noise, do you think I wanted it to come?"

The mother of Gulu was quiet. She blinked her eyes: rapidly she blinked them.

"In Lahore," he said, "I was there—I was there as well. I had my house, my children. Why when I was small …"

The mother of Gulu was quiet. She walked to the back. She returned with a tray, some tea on the tray, some cups. "Take," she said.

The man accepted the tea, he drank it from the cup. He poured some of the tea into a saucer—he drank from the saucer as well.

The next thing we knew, the old man was showing her a picture of himself as a child.

"The only one," he said.

Another picture he showed her.

"My sister," he said.

A third picture he showed her (a fourth).

"TB," he said.

He showed her a shawl, he showed her a tea set. He showed her a bracelet—he showed her that as well.

There they sat, the two of them, they sat into the night.

137

He gave her toffees, he gave her biscuits. And there they sat, the two of them, they sat into the night.

We called to them.

No answer.

We called to them.

No answer.

And there they sat, the two of them, *they sat into the night*.

***

Who was this man, we did not know. Why he was there, we did not know.

But we thought that he was a holy man. We thought that now a change would come over the mother of Gulu.

(And did it?)

We were excited, we ran around the kothi. We wanted to see the mother of Gulu, we wanted to see if this change had really come.

(And had it?)

The next morning we saw the mother of Gulu, she was lying on the steps—the steps outside her house.

"The steps are hard (so hard), they will hurt you," we said.

"Yes," she said.

She rose from the steps. She went to the bushes.

"The bushes have thorns, they will cut you, they will make you bleed."

"Yes," she said.

She rose from the bushes. She went to the middle of the kothi, she lay down on the ground (she lay down right there).

"But the sun is strong," we said, "it will burn you, it will hurt your head."

"Yes," she said.

The mother of Gulu blinked her eyes. Rapidly she blinked them.

"But the old man was there last night. Did he not teach you—teach you?"

The mother of Gulu blinked her eyes. Again she blinked them (and again!).

***

The next day we saw the mother of Gulu, she was in the back of the kothi. She was sitting on the string cot, she was rocking back and forth.

"1947 it was."

"Yes."

"Partition it was."

"Yes."

"And the seven (did I tell you) …"

It was back (don't you see)—it was *back to the same thing*.

The other women were there. Some of them knitted their sweaters. Some of them ate peanuts, threw the shells on the ground. Some of them picked the lice—they picked the lice from the children's hair.

"1947 it was."

"Yes."

"Partition it was."

"Yes."

"And the seven (did I tell you) ..."

It was back, don't you see—it was *back to the same thing*.

The days would pass, the months, and it would always—it would always be the same thing.

The old people would nod, they would not; they would purse their lips, they would not. They would listen to the tale, they would tire of it (they would look away).

The mother of Gulu would leave the old people, she would come to us. She would rock back and forth (like this, like this!). She would blink her eyes (like this, like this!). And she would tell the tale (she must, she must). And we would listen (how could we not)—could we just turn away?

"1947 it was."

"Yes."

"Partition it was."

"Yes."

"And the seven (did I tell you) ..."

"1947 it was."

"Yes."

"Partition it was."

"Yes."

"And the seven (did I tell you) ..."

It was a good tale (we liked it). It was a good tale (we loved it). And could we just ignore it? Could we *just turn away*?

Raghavendran Ramachandran

Raghavendran Ramachandran was from Madras in South India. He had been in America for eighteen months doing graduate work in chemistry. This was his first date and he was excited.

"Tell us where you're going," said the roommates. They were Indians as well, just like him.

"To see some friends."

"But what kind of friends?"

"Just friends."

Raghavendran blushed and lowered his head. His face was hot, he could feel it getting hotter. He walked with quick steps and closed the bathroom door behind him. He brushed his teeth, showered, and rubbed talcum powder all over his body. When he came out his roommates were waiting for him.

"Don't *you* smell nice," they said.

Raghavendran hurried towards his room. As he looked at the full-length mirror there, he felt ashamed. He was short, about five feet four inches.

He was dark-skinned. Americans were tall and fair-skinned. They were handsome and pretty. Why could he not be like them?

He put on black slacks, an orange shirt on top. His hair was combed down but was it combed down too much? In India the hair may have been acceptable, but here it looked greasy. Greasy and wet.

Vinay arrived at six. He was the ride for the evening, the confident one. He was the one who had set up the double date.

Vinay was tall, almost six feet, with brown hair and a dark brown mustache. He was wearing khaki pants, a collared shirt, and a navy blue jacket. When he saw Raghavendran, he smiled.

"Are you ready?" he said.

"Yes," said Raghavendran. "Should I get an umbrella? It might rain."

"Forget the umbrella," said Vinay. "We have a car."

Hearing Vinay's voice, the other roommates gathered in the living room.

"So how are you, Vinay baby?" said Satish.

"Not too bad. How's the dissertation coming?"

"It comes along. But you know me—too lazy to go to the lab, too lazy to go to the library. All I like to do is sleep."

"The Kumbhkaran of the Chemistry Department, I know. Sleep six months a year, stay awake six."

"That's right. But listen, Vinay—maybe you and I can double date some time. More fun that way. Raghu there ..." He did not finish the sentence.

Raghavendran was right there, just a few feet away, but he pretended not to hear. He had heard the comments before. Perhaps he was used to them.

"Don't forget me," said Dilip. "I'm new in this country, too. Just six months here. Somebody's got to show me around the town."

"Preferably a red-blooded American girl," said Satish laughing.

"Or a blonde," said Dilip. "I love the blonde girls."

"The blondes, the blondes," said Dilip, puckering his lips and rolling his head in small circles. They all laughed.

"Well, we better be going," said Vinay. "Are you ready?" he called towards the back of the room.

Raghavendran had gone to the back, perhaps to look at the mirror one last time.

"I'm ready," said Raghavendran, walking towards the group. Satish and Dilip smiled.

"Well good luck, Raghu," they said. "Be easy on the girls."

"I'll see you later," mumbled Raghavendran, and began walking down the steps.

They arrived at the car. "Are you sure this is a good idea?" said Raghavendran.

"Sure it is," said Vinay. "Just relax. It takes practice. Just practice."

They began getting into the car. "It may be a good idea," said Vinay, "to tuck the shirt-tail in."

"But I always wear it this way. I like to wear it on the outside."

"I know. But just for today. It may be better the other way."

***

They got in the car, a Ford Maverick, and drove the four miles to the destination. Vinay was also a graduate student, but not in the chemistry department but in economics. He had met Raghavendran in the university cafeteria some six months earlier. They had talked, taken a liking to each other. They had gone to a movie together, to a concert of classical Indian music. This was their first time on a double date.

"The girl's name is Anne," said Vinay. "Your friend. My friend's name is Cheryl. They both go to City College, they're both juniors."

"Where did you meet them?"

"I met Cheryl at a party. Anne, I've never met before."

They drove, they drove. At last they came to some nice residential area. There were rows and rows of colonial townhouses. Vinay pulled up the car in front of one of the houses. "Looks expensive, doesn't it?" he said.

"Yes," said Raghavendran. "But do they actually own it?"

"Nah," said Vinay. "Four of the students rent the place together. You wait here—it's not really legal to park. I'll be right back."

He went to get the girls. Raghavendran's heart was pounding. He took his comb and quickly tried to fix his hair again. "But what's the use?" he said. He put the comb away.

When Vinay and the girls came back, they were all laughing. Apparently someone had just told a good joke.

Raghavendran got out of the car and the introductions were made. Raghavendran smiled but he could hardly get the words out of his mouth. His face felt hot.

"Raghu," he said. "Please call me Raghu."

"Nice to meet you, *Ragu*." This was Anne and she missed the *h* in the name. But it was a subtle difference in sound, she could hardly be blamed.

She was a short girl, perhaps Raghavendran's height, perhaps an inch taller. She had short brown hair. Her friend was blonde, a little taller. Both wore mid-length skirts, a light cardigan sweater on top.

Raghavendran bowed, Anne offered her hand. Instead of accepting the hand, Raghavendran bowed again. Anne offered a hand—half a hand this time. No contact of the flesh was made.

Raghavendran began to sit in the front seat with Vinay. He had done so on the way here. Why shouldn't he do it again?

"Why don't you sit in the back?" said Vinay.

"Oh," said Raghavendran. He got in the back seat and closed the door behind him. He realized that he had left Anne outside. He unlocked the door from the inside and scooted over to the left, all the way to the other end of the car.

He sat there, immobile. Anne got in, sat on the other side of the back seat. It was not an auspicious start, but perhaps things would get better. Of course, they would.

They made their way to the restaurant. They were going to an Italian restaurant for dinner. Then to a movie. *Serpico*, with someone named Al Pacino.

The front seat of the car was talkative. The back seat was silent.

"Raghavendran is studying chemistry," said Vinay finally over his shoulder.

"Oh," said Anne. "One of our roommates— Patrice—is taking a class in chemistry. Sounds pretty hard to me. Too much math."

"Not too hard," said Raghavendran. These were the first words he had spoken in the car. He spoke the words but did they actually come out of his mouth? Did anyone hear them?

There was a long pause.

"What are *you* studying?" said Raghavendran at last. Again he had spoken the words. They were half speech, half mumble. He was amazed that a sound came out—any sound at all.

"I'm studying philosophy," said Anne.

"That must be interesting," said Raghavendran. His lips were warming up now. He must be getting better. He must!

146

"It *is* interesting," said Anne. "I especially like Eastern philosophy. Buddhism, Hinduism."

There was another pause.

"You *like* them?" said Raghavendran at last. He spoke with genuine surprise.

"I really do," said Anne. "I'd like to go to the East some day. Too much competition in the West. In the East it's much better. More relaxed. You're into your own soul, your own energy."

Another silence—this time a long silence—followed. Raghavendran wanted to say something, but he did not know what to say. He was amazed at the girl's words. How many words there were: how easily they came from her mouth. And the girl liked the East, she actually liked it!

But Raghavendran was from Madras—how far away the place was. He was short and dark. What do short and dark men really know?

Vinay began to speak up. He spoke about the restaurant—he had eaten there once before. He spoke about the movie—he had heard good things about it. The girls agreed.

They continued on their way to the restaurant. It was not a great beginning. But things would get better—of course they would. They often did.

***

They arrived at the restaurant parking lot. Raghavendran got out, closed the door behind him. He thought that perhaps he should go to the other

147

side, open the door for Anne. He rushed over, but the door was already open. "Please," he said, bowing again and holding out his hand slightly.

"Thank you," said Anne.

He closed the door after her. But apparently the door did not close shut all the way. The others were already walking towards the restaurant.

"Vinay," he called softly.

He did not seem to hear.

"Vinay," he called again, more loudly this time.

The other turned.

"The door," he called out, his words barely audible. He gestured with his hands. How forlornly—how desperately—he gestured. "The door, the door ...," he tried to say.

Vinay understood—at last he understood. He walked back to the car. He put in his keys, unlocked the door. Then he closed the door—simply, firmly.

What a confident boy Vinay was. Raghavendran admired him. How could he not? Were there really people like this in the world? And not just Americans—that you could understand. The tall Americans, the handsome Americans. But Indians—Indians as well.

***

They arrived inside, they sat at the table. It was a small round table in the back corner. Boy, girl, boy, girl. Raghavendran did not know what to do. He looked at the red tablecloth—he liked the dark color.

148

He looked into the air. He looked at the far corner of the restaurant. He lifted the tablecloth slightly, looked at his shoes. From somewhere some water came, glasses with water and ice. He lifted one glass, drank a little. His throat felt better. Or did it?

He liked the glass, he liked holding it. When he held the glass, his hands were not idle. He lifted the glass, drank from it several times in small sips. When he drank from the glass, his mouth was not idle. It was occupied and he was not required to speak.

But could he hold the glass forever? Could he drink the water forever as well?

Raghavendran again looked at the tablecloth. He wanted to talk about the things he knew. But who would care? Boyle's law of gases. What a simple and perfect law it was. Cells and molecules and the new computer technology that was changing everything. But who would care? He wanted to talk about polymers and peptides—sometimes they were stable, sometimes not. They were important to enzymes, to antibiotics, to medicines. But who would care?

"Do you like movies?" Someone had spoken to him. Who had spoken? It was Anne again. She was a polite girl. Or was she just laughing at him?

Raghavendran had seen a movie with Vinay two months earlier. *Live and Let Die*. Did that count?

He mentioned the movie—he mentioned that he had seen it two months ago.

"The James Bond movie?" said Anne with some surprise. "You like James Bond?"

"It is the first movie I have seen."

149

"The first movie ever?"

"No no, the first movie with Mister James Bond."

Mister James Bond. Anne smiled. Cheryl and Vinay smiled as well. How strangely he put it, how quaintly.

Vinay said that Roger Moore was in the movie, not Sean Connery. It was the first movie with the new James Bond.

"And what did you think?" said Anne, again addressing the quaint one. "Did you like Roger Moore?"

"Yes," said Raghavendran. "He is a handsome man. Very handsome."

Again Anne was surprised at the response. "And the *acting*?" she said. "Did you like the acting?"

Here Raghavendran was at something of a loss. Roger Moore was a handsome man. So was James Bond. They were dashing and confident. So confident with everything, especially the women. But that he was an actor. That he was acting …

"I would like to see other James Bond movies," said Raghavendran.

Anne was intrigued by the answer. Perhaps the others were intrigued as well. Raghavendran spoke with honesty. Was it so bad to be honest? Was honesty not needed in the world?

The garlic bread and breadsticks came. They nibbled on them. The drinks came—the girls and Vinay had cocktails, Raghavendran had Coke with ice. How he loved the glass again, how he loved the ice. The bigger the glass, the better. The more the ice, the better. You could drink and drink; you could chew and chew.

America was not an easy place. There were people and people around you—so many handsome and pretty people. There were girls around you—so many pretty girls. What were you supposed to do with them? What exactly were you supposed to do?

The main food came. Thank God it came. Raghavendran picked at the food. He struggled with the spaghetti—he had eaten spaghetti only once before. How hard it was to wrap it around your fork. How hard to put in your mouth. But he tried; he tried.

His face was hot. Sometimes he felt it getting hotter. But as long as you were eating, you did not have to talk so much. And was that so bad?

Was that really so bad?

***

The meal went on, Raghavendran survived the meal. The food was there—it kept you busy. Vinay was a dashing boy, he told good jokes, good stories. Perhaps if he were fair-skinned—just a little more fair-skinned—he could be in the James Bond movies himself.

The meal kept them busy, there was no time for dessert. It was almost eight-thirty, the movie began at nine.

They left the restaurant and they hurried to the movie theater. Vinay drove and told jokes; he drove and told jokes. He told a joke about a man who went to the market to get some rice. The joke had something to do with pronunciation: "nice" and "mice," "nice" and "mice." He told a joke about a farmer who raised sheep. What a talented boy he was. He could do so many things at the same time. If Raghavendran had one-tenth his talent, one-hundredth ...

Raghavendran felt something on his knee. Did it happen? Did he imagine it? Raghavendran was sitting in the back, the same place on the left side, his hands resting beside him. A hand had reached over—what hand? It had rested on his knee.

They say that dark men cannot get darker. Do they really know? They say that dark men do not blush. Do they really know? The hand rested there for two seconds, for three. Vinay swerved the car to make a sharp right turn; the hand was removed.

Raghavendran sat there in the darkness. He sat immobile. Was the hand really there? Why? Was it removed? Why? Perhaps he was expected to do something in return. What was he expected to do? Vinay had not told him. He should have told him. He was a talented boy, so talented. And yet. And yet ...

***

They arrived at the movie theater, they made it just in time. They had just eaten, no one was in the mood for popcorn. They sat four rows from the back: boy, girl, girl, boy. Vinay and Raghavendran were each at the end, the girls in the middle. Raghavendran felt lost. Vinay was his friend, his lifeboat, his savior. Why was he so far away? What would he do with him so far away?

But thank God they were at a movie, an *event*. Something was in front of them. They were not expected to speak—or were they? It would be rude to speak.

The trailers came on. Every so often Vinay whispered something to Cheryl, Cheryl to Anne. Raghavendran sat in the darkness, immobile.

The trailers were over, the movie came on. It was a police story. Al Pacino—a handsome man. As the movie went on, he grew a beard and looked even more handsome. Raghavendran had never grown a beard. Should he grow a beard? But it would be black, pitch black, not like the brown beard of Al Pacino. Would the girls like it? Of course they would not. They were pretty girls, white girls. Why should they?

Al Pacino was a policeman. There was corruption, there were bad policemen. In one scene a woman was being raped and they briefly showed her breasts. Raghavendran blushed. In another scene the hero and his girlfriend were taking a bath together. Again Raghavendran blushed. He was glad that it was dark in the theater. No one could see him blushing.

But his breathing became hard. Could they hear his breathing? Were they laughing at him? Was *she*?

The bad scenes were over, thank God. There were other, better scenes. Scenes in the police building, scenes on the streets. Al Pacino spoke—he spoke with such a nice, confident accent. Were there really people like this in the world?

The movie went on, went on. They sat in the darkness and it went on for over two hours. There was a girl next to him. A *beautiful* girl. In the car she had put her hand on his knee—or had she? Was he supposed to do something? To hold her hand—the tips of the fingers, just the tips. Or to press her hand against his cheek. Would it begin to burn? Was it burning even now?

He heard whispers to his left, soft and delicate. They had something to whisper about. They knew how to do it.

He sat there by himself. He was from Madras, the famous college there—Presidency College. Third in his class, near the top, the very top. But how far away Madras was. How small he sometimes felt. How small.

The movie ended, the credits began to come on the screen. Some of the lights, but not all, turned on.

"Did you like it?" said Anne.

"Yes yes, a good movie," said Raghavendran. "Very good."

Anne asked the two people on her left. They liked the movie as well.

They all liked the movie but now it was time to leave. They made their way to the exit.

***

Vinay and Cheryl walked ahead, Raghavendran and Anne followed. The confident ones were holding hands now. Had they been holding hands in the darkness as well?

Raghavendran watched Vinay and Cheryl in awe. How effortless they were, how natural. Perhaps it was an art. One must study it for years and years. Or perhaps it came naturally. It came only to a handful—the chosen few. And the others, the others …

They arrived at the car, they returned to their seats. Raghavendran thought that he would sit in his usual place but Anne had already sat there, on the left side. Why did she do it—was there a reason? Things happened so fast. Sometimes they happened so fast your head was spinning. But perhaps this was America—or perhaps even the world. Nothing stayed the same. Nothing ever stayed the same.

They talked about going out for coffee. At first the girls said yes, but then Anne said that she was tired. It was almost midnight, they would do it another night.

Raghavendran was not stupid, he knew. It was because of him. Of him.

They drove up to the girls' house. The girls got out, Vinay got out as well. Raghavendran was lost, he did not know what to do. He began to get out but Vinay and Cheryl were now standing outside, kissing; Anne was standing outside his side of the door—he could not open the door without hitting her. He stared straight ahead at the windshield. Then he thought he should at least lower his window, say a polite goodbye to Anne. He lowered the window a little, it made a squeaking sound. It was not much but it was there. Vinay and Cheryl were startled, awakened from their embrace. They looked at Raghavendran. At last he rolled down the window a little more.

"Thank you, Anne," he said. "Thank you for a nice evening."

Anne held out her hand. "Thank you, Ragu."

Raghavendran was sitting, the window was just partly open. He could just get part of his hand atop the window glass. The hands did touch this time. But just the tips of the fingers, no more.

"Goodnight, goodnight," everyone said again and the girls walked up to their house. Vinay walked them to the door. Raghavendran stayed in the back seat. He thought again of getting up, of saying a more proper goodbye. But it was too late.

***

When Vinay returned to the car, Raghavendran was still in the back seat.

"Time to go," said Vinay, his voice cheerful.

"Should I come to the front?" said Raghavendran.

"Yes yes, of course, of course."

They drove for a short time. "The girls are nice," said Vinay.

"Yes," said Raghavendran.

"They live in a nice neighborhood—don't they live in a nice neighborhood?"

"Yes," said Raghavendran.

They drove for another few minutes. "I am an idiot," Raghavendran said at last.

There was no answer.

"I am an idiot," he said again.

"Oh cheer up," said Vinay. "You were fine, just fine. It takes practice. Just practice."

What a confident boy Vinay was. How nice. How reassuring.

They made their way home.

When Raghavendran arrived, the roommates were asleep. Thank God they were asleep. He went to his room, he changed. He went to the bathroom, he threw water on his face. He washed his face with soap and water, he rubbed and rubbed. He threw water on his face, more water.

"I am an idiot," he said again.

He walked back to his room. "But the knee," he suddenly remembered. "Was it my imagination? No no, it wasn't. But what was I supposed to do? What?"

America was a confusing place. No no, the world was confusing, the whole world. He was getting his PhD in Chemistry. Chemistry, ha! He knew so little about the world, the real world.

Raghavendran lay in bed that night, awake for hours. He thought about Madras—how far away it was. He thought about America—what a difficult place it was. He thought about Anne. She was sweet, she was kind. He was an idiot, but she was not. She was sweet, she was kind.

There were so many things he did not know. So many.

"I will go out tomorrow," he suddenly said out loud. "I will go by myself, I will order spaghetti. I will practice and practice. Is that not what Vinay says?" And then, more softly: "Eating spaghetti isn't hard. I will learn. I will learn."

The next night Raghavendran Ramachandran did indeed go out by himself. He walked to a restaurant almost two miles away. He went to eat spaghetti. He had so much to learn.

He sat at the table, he rolled the spaghetti around in his fork. Again and again he did it. "And the knife," he reminded himself. "Don't forget to use the knife."

He was short, he was dark. But what did that matter? He was not James Bond, he was not Al Pacino. But what did that matter? He would practice, he would practice. And he would get better. He would, he would!

D.K. Choudhary

He went to the State Bank of India (or was it the Indian Bank?). It was in Defence Colony—across from the Minar Hotel.

He climbed the narrow, and winding, steps. He went to see Mister D.K. Choudhary. He worked in the Pension Department.

But Mister Choudhary was not there.

"Where is he?"

"Out to lunch."

"When will he be back?"

"He did not say."

"There is a chair here, the cane bottom sagging. Can I sit in the chair, can I wait?"

The other did not say anything. He took that for assent. He lowered himself carefully, he sat down.

The other seemed even, and perhaps suddenly, to have grown sullen. He lowered his head to the work in front of him, he returned to this work.

Work—what work did he do? There was a ledger open in front of him. It was a wide ledger, not so long but wide. There was a left side: a green page with criss-crossing lines. There was a right side: a blue page with crisscrossing lines. There was a wide column to the left, with some words written in the column. Perhaps these were the names of people, of accounts. Next to the wide column there were narrow columns—three or four—with numbers in them. Perhaps these were the amounts—or "entries."

The visitor looked at the man with the ledger, he looked at him with interest. Who was the man, where did he come from? Was he educated, was he not? Was he married, was he not? Was he happy with his life (he did not seem to be), was he unhappy?

The visitor sat on the cane chair, he looked at the man. He sat there for a long time. But where was Mister Choudhary? Where was he—would he ever return?

***

The visitor had arrived at the bank at a few minutes before one o'clock. The clock struck one-thirty, then two. Two-thirty, and then two-forty. At last a man—a middle-aged man with a sallow complexion—began walking towards the desk.

"Mister Choudhary?" he whispered, looking at the man hunched over the ledger.

The other looked up, screwed his face—pushing out his right cheek. But he did not say anything.

The newcomer approached the desk, turned sideways, and, somehow, squeezed his way through to the chair.

"Mister Choudhary?"

The newcomer looked up quizzically (was it with disdain?), as if to say, "Who wants to know? Who could possibly be asking?"

"I am Kumar," said the other, "V.V. Kumar." And having said these words, he seemed to have a lump in his throat, he seemed to have exhausted himself—he suddenly stopped.

The newcomer, it turned out, was indeed the awaited—the esteemed—Mister Choudhary. He was a man of medium height. He had a small and slightly round face. But what stood out was not the size of the face or the roundness but the stubble—the white hair—on his face.

He had not shaved, it seemed, in days.

He wore green or greenish-brown pants. They were in the old style, cut very narrowly at the bottom. He wore a striped shirt, with vertical blue and yellow lines. The shirt hardly went with his pants—or with his complexion or his face.

But this is the kind of man he was—he seemed to be.

He worked in the Pension Department. It was not an exciting position; he hardly seemed to be excited—or was it even alive?—himself.

"I am Kumar," said the other, "V.V. Kumar. I have come to see you about a matter."

"A matter": this is just how he phrased it. It was quaint English, old-fashioned English. But the manner of the English—or the very fact that he spoke English to begin with—all this told a great deal perhaps about the visitor.

***

So he was there, at the Pension Department. He had waited for Mister Choudhary—waited for a long time. Mister Choudhary had arrived—arrived at last.

And what now? What next?

The visitor had brought a bag, four shirts in the bag. They were new shirts—shirts from America, imported shirts. Could they help him—help him at all in the matter at hand?

He took the bag from the floor (where he had rested it quietly), he offered it to the other.

"A small token," he said.

The other looked at him.

"Shirts. There are four of them, new, *imported* shirts." He emphasized the next-to-last word but only slightly, discreetly.

The other opened the bag a crack, looked at it for an instant. His face, the tight muscles, seemed to slacken. He opened the bottom drawer, on the right—but quietly, only a little—he put the bag in the drawer. Discreetly, just as discreetly, he closed the drawer.

There was a moment of silence. An awkwardness seemed to follow.

"Pension," said Mister Choudhary—he said at last. "So it is a matter …"—and he suddenly stopped short, in mid-sentence.

Another moment of silence—of awkwardness—followed.

Mister Kumar was at a loss, was hesitant. But he was the one who had come, he had to say something. Was it not expected—his *duty*?

And his tongue loosened, he began to speak. He explained the details—all the details of the case. The case (the papers) had been filed: such and such papers. The person had retired: such-and-such a date. Everything was legal (in duplicate, even in triplicate): "We have an STD and cyclostyling shop nearby—it is very reliable; everything is legal, it has been properly attested."

"So what is the problem?"

Mister Kumar seemed to be taken aback. He hesitated, he stammered. At last he blurted out: "The money."

"The money?"

"No money, no sums"—the very word he used—"no sums have been received. And it has been six months now." His voice seemed to trail off. "*Six* months," he added, as if to emphasize the time. But the words came out weakly—he was hardly audible.

Mister Choudhary looked at his visitor, his *petitioner*. He was struck by his discomfort but perhaps he was impressed—emboldened—by it as well. After all, was it not a compliment to him? The petitioner had come to see him. He was the man of authority, of power. It was to him that the petitioner turned; so much depended on him, on *him*.

***

That evening Mister Kumar came home, he told his family what had happened.

They were happy, they were hopeful. The children jumped up and down, the wife allowed herself a smile. Perhaps now the pension would come.

And did it?

That evening Mister Choudhary went home as well.

The children came running out, they asked for toffee. He reached into his pocket, he took out one.

His wife stood in the back, at the stove in the kitchen, her head covered with her sari.

He called her to the room and showed her the bag. He pulled out the shirts.

"Four," he said. "*Imported*," he said.

She did not know where the shirts were from. But she could guess.

She was pleased.

***

This was the beginning then, the early days. And what happened then, what happened next?

Mister Kumar waited for the pension check; every day he waited.

And did the check come?

He waited, he waited.

And did the check come?

Mister Kumar dressed, he put on his jacket and tie. (Should he not look respectable?)

He put on his respectable clothes and he went to Defence Colony. He went to the bank. He went to see Mister Choudhary.

"He is not here."

"Not here?"

"He is out of station."

"Out of station?"

And then the simple, the common: "He is not available."

Not available, not available. They say that Mister Choudhary was not available, he was *never* available.

They say that Mister Choudhary was not a bad man (not really). But he was not the most thought-ful, or most sensitive, man either. And when you are not thoughtful, you can become thoughtless. You can hurt others.

Mister Choudhary hurt—he hurt the life of Mister Kumar, of Mister Kumar's wife, of his children.

Was he aware of this?

Did he care—did he even *care*?

***

The days passed. Mister Kumar became sad. Mister Kumar became despondent. There was the sum, the matter of the "sums"—but these sums, where were they? These sums, would they ever arrive?

He had worked for the office, worked there for thirty-five years. He was entitled to the sums. He had earned them. It was not as if they were doing him a favor.

But these sums, where were they? These sums, would they ever come?

Many days passed. A relative—a relative of a relative—said that Mister Kumar was being too weak. He was, as the relative put it, "playing into the hands" of the others. He was being meek, playing the petitioner, playing well—"too well"—the role of the petitioner.

"Write them a letter," he said.

"A letter?"

"I don't mean any letter. I mean an official letter, a *harsh* letter."

Mister Kumar was taken aback by the words. A harsh letter—what kind of talk was this?

The relative went into the details. The letter should be typed, not handwritten. The letter should be sent by registered mail. The letter should indicate how many trips Mister Kumar had already made to the bank—how many personal trips, without avail. And most of all, said the relative, copies of the letter—copies should be sent to the headquarters bank in Tamil Nadu—to the Reserve Bank there as well.

Mister Kumar was aghast at the suggestions.

"It is done," said the other, "done all the time. They realize you mean business. It is the thing that works—it is the only thing that works."

***

Mister Kumar was a timid man. "Chicken-hearted," the others used to call him. It was not in his nature.

But he did what the relative had asked. He wrote the letter.

He wrote the letter, he took it to the relative. The relative looked at the letter, he laughed. "Please," "your Excellency," "if you could," "may I kindly," "may I humbly"—the letter was filled with these words, and words like them. The relative took the letter, he tore it into pieces (eight). He took the pieces, he threw them into the dustbin.

"Let us begin," he said, "let us begin again."

The relative dictated the new letter, Mister Kumar wrote. He dictated, Mister Kumar wrote. When they were done, Mister Kumar took the letter to the type-writing shop (the one in the market)—he had the girl there type it.

He sat in the corner, he proofread the letter. (How strong the words were.) His heart beat. (How loudly it beat.)

He came home, he proofread the letter. He proof-read it a second time, a third.

He showed the letter to his wife—she marveled at it.

He kept the letter at home—he kept it there for ten days. At last he gathered the courage. On the eleventh day, he took some glue, he sealed the letter. He took the letter to the post office—he mailed the letter.

Copies were to be sent to the important places. He had copied ("cyclostyled") the letter two days earlier. He put the copies in separate envelopes, he mailed them as well.

***

He mailed the letters, he felt a sense of relief. He arrived home, he was filled with hope.

But that afternoon—not surprisingly—the panic came. Send these letters, these "harsh" letters—what had made him do it? Was he sick, was he mad?

The panic left. He went to his wife, she comforted him. The panic left, it returned. The panic left, it returned.

And Mister Kumar waited (he waited). He waited for the answers. He waited to see what would happen now—what would happen next.

Mister Kumar waited. He waited for weeks, he waited for months.

No answers came.

He waited, he waited.

No answers came.

One day he received a package in the mail. He opened the package, wondered what was inside.

But the package was empty. (There was nothing inside.)

One day he received a package in the mail. He opened the package, wondered what was inside.

But the package was empty. (There was nothing inside.)

One day he received a package in the mail. He opened the package, wondered what was inside.

There were three books. *A Sanskrit Primer* (by E.D. Perry). *10,000 Urdu Words* (by Sultan Nathani). *Cosmetology* (no author). What strange books they were—what a strange *combination* of books.

He looked at the return address on the package: there was none. He looked—he tried to look—at the postmark. He had difficulty making out the words. But "Tamil Nadu"—did they not say "Tamil Nadu"?

He was getting old, his eyes were weak. He took the package—took it to his wife.

She was younger, but only by three years. She had difficulty making out the words as well.

He took the package—took it to the children.

"Tamil Nadu," they said. "Papa. Tamil Nadu."

He had sent copies of the letters—sent them to headquarters. The people at headquarters had replied. But this, was *this* their response? The response meant something, had to mean something. But the response, what did it mean? What *could* it mean?

***

Sanskrit is an ancient language. It is a difficult language. Not many people can understand it—can dare to understand it. There are roots and stems, *visargas* and *anusvaras*. But for those who do understand it, secrets are inside. Sometimes—with effort—the secrets are even revealed.

Mister Kumar was a hopeful man. Would the secrets be revealed. To him, to *him*?

He looked at the Sanskrit book. He looked at the other books as well. He put the books on top of each other. He put the books in the corner.

Sometimes he opened the books, glanced through them casually. Sometimes he read the books—read them from the very beginning: letter by letter, page by page.

And the answers that he was looking for—the secrets—did he find them? The secrets, were they revealed?

***

One day a man came to the house.

(Who was this man?)

He was an old man, he walked with a stick. He was dressed simply, in a white shirt, white pajamas.

He knocked on the door.

"Yes?"

"Have you understood?" he said.

"Understood?"

"A package was sent. Have you received the package?"

One day a man came to the door. He was an old man, his face was smeared with ash.

"One must see—it is not always easy."

"Easy?"

"But one must try—one must try."

One day a child came to the door. He had a toffee in one hand, a paper—a small piece of paper—in the other.

He kept the toffee (how could he not?)—he held out the paper.

Mister Kumar reached for the paper.

The child dropped the paper. He turned, giggling, and ran away.

There were words on the paper, they were printed in small, faint letters.

"Have you understood?" they said (they seemed to say). "Have you understood?"

***

Mister Kumar was a simple man—there were many things that he did not understand. A package had been received, yes. But this package, what did it *mean*?

He had asked for "sums"—were these the sums? He had asked for sums that were due to him—sums that had not been paid (that were in "arrears" now for years). And these—were *these* the sums?

One day Mister Kumar rose, he turned to his wife.

But she was a simple woman. What did she know?

One day he rose, he went to the Pension Department.

Mister Choudhary was there, he looked at him. Mister Kumar babbled, he explained, he tried to explain.

Mister Choudhary was a busy man. Do you think he cared?

One day he rose, he went to the relative—the "kind" relative—who had helped him write the letter.

"Has a response been received?"

"Yes."

"Is there a postmark?"

"Yes."

"One must not be greedy."

"Greedy?"

"One must receive what is due—nothing more, nothing more."

"Nothing more, nothing more." What strange words they were.

But Mister Kumar was a simple man. What did he know about the world—what did he really know?

***

That night Mister Kumar had a dream. He dreamed that he was in an office (or perhaps in a cell). There were ledgers around him—all kinds of ledgers. There were words in the ledger, there were numbers. How neat they all were, how clean.

He bent down, he tried to make out the words: he

could not do it. He bent down, he tried to make out the numbers: he could not do it.

But how clean the words were (the numbers): how clean, how *clean*.

Mister Kumar rose from his dream, he felt an emptiness in his stomach. He rose, he felt an emptiness in his heart.

But he should be strong (should he not). Something had been received, something. And was that not sufficient? Something had been received (something). And was that not the key?

One day he opened the Sanskrit book, there were some words inside (on page 3):

> *By the water which drops*
> *from the clouds*
> *upon the fields*
> *the grain grows tall.*

Were these the words, the secret words?
He turned to another page:

> *In a kingless land the rich do not sleep.*

And again:

> *Having sipped water thrice, one wipes the*
> *lips twice; according to others, once.*

Were these the words, were *these*?

He looked at the books—how nice they were. He looked at the package—it was a nice package. He looked at the postmark—how nice it was, how nice as well.

One day he went to his wife, he lay down at her feet.

Do you think it helped?

One day he went to the temple, he prayed.

Do you think it helped?

One day Mister Kumar rose, he went for a walk. It was an overcast day, he walked for a long time.

There were some birds in the sky: how happy they looked. There were some children in the distance: how easy their world was, how free.

"A response has been received?"

"Yes."

"One must not be greedy."

"No."

"One must receive what is due—nothing more, nothing more."

They were odd words, what odd words they were. But Mister Kumar was a simple man—there was much that he did not understand. He was a simple man—there was much that he did not see.

One day he opened the book, *10,000 Urdu Words* (the inside cover):

> *Due to his hard work, integrity and fore-sight he rose to be a leading industrialist.*

He turned to *Cosmetology* (p. 91):

> *The hair must be kept dry—especially*
> *before retiring to sleep.*

He turned, again, to *A Sanskrit Primer* (various pages):

> *All guilt departs from one-who-has-done-*
> *penance.*
> *Iron is lighter than gold, but heavier than*
> *wood.*
> *The gates of the city were shut fast; the*
> *citizens equipped themselves for battle.*

Were these the words, were *these*?

Mister Kumar rose, he went to the market to buy vegetables. He left the market, he went to the chemist. He left the chemist, he went to the store.

He came home, the gates were shut (what gates?). He came home, the citizens were equipped (what citizens?). He was told the battle would be fierce, that it would last for a long time.

(Battle—what battle?)

They say that the battle is a nice battle. Sometimes you win, sometimes you lose. Sometimes the rules are clear, sometimes they are not.

But it is a keen affair; it is joined; it is fun!

In *Cosmetology* (p. 214), there are the words:

The wayfarer was troubled and spent a sleepless night. But he combed his hair (he combed it thrice). He parted it in the middle (exactly there). And he was at peace again—he was again at peace.

Mister Kumar was a simple man (how simple). He was a timid man (how timid). Perhaps one day he would be wise. Perhaps one day he would understand. Perhaps one day—one day he would see.

Notes of
a Mediocre Man

I am a product of my age: mean, jealous, vindictive. I hate my neighbors, I hate their successes. I hate Justices of the Supreme Court: I find them dull. I hate schools of government: I find them silly. I hate law schools: I find them limited. I hate Aristotle: he would, if living, be a professor of law—at least on a part-time basis. I hate the black and women's movements: I find them aggressive. I hate movements in general: I find them vulgar. I hate *The New York Times* and *The Washington Post*: I find them smug. I hate people who ride bicycles and go to museums: I find them phony.

But of course, of course, I must stop. I am, by nature, a shy, a deferential person. And I do not wish you to misunderstand. If I say the above things, it is only to catch your attention—to get you to stop by and chat, as it were, for a few minutes. I never have company anymore. The last visitor I had was Nankua, but that was over ten years ago. And of him, I can only speak later.

I really did not mean to offend you. But perhaps I presume even to think that I *could* offend you. And for that, too, I apologize. The differences in our positions are, after all, so great. You rule the world or, at the least, live in it. I neither rule nor live; I merely exist, on the fringes.

But I say this not to invite your pity. I am, in my own ways, a proud man. And even in my despondent, my pitiful, state, pity is something that I will not tolerate. It is the one thing that still sets my teeth on edge. And, as the doctors say, that is not good for me, not good for my heart condition.

I will be forty next month, but I look more like fifty-five, even sixty. I have always looked older than my years, but the situation has—I suppose—never been so bad. In my youth, it was not uncommon for people, even those my age, even girls on whom I may have had other, more sublime, designs, to address me as "Sir." But girls are with me a sensitive, delicate topic, and I would like, with your permission, not to get into it. Actually I don't need your permission not to discuss the topic; it is one that I could not even be dragged into. But I thought that, just to be polite, just to be civil, I would ask.

Perhaps you think that by mentioning my pride and through refusing to discuss certain topics, I am trying to reassert myself, that I am really a cunning and duplicitous creature. If that is the impression I have created, then, my friends—I hope that you do not mind me calling you that—then, my friends, I am truly sorry. What you take for duplicity is probably just awkwardness, social maladroitness, on my part. I am so out of the habit of talking to people, *real* people that is. I do talk a lot to myself, to my doctors, and to the birds outside my window, but that isn't quite the same.

With doctors, for example, you cannot really discuss anything important. The conversation is always so one-sided: "Take care of your health," they say. "Do you want to die an early death? Run, walk, exercise. And for heaven's sake, no, for *your* sake, improve that terrible posture. Why must you always walk with that stoop in your shoulders?" Doctors don't understand that to improve your posture, you need something to improve it for. "Improve it for yourself," they'll say. If it were only so simple!

Doctors tell you, too, to get a lot of fresh air. They do not realize that if there is no incentive, there is, again, no point to it. "No point to it," they'll say. "So you want to wilt and wither, that's up to you." To them everything is medicine, medicine and more medicine. They know so little about *real* life.

With birds, one can discuss music, even a little philosophy. But they are so busy with their own activities. And besides, their attention span is so short. They have no compunctions about leaving you in the middle of a sentence, about flying away to wherever it is that suits their momentary fancy.

To discuss real things, one needs real people. People who live real lives. And that is why it is so good to have you here.

***

I am an average man, limited and insecure. And that is why I said above that I do not like newspapers. Especially certain kinds. Newspapers always talk about successful people, about people who are "newsworthy." And yet, what do these people have to do with me? I am almost forty years old now and in my life I have done nothing. Till two years ago when a distant relative left me an inheritance, I worked as an accountant for a major multinational corporation. The corporation may have been major and multinational but I wasn't; I was only an accountant. In my eighteen years with the corporation, I received only two promotions. And even they were very early in my "career."

For the past two years I have not even been an accountant. I have been, in your language, a "has-been." But no, even that implies that once, somewhere in the past, I was something. And I *never* was anything—except perhaps in my dreams. Of dreams I had quite a few but I learned, with the years, that I was only fooling myself. By dreaming, an average man is only asking for trouble. He is creating expectations, even great ones, that he can never meet. And, like me, he will end up disappointed, an angry and embittered man.

Newspapers talk about Kings and Queens, about Presidents and Prime Ministers. They talk about Senators and Congressmen, about Secretaries and

Assistant Secretaries. And what do these people have to do with me?

"But newspapers are also the voice of the people," you will say. "If you are dissatisfied with the way they are run, then write and let them know."

Well, I did write to newspapers several times in my youth, perhaps as many as a hundred. And not once did they print my letters. Worse: they did not even acknowledge them. It was as if I never existed!

On two occasions, I even sent long articles to newspapers. One time I spoke about the aesthetics of the rise and fall of the Roman Empire. The other time I proved, beyond the shadow of a doubt, the hypocrisy of our ways. But both my articles were turned down. This time I did receive acknowledgments from the papers, but it would have been better if I hadn't. The papers maintained that my articles were "reactionary," "nonsense," "a practical joke." And I had put so much of myself, my soul, into them! Though exhausted and drained from my job, I had toiled through the nights working on the articles. They were to have been my *début*, my *bonjour*, as it were, into the world of letters. But the papers would have none of them.

I especially used to enjoy reading the sports sections of papers. I had, over the years, my baseball heroes, my football heroes, my boxing heroes. I read of my heroes with relish; I relived, with childlike delight, every one of their exploits. But that was all right as long as I was young and these heroes were older than me; as I got older and the heroes became—or seemed to become—younger, my affection for them vanished. All of my dreams, you see, have always been based on comparing myself with those older than me. If others know or can do something that I cannot, that is, I tell myself, understandable; I am, after all, younger than them. I am in training, preparing for the future when I will *really* show them. And if *I* know something that others don't, I am ecstatic. How quaint, how remarkable I tell myself. I know more than my fellow men—and I am so much younger!

And so, in my youth, I worshipped my heroes: safely, unthreateningly, from a distance of age. I read the sports sections with passion, like a famished mouse set loose upon cheese. But, of course, it is too late for that now. I am old and I can no longer fool myself. As long as the birth rate is greater than the death rate—in this day and age an incontrovertible fact—both the number and proportion of people older than me will inevitably, inexorably, keep decreasing. In the freakish case that all deaths are consistently of those *younger* than me, the number of people older than me will stay constant; the proportion of such people will still decrease. It is a mathematical law, I cannot deny it. Fairly soon, I will have no seniors to compare myself with!

And so, with the same zeal with which I once devoured the sports pages, I now avoid them. And, too, sports pages have developed a new habit nowadays of telling which athletes went to which schools. Perhaps it is an old habit, one that I simply never noticed before. But old or new, why they must get into it at all, I do not know. Perhaps they do it simply to spite me. They know that I went to a state university; and vicious devils that they are, they will not let me live it down.

***

But it is not only the sports pages that are after me. On the more "serious" pages—the editorial pages, for example—they always have articles from professors at certain schools: Harvard, Yale, MIT. Professors of government, professors of public policy, professors of economics, professors of physics. What in Lord's name have I to do with any of them? On the "news" pages they speak of the rising costs at certain other schools. What in Lord's name do I have to do with rising costs and admissions policies? I have never charged anyone an exorbitant price and I have never been admitted anywhere.

Even my once beloved matrimonial pages are no longer safe. In my youth—my wondrous youth—I used to dream of women and love and matrimony. I vowed above never to discuss this topic, but I will mention it here, just this once, to show, if nothing else, how far *all* my dreams have been shattered. In my youth, full of hopes and plans, I used to read the matrimonial pages with awe. Would I, too, share some day the bliss of these loving couples? There was always such pride in the smiles of the grooms, such twinkle in the eyes of the brides. Now, an old and broken man, I know that I was only fooling myself; conjugal happiness was never fated for me. But must papers compound my misery, must they add salt to my wound, by telling me that groom A went to Dartmouth and bride B to Vassar? That groom X received his law degree from Chicago and bride Y her PhD from Princeton? Isn't it enough that these couples are happy, that they are couples, and that I am unhappy, *single*?

"But," you will say, "matrimonial pages always mentioned school degrees, only you never noticed them."

Perhaps I didn't notice them, but cannot newspapers be a little considerate? Cannot they appreciate, just once, the plight of an old and average man, a man who went to a state university and is tired of being belittled?

But of course, of course, it isn't only the newspapers. Magazines and television networks are at it, too. Top ten law schools, top ten medical schools, top ten graduate schools, top ten MBA schools. Starting salaries for law school graduates, starting salaries for B-school graduates. And, too, the neighbors: my son the salutatorian, my daughter the valedictorian; my daughter-in-law the medical student, my son-in-law the dental student.

What, I ask again, has an average man to do with such matters? They are the stuff of kings and queens, of aristocracies and meritocracies. I am willing to admit that others are more intelligent than I am—I cannot but admit it—but must such intelligence always be displayed at the market place? Cannot it be kept at least a little private?

A few years ago *The Washington Post* had a running "debate" between two columnists on which school, Harvard or Oxford, was better. My Lord! One columnist, a Harvard graduate, defended—naturally—the crimson point of view. The other, an Oxford graduate, spoke for the Oxford side. Each spokesman introduced apparently serious arguments but the debate was too good-natured, too much of a charade. And what, I ask you, was the *real* purpose of the debate? But, of course, to allow *both* columnists an opportunity to reveal, and to bask in the glory of, their alma maters. And the unstated, but clear, presumption? That, of course, *both* schools are not only good, but exceptional!

I have a fantasy—when my dreams fail me I turn to fantasies, you might say, but what else is an average man to do?—I have a fantasy that one day an edict is passed that prohibits, absolutely prohibits, people from revealing the schools of their past. Violation of the edict is punishable by life imprisonment. People must complete resumes without mentioning the names of their schools; they must seek jobs and undergo interviews under the same constraints; they cannot even mention their schools in casual conversations. Even mentioning geographical locations—Cambridge, Palo Alto, New Haven—in suggestive ways is prohibited. The enforcement of the edict is absolute; the inspectors show no mercy. What would happen under such a rule?

"All nonsense," you will say, "a madman's hallucinations."

But what, my friends, *would* happen? Would not the whole society, especially the elite-aristocratic-privileged component of it, stand on the brink of collapse? Would not many, unable to bear such a state, a state in which they cannot reveal their precious backgrounds, take their lives?

"But only a handful," you will retort, "only a fanatic handful."

The others would hold out, then, but *for how long*? No degrees, no easy identifiers to distinguish themselves from the masses. Always the need to prove and reprove themselves. No *presumption* of intelligence. Would not the torture get, after a while, too much? Would not they, too, commit suicide? Or go insane? Or, for the opportunity to proclaim just once, just once more, their separateness, their superiority, would not they readily risk life imprisonment? Or life imprisonment ten times over?

"Nonsense," you will say, "all nonsense. You are a fanatic, a madman, a sick man. You invite us over on the pretext of a chat and then you embarrass us with your ravings. *Fantasies*, you call them. If you went to a state university that is *your* problem; you should have been more intelligent. If you have insecurities, take them elsewhere: to a doctor, a psychiatrist—or to one of your precious birds. If you have dirty laundry, bare it in the washroom. But leave *us* out! Our patience has a limit!"

But of course, gentlemen, ladies—my friends—I did not mean to offend you. I was, as you say, only raving. I *am* insecure, and old and lonely. And sometimes my thoughts get away from me. I went to a state university and I *do* feel inferior. And though I may claim to speak for all the dispossessed, and lonely, and forgotten—all the others who never made the elite—I speak, really, only for myself. What concern have I for others? What have they ever done for me? Just accept *me*, somehow, in your group, and I will be your slave for life. I have, you see, a little cash, a little money that I would not be unwilling to share.

But no no, you must forgive me; I see that you are getting angry again. I really did not wish to offend you. It just slipped out, as it were. I am, my friends, so out of practice. I have not spoken to anyone for so long. You must forgive me.

***

Not that I wish to beat a dead horse—I could not beat anyone really even if I tried; I am, after all, so frail and weak now—but nonetheless the questions do gnaw at me. Why was I left out? Why was I excluded from the elite? Was it my receding hairline? My effeminate voice? My snubbed nose?

"There you go again," you say, "still harping on the same issues, now beating not one but a stableful of horses. You were left out because you were too stupid, because you did not cut the mustard; because you struck others, as you strike us, as unstable, mad. But finally, when it comes down to it, we do not care *why* you were left out. It is your own private problem; even raising it is in bad taste."

Thank you, my friends, for your honesty, pierce me though it may. Forthrightness is something that I have always admired in you, even tried to emulate. But one more question, my friends, or perhaps two. Not about myself this time, for that is in bad taste, but about society. The laws of society are so much more impersonal, even scientific. To take, therefore, a societal law at random. Why, my friends, must society assume— no, *pre*sume—the intelligence of people from certain schools, and put that, of others, always to the test?

"More nonsense," you say, "cryptic utterances. More ravings of a madman."

But let me explain, my friends, let me explain. Do you not, my friends, *pre*sume the intelligence of my neighbor, the Harvard graduate, and ask me repeatedly to prove mine? If my Harvard colleague works at a job that is, shall we say, intellectually undemanding, you say, "He chooses to." But if I work at the same job, you note, "He couldn't but work there, he had no choice. It was the only thing that, given his intelligence, he could find."

"But I judge a man by his ability," you will retort. "Hell, I've known a lot of stupid people from Harvard."

But of course, my friends, how well, how *poetically* you put it. And if you find my Harvard colleague stupid, don't you add, at least mentally, at least silently:

"I wonder how he got accepted there; it must have been a mistake." Don't you, my friends, presume that the Harvard norm is intelligence and don't you seek reasons, extenuating circumstances, to explain, to justify—mostly to yourself—any seeming deviations from the norm?

"But suppose I do," you say, a bit more excitedly, a bit more angrily now, "suppose, for the sake of argument, that I *do* presume the intelligence of the Harvard man? Would not I, as a rule, be right? Harvard is the archetype of our meritocracy, our way of separating the wheat from the chaff. The archetype may be imperfect, and we may not always choose the most intelligent—or we may not even know what intelligence is to begin with, in fact we may have it all wrong—but the archetype *is* something. And certainly it is better than anything you can come up with."

But I have my doubts, my friends, my several doubts. I am like Thomas (one of the twelve, called Did'-y-mus) a skeptic. I maintain that the differences between the Harvard representative and the others are minimal. Fortuities, circumstances, accidents of birth: one had the opportunities, the parents, the counselors, the other did not. But then again, my friends, what am I talking about? What do I care about others? My concern is not societal laws, but myself, only *me*. And besides, what is in a name? Nothing! And even if there were something, why should I let that obsess me? What should I care what others think—about schools, or meritocracies, or about anything else?

"Precisely," you say, "precisely. You keep harping on the same tedious points because you cannot get them out of your system. For all your postures, your alleged disclaimers, you probably believe, no, you *do* believe, more in names, in elites, than all of us put together."

Of course, my friends, you are right. I *do* believe in names—in a name, everything! Include me in your choice group, give me a T-shirt, a decal, and I will— I have said it once, I will say it again—be your slave for life.

But then again, my friends, will I? Perhaps I say the above only for show, for dramatic effect. Though I beg for membership in your club, perhaps I am only rehearsing, putting on airs. For, when you think about it, what good would it do? With your praise and applause, I might learn to shed the old skin and claim, like Augustine, to be a new man. But I would only be fooling myself, wouldn't I? Because, my friends—and this is the *real* point—if I *really* had the ability, if I *really* cut the mustard, I could do it even without your club, without you, without any of you. My genius would come out—somehow. Fortuities, accidents, circumstances of birth: I would overcome them all.

The latter are, of course, not completely irrelevant. If they are so stacked against you that you die, for example, an infant death, then you will, obviously, never get anyplace. But if the fortuities and circumstances are within *reason*—within *limits*—then a genius will manifest himself, regardless of others. It is a law of nature; it cannot be denied.

And *that,* my friends, is my torment, my beastly burden. The knowledge that even if I were admitted to the world's choicest group, I would—even with all my effort—be, at best, only an ordinary member. No, perhaps even a good member, even a very good one, but—and this is the key—*never* the exceptional one. Not Marx, not Einstein, not Shakespeare. Not even an exceptional professor who writes to newspapers. Finally, in the ways that matter most, only an average and mediocre man. Nothing.

***

An average and mediocre man. Nothing.
An average and mediocre man. Nothing.
An average and mediocre man …
But the question remains, my friends, it remains. An average and mediocre man in this society, just what does he do? All this success and publicizing of success around him. What exactly does he do?

You do not care, my friends, I know you do not. But hear me out—do hear me out. Your lives are full, are happy. You are part of the elites. You go to Venice, you go to *Chez Panisse* and have your Merlot or Pinot Noir. But if you do not want a revolution in your hands—chaos, chaos—should not something be done?

I am an average and mediocre man. What should such a man—what should *I*—do?

Do I join the ranks of the worshippers, those who praise the successful ones? Do I say, like Eliot's

Prufrock, that I am not Prince Hamlet, nor was meant to be? That my role is to show up at the parade, to applaud, to applaud? To "swell a progress"?

Do I seethe in resentment, in rage, perhaps even plotting my "revenge"?

Do I retreat to a monastery and hide myself?

Do I resign myself to the facts, the cold facts, in front of me? Learn to keep a stiff upper lip? (And so on.)

Just what, my friends, just what do I do?

You do not care, my friends, I know you do not. But is it not in your self-interest to care? Revolution, chaos, is that what you want?

I have an idea, my friends, just an idea. I lie in bed, I think of these ideas. I live in my mouse hole, I think of these things. My idea, my friends, it is this. What if a law is passed that limits the publicizing of success? Or better yet, a law that limits success itself? Oh I admit, my friends, that the law would hurt a few. The gifted, the talented, the lucky—all those who, for some reason or other, have successes up their sleeve. But what about the rest, my friends, what about the rest? With the new law—the silence, the *curfew* on successes—the rest, the majority, would no longer feel so small or little. Or at least not to the same extent. So some would be hurt by the new law but many would be benefited—and we have to think, you know, of the greatest good for the greatest number. Yes yes, my friends, the greatest good for the greatest number, isn't that the key?

The many might realize at first that they were living with a lie, that those with successes up their sleeves, the gifted, were being muzzled, that their spirit was being broken. But what of their *own* spirit? What of their own spirit that had always been crushed, humiliated? And with time, you know, the passing of generations, even the "lieness" might disappear. Through atrophy, through disuse, the talents of the gifted might in *fact* become dead.

Yes yes, my friends, I am convinced that this is the answer. The only answer!

I see, my friends, that you are upset. "He wants to get rid of success," you say. "The madman wants to get rid of success. Is there no end to his ravings? Success is a good thing, but he wants to end it. He wants to pass a law, an actual law, to limit it. Does he think that it is actually possible? Does he think that it is good, actually good?"

It *is* good, my friends, of that I am convinced. All this success and this publicizing of success around a person. It makes people go mad. It creates new madmen every day.

But can it really be done, my friends, that is another matter. There are other average and mediocre people in the world. But will they join me in the push for this new law, really join me? Perverse beings that they are, they may (like me?) be more elitist than the elite themselves! "We need the exclusive clubs," they might say. "We need something to look up to, to strive for." Like the proletariat, they may, at times, be more capitalistic than the capitalists themselves (something Marx did not see). They do not want to get *rid* of management, you see, only to replace it with a better one. Or to make *themselves* the management.

No no, my friends, it will not be easy to bring about the new law. You will object; the masses might object as well.

But I have another idea, my friends. I lie in my mouse hole, I think of these things. I think, I think. If the success-limiting law is too extreme, is not another law—a *compromise*—possible? Yes yes, if the law is too extreme—anathema to the gifted, unacceptable to the ungifted or the forgotten—then we could, you know, choose a middle ground. We could be a bit more lenient, we could allow *some* successes. We could do it fair and square, not the way they do things in Russia, or in China. No no, we could do it by the lottery! The lottery would be held periodically, every year or so. Everyone would be allowed to enter, everyone would be allowed to participate, but—and this is the key—only a few people in each profession (law, literature, science, economics, you name it) would be chosen. Only *they* would be allowed to pursue success and, if successful, to *reveal* their successes. We wouldn't abolish the success stories, even the successes, but we would, at the least, *limit* them.

And something, you know, is better than nothing. We do need to limit—that, if nothing else.

You stand there, my friends, you listen to me. But are you convinced? Are you really convinced? I see that your nostrils are getting big, you are not really happy. But you are considering it—I can tell, I can tell. And that *is* encouraging, my friends. Is it not so?

I was thinking just recently, my friends, of the ancient Hindu texts. (Stay with me, I think of many things.) In these ancient texts, the name of the author is almost never given. I think they did it on purpose. On purpose, I say! It was the deed that mattered, not the doer, or the celebration of the doer. In Sanskrit the verb "to have" does not exist. Possessions (success, fame, etc.) are bad, they ensnare you, they corrupt you. They make you mad. The sentence "I have a house" does not exist, it cannot exist. It becomes, in Sanskrit, "With me a house is." The subject is the house, not the self; the verb is the simple verb of being. There are so many other examples in Sanskrit and in the other Indian languages—but I will not bore you with them.

No no, not that.

Your nostrils are still flaring, my friends, the blood has rushed to your head. I am not stupid. I can see, I can see. But think about the law, my friends, just think about it. The lottery, my friends, think about it. Peace is possible in our times. It is, it is! Happiness is possible as well!

You know where I live, my friends—the basement, the underground. The mouse hole (ha!). You know where to find me.

I am a simple man, a mediocre man. My hair is balding, my nose is snubbed. But you know where to find me, my friends. You know where I live. You know exactly where I live.

The Boy

It was a nice day. I was wearing my white shirt, my white pants. I was wearing a red tie, a clip in the middle.

The people in the office even made remarks about it. "You look so handsome, Pushkar," they said. "You look so content."

Perhaps they spoke seriously; perhaps they spoke in jest. But I took their words at face value.

Did I not do the right thing?

I came out of the office. I lit my cigarette. It was a sunny day—a nice blue sky, a light breeze. I took a puff from the cigarette and watched the smoke rise in the air.

There was a park, the green grass of the park all around. I felt in a good mood, I decided to indulge. I took off my shoes (and why not?). How nice it was to walk on the green grass. How nice to walk in my socks!

I felt tempted, I decided to take off my socks as well. I felt so light, so free.

"You are a serious man, Pushkar," my manager had once told me. "If one is serious, sometimes one cannot be free."

I remembered the words of my manager. I remembered the words as I now walked on the green grass—walked in my bare feet.

***

There was a tree. A boy was sitting under it. He was a poor boy, he had a shoe-polish kit with him. Every few seconds someone walked by, he called after the person. "Shoe polish, sir, shoe polish!"

As I walked on the grass, the boy called after me. The shoes were in my hand, not on my feet. I looked at them, noticed that they were indeed dirty. But there was so much dust in India, they would always get dirty. Still I felt in a good, a liberal, mood. I decided to give the boy some business.

"Come come, sir."

I walked towards the boy.

"I will do a good job, sir."

"I know you will." And then: "These are nice shoes. You *better* do a good job," I joked.

I arrived at the tree. I handed the shoes to the boy.

The boy took the shoes, he laid them on the grass beside him. He took one of the shoes, he laid it on top of the metal stand before him. He began to open his can of shoe polish.

He looked up at me, smiled.

"You work in the office, sir?"

"Yes," I said.

"Your sir is good?"

"How is that?"

"Your sir, sir—the man who gives you orders—is he a good sir?"

I found his remarks amusing, but I found them impertinent as well. Who was he to speak to me in this way?

Still, I was in a good mood. I did not lose my temper. I ignored—I simply ignored his remarks.

He rubbed the shoe with his brush, rubbed it vigorously. As he rubbed, he began to hum a tune. It was a slow tune, one I did not recognize. Most poor boys sing the tunes—often crass and vulgar—from the latest film songs. But this was a different tune. Perhaps it was from some hymn; or perhaps from some folk song.

"Do you like the tune, sir?"

"How is that?"

"It is an old tune, sir, my mother taught it to me. She would go to the room inside (it is the only room we had). She would sit there, she would sing."

"Sing?"

"It was raining outside. She would sit there huddled all night. She would sit there damp and wet. And she would sing."

What strange words he spoke. He was sharing the words—why was he sharing them with me?

"My mother, sir, she was a good woman. She is dead now—they put her on a string cot, they took her to the Jumna River. When they took her, people were singing the tune. I had nothing better to do (it is true sir, ha ha)—I had nothing better to do. I went along, I sang the tune as well."

They were strange words. They were odd, they were disjointed. Were they mocking words as well?

He was telling me about his mother—why was he doing it?

"You work in the office, sir. Do they have water there, do they have soap? Do they have water and soap to keep you clean?"

"Water? Soap?"

"My mother died. There was so much pain (and so much dirt). They looked for water, sir, they looked for water to make her clean.

"The old women came, they came to clean her. But they did not have water, they sent them away.

"A man came to the house, a stranger. He had soap in his left hand (it was red in color), he had a bucket in his right. They were happy to see him. 'Come, come,' they said, and they pressed their backs to the wall to let him pass. 'Come, come,' they said, 'a nice man is here. He is here at last.'"

In this way he spoke—he continued to speak. I had stopped for a shoe polish—a simple shoe polish—and *these* were the words that awaited me.

I was in a good mood; I did not want my mood to be spoiled. I knew that I was being vain, that I was being selfish. But this was my one day of freedom. And who was he to spoil the freedom?

"Hurry up with the shoes," I said, my mood no longer so generous. "I am an important man (can't you see it?). I am an important man, I have places to go."

The boy looked at me. He grew serious, he grew quiet. Was he hurt as well?

***

Important man—ha. Was I really such an important man? Places to go—what places were they?

Sometimes I walked the streets. Sometimes I walked the alleys. Were these the important places to which I had to go?

The boy polished my shoes. Vigorously he brushed them—back and forth, back and forth.

"Finished, sir."

He was quiet, he was formal.

The charm of the moment—charm, what charm?—had been broken.

I tried to be nice to the boy. He was silent. I tried to make a joke. He was silent. I tried to give him a tip. But actions, real actions, speak louder than words. And had not my actions spoken for themselves?

The boy took the money—the fee for the shoe polish, not a penny more. He bowed silently.

He collected his things—with such purpose he collected them. He rose, he left.

I had come to the park—come with dirty shoes. My shoes were no longer dirty. But my soul, what of that?

My soul, what of that?

***

Some time passed. I thought of the boy—I felt low. I thought of the office—the praise, the flattering words—how silly it all seemed now, how pointless.

I went to the park looking for the boy. There was no sign. I walked the streets, the alleys. No sign.

Such a small boy he was—seven years old, perhaps eight. He wore those small shorts, brown, a small shirt that hung over the shorts. The shirt, originally white, was now covered with polish marks. He worked hard, he worked hard. He was a good boy—how could he not be?

Days passed, weeks. Weeks passed, months. I had forgotten the boy (or had I?); I had moved on to other things.

One day I saw the boy—I saw him again.

There was a long and narrow alley. There were open drains on both sides. Children played in the alley. They were poor children. Some of them wore clothes, some of them were half-naked, their genitals exposed. All of them were covered with dust.

The girls jumped rope. Some of the boys played with a ball. It was a pink rubber ball. One of the boys threw the ball, the other missed. The ball went over the other's head; it went into the open drain.

There was some shouting—some curse words were exchanged. The open drain was dirty, the ball would be dirty. No one wanted to go to the drain, to pick up the ball.

And there he was—the shoe-polish boy. He must have been standing in the corner (or perhaps in the shadows). He must have seen it all.

He came to the front. He walked—quietly, simply—to the open drain. He picked up the ball— picked it up between his thumb and his forefinger. He carried the ball—the water dripping from it—carried it this way for a few feet. Then he squatted on the ground. He took the ball, he rubbed it in the dirt. He rubbed it, he rubbed it—he did this almost for a minute.

The others looked at him—looked in awe. They were afraid. He was a brave boy. He was *not* afraid.

"Well done! Well done!" one of them said at last.

"Yes yes, well done!" said another.

Now all the others joined in as well.

A boy came from the far end of the alley. He was pushing a bicycle tire—pushing the inner rim of the tire with a stick. He pushed the rim with such interest—with such concentration.

But when he saw the boy with the ball, he paused. He held the rim with one hand. He seemed to be filled with admiration—even he.

The boy—the shoe-polish boy—was not quite done. He reached into his kit, he took out a small towel (it was torn, it was green). He rubbed the ball with that now, rubbed it vigorously.

Back and forth; back and forth.

"It is clean now," he said at last. "The ball is clean."

A cheer—another cheer—rose from the children.

One of the children came running. He went to the ball, grabbed it. He held the ball in the air.

"Time for *pithoo*!" he said (a popular game).

The other children watched him, they cheered as well.

"Time for *pithoo*!" they said.

The boy ran with the ball—ran into the distance.

The other children went running after him.

***

The scene was forgotten, the children had moved on. And there he stood, the shoe-polish boy (the "hero"). He stood by himself.

I emerged from the shadows, I walked towards him.

He saw me—did he recognize me? Some seconds passed.

"I will clean the towel, sir," he said at last. He was referring to the towel he had used to clean the ball. "I will not use it for shoe polish. I will clean it, sir—I will, I will."

"I will, I will." Was I some kind of policeman, some inspector? Did he have to justify his actions to me?

"My mother was a good woman, sir."

"I know."

"She loved me."

"She did."

"She said that it was important—important to be clean."

In this way the boy spoke—simply, calmly. Was it with passion as well?

His face was small and black. His eyes were small and black. He looked at me—directly he looked.

"Do you have a mother, sir?"

"A mother?"

"Is she good?"

"Good?"

"Does she tell you, sir, tell you to be clean?"

In this way he spoke. On and on he spoke. They were strange words. But he believed in his words. He believed in them, he believed! And was that not the key?

"The ball was dirty, sir—I cleaned it."

"I know."

"I cleaned it, I cleaned it. Did I not do the right thing?"

Clean, clean, how he insisted on that. I tried to explain to the boy—explain about that day. But how far away it seemed. I tried to apologize to him. But how silly it seemed. He knew about the world, he knew what was important—or did he? Did he have time for such things?

"There are good people in the world, sir."

"Good people?"

"There are bad people in the world, sir."

"Bad people?"

"My mother was a good person. The sir is an important man. Is he a good person as well?"

"There are wise people in the world, sir."

"Wise people?"

"My mother was a wise person. The sir is an important man. Is he a wise person as well?"

In this way he spoke. On and on he spoke. He spoke with pride. He spoke with feeling. Was it with insolence as well?

It was twilight now, the sun was beginning to set. Soon it would get dark (but did the boy care?). There was a reason for his words (what reason?). There was a meaning to his words (what meaning?).

"My mother was a wise person. The sir is an important man. Is he a wise person as well?"

In this way he spoke. On and on he spoke. The minutes passed. Perhaps, at last, the boy grew tired. Perhaps, at last, he had exhausted himself. He looked at me, he smiled. He looked at me, he stared. Then he bowed. He picked up his things—his shoe-polish kit, his old green towel. With such purpose he picked them up, with such concentration. And he continued on his way.

Ahmed

A hmed was a short dark man and he went to work. Others made fun of the work (they said it was simple, low-class), but let them say what they would. It was his job, he did it. He went to work.

It was a simple store in a shopping mall—a 5 and 10. The work was hard, the pay not much: two dollars an hour. But it kept him busy. It gave him something to do. It helped him pay the bills.

Some people drove to work. Some people took the bus. He rode on his bicycle. It was an old bicycle with a basket in the front (he kept his lunch there in the brown bag). There was a silver bell. He liked the bell especially. He liked to tinkle the bell.

"Where are you from?"

"From Yemen, sir."

"You will work hard?"

"I will."

"Your father?"

"Nasser is a bad man, sir. He killed my father— many years ago he did it. I have no respect for Nasser.

But other men I respect. I will work hard, sir. I promise. I will work hard."

The manager was Mister Mundy. He did not know who Nasser was, did not really care. But Ahmed seemed like a nice man. His face was dark—perhaps too dark. But his black hair was short and not like that of those crazy hippies. He was dressed in clean clothes, he wore a grey sleeveless sweater on top. Should he not give him a chance?

Ahmed went to work. They told him to work in the stockroom—he worked there. They told him to sweep the floors—he swept the floors. They told him to help the cashiers with the bagging—he helped the cashiers with the bagging.

The customers were many, the lines long. The customers' demands were endless. Should not the lines be kept down, the demands met?

A child came to the store and threw up. There was vomit and vomit all up and down the aisle. They called Ahmed and asked him to clean it. He took a mop and a bucket, he cleaned it.

It took one hour to do it. Then he spent another hour trying all kinds of ways to take away the smell. They asked him to go to the electric store and buy a fan (it came out of petty cash). He turned on the fan and he kept it on for hours. At Mister Box's direction—he was the Assistant Manager—he even left the fan on at night when they went home.

This was Ahmed's job, he did it. He did it and he did not complain.

***

Ahmed was a simple man, a Muslim. Sometimes he went to the mosque and he prayed to his Lord, to Allah. The people at work did not know who Allah was and they did not care. They were too busy with their own lives. To them Ahmed was an outsider, a strange man. And sometimes they were intrigued— just that.

"What is your name?" they said.

"Ahmed," he said.

"Why don't you change your name?"

"Change it?"

"Change it to something simple. Something American. Change it to Al."

Ahmed liked his name but perhaps there was truth to what they said.

Ahmed did not eat pork.

"Pork is good," they said. "Bacon. Ham. You should try it sometime."

The national elections were going on, he was fascinated by the elections. In Yemen Nasser had been in charge and the elections had been a farce. Yes, the elections were going on in America—sometimes he talked about them. But to the others they were of little interest. "Nixon, Humphrey, Wallace—who cares?" they said. "It is the same. It is all the same."

Ahmed went to work. There was a woman there, Helen Bender by name. She was in charge of payroll. On Thursdays she paid you cash placed in a small brown envelope. Ahmed counted his money and then he bent down and put the envelope inside his shoe—sometimes even inside his socks. When work ended it would be night and he would have to ride his bicycle home in the dark. He did not want anyone to steal the cash.

Helen Bender was a strict woman. She was fifty years old, maybe fifty-five, and she had grey hair. She was short, no more than five feet. She wore thick stockings and thick round glasses. There was a wooden booth in the middle of the store—there were two steps and you climbed the steps—and she worked inside the booth.

There was a lock on the inside of the booth. If you wanted to talk to her, you had to knock on the door. There was a sliding window there and she pushed on the sliding window a bit. "Who is it?" she said. You introduced yourself. If she recognized you, she opened the window some more. If she did not recognize you, she continued to ask questions.

There were ledgers inside—she worked on the ledgers. There was cash inside—she worked with the cash. And open the door just like that, how could she do that?

Helen Bender was a strict woman and she had high standards as well. She said that she liked men with big cars.

Ahmed said that he did not have a car. He had a bicycle.

Helen Bender was not impressed.

Helen Bender said that she liked men with big muscles.

Ahmed said that he was a small man—he did not know much about these things.

Helen Bender was not impressed.

Helen Bender said that she liked men who could tell good stories.

Ahmed knew a story about Yemen, he began to tell it. "I had a father," he began, "he lived in Aden. One day Nasser came—he came with his soldiers."

But the phone rang and Helen Bender had to go and answer it. The story was left dangling. It was a good story (or so Ahmed thought) but the people were busy. They did not have time for such things.

***

The days passed. Ahmed went to work, he came home. He went to work, he came home. He was from Yemen, a world far away. Sometimes he missed the old world—but why think of these things? The children there played soccer, there were cinema halls with ceiling fans inside. But it was an old and ancient world. Why think of these things?

He had come to America as a refugee with his mother and sister. His mother had died three years ago. His sister had married and moved to Cincinnati.

He lived in a small rooming house with people who came and went. It was not an easy life. But one must be strong. He had finished high school, perhaps one day he would go to junior college, even to college. And then things would be better—was it not so?

Sometimes the people at work asked him questions.

"You want to be a movie star?" they said.

He did not answer.

"A bank manager?" they said.

He did not answer.

"A computer programmer?"

They were strange words, what did they mean? But perhaps they would come true. He would work hard, he would. And then good things would come to pass.

Ahmed worked hard. And did these good things now happen—did they now come to pass?

They gave him work to do. He was good at some things, he was not so good at others. They asked him to put up a shelf; the shelf fell. They asked him to blow up balloons on the machine; he blew them up, but then he did not know how to tie the knot. They put him in the pets section and the people came to buy goldfish. He filled the plastic bag with water and he put the goldfish inside. But sometimes he put in too much water, sometimes too little. And then the knot on the top of the bag with the plastic strip—he always had trouble with that.

They put him behind the cash register—he was not bad. They put him in the stockroom—he was not bad. Mister Mundy, the Manager, spoke to Mister Box, the Assistant Manager.

"But he has a good attitude."

"He tries."

"He's not terrible at everything, you know. There are a few places we can use him. It's not all bad. No no, it's not all bad."

Sometimes Ahmed was embarrassed at his clumsiness, sometimes he was ashamed. But he was willing to try. And was that so bad?

***

The days passed. The people at work were white, they were pretty. Was Ahmed the same way? The people had dreams—they spoke about their dreams. Was Ahmed the same way?

"I want to be a movie star."

"Yes."

"A singer."

"Yes."

"I want to be a millionaire."

"Yes, that as well."

Ahmed listened to their words, perhaps he even marveled at them. But was there not work to do? Must he not return to the work?

Sometimes Ahmed thought about home, about Yemen. He thought about his mother and his sister—how far away it seemed. He thought about his father—how far away it seemed. He thought about the bad man from Egypt who killed his father. Nasser was a tall man, he had a grey mustache. His picture was often in the newspaper. He gave speeches, the people cheered him. He walked the streets, the people waved or gave parades in his honor.

But did the people know what he had done? Did they even care?

"He asked my father to come to his house. My father went. He threw water on my father's shirt."

But did the people care?

"He asked my father to join him for a drink. My father went. He threw whisky on my father's face."

But did the people care?

"'I am a general,' he said. 'And you? My picture is in the newspaper. Is yours?'"

***

There was a woman at the store, Hortense by name. She was a simple woman but quite attractive as well. She was thirty-five years old, maybe forty. She had streaked blonde hair, a mole on her right cheek. She had nice firm legs. She wore light brown stockings—they were pleasing to the eye.

One day Ahmed tried to tell her the story. But did he succeed? Did she care?

Hortense was a saleswoman and she worked in the fabrics section. Curtains, raw cloth—those kinds of things. She saw Ahmed, she seemed to develop a great interest in him. Or perhaps she just felt sorry for him. She pitied him, that is all.

"My father was a simple man," said Ahmed.

"Yes."

"He was not a general. His picture did not come in the newspaper. But he knew what was right."

"Yes."

"He loved his family, he loved his country."

"Yes."

"And the tall man from Egypt—the one with the grey mustache—could he ever understand?"

She looked at Ahmed—she looked at him for a long time. And then: "The world is a hard place," she said. "America, Yemen, it is all the same. But a few people find happiness. One out of a hundred. Sometimes one out of a hundred and five."

Ahmed listened to her and was intrigued by her words. Happiness, happiness—what was all this strange talk about happiness? Where did it come from—what did it mean?

One day Ahmed was outside sitting on the bench. He had a brown bag with a sandwich inside. He had a small soda that he had bought from the lunch counter. Hortense was on her break and she had come out to take a smoke.

She saw Ahmed on the bench and she approached him. She was a simple woman and not very educated. But they said that she was a special woman with special powers. They said that she had hypnotized people and that she could do it again. You went back to your childhood, to your past lives. If you had a guardian spirit or angel, you could get in touch with them.

One time she herself had been hypnotized and she had traveled back to her childhood. Another time she had gone back not only to her childhood but to a past life. It was the life before the last one: she was a schoolteacher in a small town in Mississippi. There was talk of giving colored people more say, even of having some colored children come to school.

The man who hypnotized her was now dead. He lived in Virginia, some twenty miles from Lynchburg, and was a successful businessman who owned two drug stores. But he discovered that he had another calling and first let others manage his businesses and then sold them altogether. He had passed on his skills of hypnosis to Hortense—he had taught her for many years.

"Both people have to believe fully," Hortense said. "The person doing it and the person it is being done to. If they do not believe, as many as fifteen things can go wrong."

Hortense was there, she watched Ahmed for some time. He was a decent person, he worked hard. Would he be willing to give it a try?

Ahmed was busy with his sandwich, at first he did not notice her. She was small with heelless rubber shoes and she walked so softly. But then he smelled the smoke of the cigarette—or was it that he first saw the small shadow on the ground?

Hortense stood there, the cigarette between her first two fingers. How softly she seemed to hold the cigarette.

She was wearing stockings—they were pleasing to the eye. It was time to hypnotize Ahmed. Was it? She asked him to close his eyes.

He closed his eyes.

To think of his past.

He thought of his past.

To think of a river in Yemen.

He thought of a river.

There was music in the background. There was a flute, there was a violin. Was there a mandolin as well?

Ten minutes passed, perhaps eleven. Ahmed awoke. How tired he was. Hortense was running her hands through his hair.

No, it did not feel bad.

Hortense asked him if he remembered anything from his rest.

"What is there to remember?"

"You were in Aden—or perhaps in Hodeida. You were there for a long time."

Ahmed was amazed at her words. She had taken him to Yemen—had she really? She had taken him to the past—had she? Was this the path to happiness? Would he be one of the lucky ones—one out of the hundred, one out of the hundred and five?

That night Ahmed went home and he thought about it. Something had happened—what had happened? What had come to pass?

***

The days passed. Ahmed thought about America—he thought about it for some time. He went to work, he came home. What a strange place this America was. To what did it add up? What did it mean?

His father was dead, his mother was dead. There was his sister—she was far away. There was Helen Bender—she was a strict woman. There was Hortense, a pretty woman.

They asked him to clean the floors—he cleaned the floors. To mop—he mopped. To open the boxes—he opened them. There were prices to stamp: he stamped them. Ahmed wanted to find happiness—or did he? What was this happiness? What did it mean?

Sometimes Ahmed felt sad, he felt alone. He went for a walk, he wandered the streets. He walked down the alleys and he saw the broken glass there, the debris. One day he went to the famous place—the one in Cheverly, Maryland. There were girls there, special girls, who came to the parking lot behind the movie theater. They were girls who had dropped out of high school, or studied bookkeeping and typing in their senior year. They had never gone to college, would never go. But they needed money. Were they not just like the rest of the world? They painted their fingernails, they painted their toenails. They got a tattoo near the right breast, or on the upper thigh. They knew it would bring pleasure to the customers, or at least be something to talk about. Did it bring pleasure to them as well?

One night, after visiting the girls, Ahmed came in to work. Mister Mundy was there, the manager of the store. He was a perceptive man—and he noticed that something had happened.

"Are you tired?" he said.

Ahmed looked at him.

"A long night?" he said.

Ahmed looked at him.

"It is dark in Cheverly, the twilights are long, the nights even longer. Is it not best to avoid such places and to stay at home?"

Ahmed did not know what to say. So in fact he checked his tongue, he said nothing. Mister Mundy was an intelligent man. But did he understand? Did even he?

***

The days passed. Ahmed used to make two dollars an hour. Now he made two dollars and ten cents. But the work, did it really change?

He wandered the streets—often he wandered them. He thought about Yemen—did it help? He thought about his mother and sister. Did it help?

One day Ahmed was in Hortense's apartment— she had invited him over for some snacks. It was a simple place with an orange rug and a sofa covered in colorless plastic. But the place had been well kept— there was hardly any dust in sight.

Hortense liked to smoke, there were ashtrays throughout the house. She smoked Pall Malls— sometimes straight, sometimes the menthol. The black mole was on her cheek; she rubbed on the mole with the tip of her index finger.

She was wearing stockings—they were always pleasing to the eye. It was time to hypnotize Ahmed. Was it? She asked him to close his eyes.

He closed his eyes.

To think of the cinema halls in Yemen, the ceiling fans there.

He thought of the cinema halls in Yemen, the ceiling fans there.

To think of a river in Yemen.

He thought of a river.

There was music in the background. There was a flute, there was a violin. Was there a mandolin as well?

There was the sound of a hammer. There was the sound of a bird, the sound of a leaf. Ahmed tried to imagine the sound. What a soft sound it was. The leaf was in the air—it was suspended, suspended. It was there for a minute—for two—it did not fall.

How relaxed Ahmed was. There was peace in the world. It was all around.

Ten minutes passed, perhaps eleven. Ahmed awoke. Hortense was running her hands through his hair.

No, it did not feel bad.

Hortense asked him if he remembered anything from his rest.

"What is there to remember?"

"You were in Aden—or perhaps in Sayhut. You were there for a long time."

Ahmed was amazed at her words. She had taken him to Yemen—had she really?

Would he find happiness now—would he find it at last?

Hortense was wearing stockings and she began to roll them down. She took out a box of Pall Malls. She tapped at the end of the box and took out a cigarette. She offered it to Ahmed. He shook his head—but then he changed his mind.

"One," he said. "Maybe for later."

"Later?"

He put the cigarette in his shirt pocket.

He had been hypnotized before—he knew what it was like. He had been to Yemen—he knew what that was like. But an attractive woman—thirty-five years old, perhaps forty; a woman rolling down her light brown stockings—for this he was not prepared.

"My husband is a good man," she said.

"I know."

"He is a good provider."

"He is."

"He treats me well, I've never had cause for complaint."

She paused. Was this the end of the sentence? Were more words to follow?

It was raining outside now, harder than before. The wind had picked up, the leaves were swirling to the ground. The leaves, the leaves—always the leaves swirling to the ground.

"The world is a long place," she said.

"Yes."

"The world is a hard place," she said.

"Yes."

"A man is away from his home. Is it not important for him to find shelter? Is it not important for him to find rest?"

She moved closer to him, he could smell the tobacco in her mouth. It was a good smell—he had always liked the smell. She put her hand in his hair. What does it mean when a woman puts her hand in your hair? She brought her mouth close to his mouth. What does it mean when a woman puts her mouth close to your mouth?

The rest, why go into the rest? Ahmed was hypnotized, or perhaps he was not. Perhaps he found shelter, perhaps he did not. That night he went home on his bicycle. And did he tinkle his silver bell (the simple man)—did he tinkle it again?

***

The days passed. Ahmed went to work, he came home. He went to work, he came home. And was he at peace now, was he at rest? Was he happy now—was he that as well?

Ahmed rode his bicycle to work. He did not have a car, he did not have a pick-up truck. So he took his bicycle. There was a basket in the front suspended from the handlebar. He used it for his sandwich, he used it for an extra jacket or sweater.

One day it had rained, the streets were wet. The bicycle skidded and Ahmed fell off and hurt his leg. His pants were torn at the knee and there was blood there. He walked the bicycle to work the rest of the way—almost half a mile. At work, he asked for some antiseptic ointment and some band aid—there was some in the small office at the back of the store. He put the ointment on his knee. He took his handkerchief, he tied it around his knee.

That night he hobbled around the store. Some of the blood was still there. And the pain, the pain, did it really go away?

One day Ahmed was not feeling well. He was downstairs throwing up. He had been working in the stockroom unpacking boxes. It was hot, it was stuffy. There was dust all around.

Ahmed recovered from his nausea. There was a simple wooden bench there and he lay on the bench. He lay there, he dreamed. He was in Florida—he was lying on the sand. He was in his room in his boardinghouse—he was sitting on the old armchair, his eyes were closed. He was in Yemen—his mother was there, his sister. He was lying on a string cot. He made a pillow with his arms, he turned to the side. The sun came—the kind sun—it came and fell on his face.

How nice it was to be in Yemen. To be at peace again, to be at peace.

He thought of his father. A sadness came. He thought of Nasser. An anger came. But then he thought again of the kind sun. And how nice it was to be in Yemen. To be home again (ha). To be home.

***

The days passed. Sometimes it rained, sometimes the snows came. Sometimes it was cold and Ahmed shivered in the wind. But he went on his bicycle, he went on. He did not yield.

One day Ahmed was called into the office. Helen Bender wanted to see him. One day he was called in. Mister Mundy wanted to see him. One day he was called in—Mister Box wanted to see him.

They asked him questions, he answered. They asked him questions, he answered. He spoke of the places in Yemen they had visited. He spoke of the "tours" with his father they had gone on—the tours to Mocha, to San'a.

Did they understand?

He spoke of the cinema halls in Yemen. The cinema halls in America were nice, they were clean. But the cinema halls in Yemen had something else. They had ceiling fans.

One day they called him in, they took him aside. They said that his work was good, but not great. They said that there were budget problems, they must let him go.

"Go?"

"We must let you go."

Ahmed protested—he began to protest—but the words stuck in his throat. What could he say? What could he say?

There were the memories from Yemen—perhaps he should think of them. There were the memories from work—perhaps he should think of them.

Ahmed went to look for Hortense at the store—she was not there. He went to her house and knocked. The door was locked, the curtains drawn. But he would go back there tomorrow, and the day after. She would comfort him, of course she would. And then things would be well again. They would be well.

It was night and Ahmed made his way home. He rode on his bicycle—he rode, he rode. The streets were wet from the rains. The streets were deserted. When he got home, it was the early hours of the morning and his hair was dripping wet.

"Where have you been?"

"Oh nothing, sir."

"Where have you been?"

"I was riding the streets, you see. I was on my bicycle, I was tinkling my bell."

No one was there, not really. An old man, a cripple man—choose anyone you wish. A man is in a strange country. Does he not need a companion? Does he not need a friend?

Ahmed thought of Helen Bender, he thought of work. And was it enough? He thought of Mister Mundy, he thought of Mister Box. And was it enough? He thought of Hortense—even her. And was it enough?

"I was riding around, sir. I was tinkling my bell."

"Your bell?"

"The streets were wet, sir. They were deserted. I was riding around—I was tinkling my bell."

A man is tired. He is no one. His father is dead, his mother is dead. His sister is far away. He rides around, he rides around. He is looking for something—what is it?

He tinkles it, he tinkles it. He tinkles his bell.

My Daughter

There is a train. It comes at midnight. You can catch it at Dupont Circle. It goes to Silver Spring (the land of the beautiful water). It goes to Rockville (the nursing home).

I tell my daughter about the train. She is afraid of the city, afraid to leave the house. But she grabs her purse, makes sure she has enough money. And she takes off for the train.

She stands at the platform, looks at the people around her. There is a man in a dress. A man with a ring in his ear.

The man with the ring approaches her. She shivers, takes a step back.

"I am from the bookstore," he says.

"I do not go to bookstores."

"It is a clean place, open on Sundays. The people come, they linger through the night."

My daughter is a shy person, timid. But she is a good person. This man is troubling her. He should not trouble her. My daughter (poor daughter), how I feel for you; he should leave her alone.

The train comes, my daughter sighs in relief. "Excuse me," she says.

"Heading for Rockville?"

"How did you know?"

"I've been there, met some Jews. I think they still live there, in the nursing home."

My daughter boards the train. She is coming to see me. I am an old man, a Jew.

I live in Rockville. The Smith-Kogod Building. But I am not the only Jew in the building. There are other people. They are old, they are Jews as well.

My daughter arrives. She hesitates at the door.

"Why do you hesitate?"

"I thought you were asleep."

"I am your father. This is my room, so your room."

I pause, consider the import of my words. My room—an old man's, a Jew's, so your room. Is that such a good thing to say?

She walks in, approaches the bed.

I push myself up onto my elbows.

"No no, Father, don't bother."

"I am old, yes. But I am still your father. Eyes open, a few breaths still inside these lungs. I am not yet dead."

My daughter goes to the dresser, she puts the plastic bag there.

"What is in the bag? A gift?"

"No, Father, just some clean socks."

"I live in old clothes. Old sheets, old diapers. Anything is a gift."

She turns, she smiles. A small smile at the right corner of her lips.

"Have you had breakfast?" she says.

"I have."

"What did they give you?"

"Toast, eggs. Cereal, fruit. I am an old man, I take two bites, I get tired. A third bite, I fall sick. But they're optimistic, they persevere."

"I have brought the bills, Father."

"Have they bankrupted me?"

"No, Father."

"I know they can't. I am a Rockefeller—I own a Chagall, a reprint, just like the rich one. I have a magic cow—it gives cash forever. I go on, go on. Old man, Jew, don't give up: I persist."

My daughter goes to the closet, she begins to look through the clothes. Shirts, pants, sweaters, socks.

"I'm old, Marie."

"Yes, Father."

"I seldom leave this bed."

"Yes, Father."

"These pants, these sweaters—all the fancy turtlenecks. Do you think I have need for these?"

My daughter is quiet. She is a sweet girl. Poor girl, what can she say?

***

There is a man (where is he?); he looks like a Jew, but I'm not sure. His back is bent, he has a long black beard. He has lit a candle and he is looking for something in the dark.

"Mister?" I say.

He does not answer me.

"Mister?" I say.

He does not answer me.

"Are they coins?"

"No."

"A letter?"

"No."

"A note, a sheet, some memory perhaps—of Poland, of New York—something from the past?"

I see my daughter, I ask her about the man. She does not know. Again I ask. She does not know.

"Is he a doctor, a priest? Is he from New York—did he go to some school, was too poor, turned away? Is he from Poland—did he sleep on the street in the darkness (three days), and sometimes under the gas lamps?"

My daughter is not sure, says she will try to find out.

She opens the door and goes outside. Construction is going on. Cement has been dug up, earth has been turned.

"You see something?" I say.

"Not yet."

"Keep looking."

"I will."

I think she will do it, too. She is a brave girl. She will go there, go in the dark. She will stay in the dark, stay all night if she has to. She will do all she can.

***

My daughter goes outside for three days (is she still there?). She tries to find this man (is he Jewish?). She tries to find out who he is, why he is here. Find out what he wants.

"Marie," I say.

She does not answer me.

"Have you found him?"

She does not answer me.

She is at the dresser, she stands in the shadows. Her back is bent. She is going through them, you see—she is going through my socks.

***

My daughter is a good girl. She is tall, a little too tall for a girl. She is fat, a little too fat. But she works hard, is a good daughter. She takes the train, she takes it to Rockville. And she comes to see her old man.

Across the hall is a piano. She helps me put on my diapers, she puts me in the wheelchair. It takes a long time but we manage. She wheels me across the hall.

"You want to play, Papa?"

"No, Marie," I say, "you play."

She hesitates, smiles. She spreads her skirt to both sides and lowers herself down.

"Kessler taught me."

"I know."

And she begins to play. It is a tune Kessler taught her—taught her a long time ago—a tune he learned in Poland.

She plays, she plays.

"Play it, Marie. Do not stop. It is good for the heart."

"The heart?"

"And for the soul (the urine is stopped, it does not come—this, Doctor, is this the medicine I seek?). Yes, it is good for the soul as well."

The night comes, it is time for her to leave. The light is dim, I cannot see. She turns on the lamp, it hurts my eyes.

Too much light or too little.

"Yes, daughter, an old man's complaint. But old men are not allowed to die. They try and they try— but no, they are not allowed (forbidden, verboten) to die."

***

So I sit here, I sit in the darkness. I lie here, I lie in the bed. I stand beside the bed, I aim for the basin. I am old and the urine sputters down my legs.

I smell phenol. They used it in the old days, in Poland. In the lavatories, in the land far away.

I remember when I was in Poland. Men stood there as well in the darkness, the cold night around, the stars above them. And the urine sputtered down their legs.

"It was a long time ago?"

"Yes."

"You were happy then?"

"Happy, not happy. What difference does it make?"

"You were a boy?"

"A boy, a girl. A child, a dead man. What difference does it make?"

The people ask questions, they ask all these questions. Do you really think they are of any use?

The days pass. Some days are bad, some days are worse. One day my daughter comes to see me. There is a tin box in her hand.

She takes the box, she lays it on the floor. She opens the box, she takes out a bottle.

"Ready, Father?" she says.

I am silent.

I sit on the armchair, she kneels on the floor. She takes my pants and she begins to roll them up my legs.

"Ready, Father?" she says.

I am silent.

She takes the green bottle, the one with the white liquid. She pours some of the liquid on her hand. She takes the liquid, she rubs it on my legs.

"How does it feel?"

"It feels alright."

She takes the liquid, she rubs it on my legs. Then she begins to massage the legs. Up and down, up and down.

"How does it feel?"

"It feels alright."

She talks to me, she encourages me.

But is it so easy—as easy as that?

"The legs," she says, "they are the first to go."

"Yes."

"You must keep them strong."

"Yes."

"You try—you must try harder."

"I will."

She tells me to try, to keep a schedule. "I am a creature of habit," she says, "I think you are too."

"I am?"

"Give yourself a schedule—keep it. Eat at this time, walk at this time, exercise at this. You need to exercise—to exercise regularly."

"I will."

"Try Father, try."

"I will."

This is the way she is. She is a good girl, she means well. She encourages me.

But is it so easy—as easy as that?

***

It was Saturday (a long time ago), we had walked to the temple. In Poland there were eight of us; now, in New York, there were only three.

We said our prayers, we came out of the temple. Some of us went to the market, some of us went to the zoo. I was tired, I begged to be excused. I went to the park (you know the one, near Washington Square), I lay down on the grass.

I must have dozed off. When I awoke the sun had already begun to sink well into the west. I lifted myself onto my elbows, I looked around me. The bushes, the grass, the statue of some hero.

How nice it was to just lie there. To lie on the grass.

The years have passed now, so many years. I sit in my room, I sit in the darkness. No one is here. No statue, no hero.

No grass.

Not even any grass.

***

My daughter comes to see me.
"The legs," she says.
"Yes."

"You must keep them strong."

"Yes."

"You try—you must try harder."

"I will."

She tells me to try, to keep busy.

"I will."

To try.

"I will."

She is my daughter, I do not want to disappoint her. I do not want to let her down.

I go to the bathroom, I try to unzip my pants.

I cannot do it.

I unzip them, the diaper is there. I tug at the elastic, the sound irritates me.

And the urine, it sputters down my legs.

I stand in front of the toilet ("commode," the good people say). And the urine, it sputters down my legs.

The doctor (he is a kind man) comes to my room. "Old man," he says.

I look at him.

"Old man," he says.

I look at him.

"Old man," he says, "here is a cup. Can you please—that is—could you please—that is—void into the cup?"

"Void?"

Void: what a nice word it is. I void—I try to void into the cup. But is it so easy?

I try again.

Is it so easy?

The urine is there. It sputters down my legs.

***

It is dusk (or is it night?). My daughter has left. I should be tired (I am not). Lonely (I am not). A black woman is in my room.

"Cecile," she says. "Sierra Leone," she says.

She says that she went to Jamaica one year. She saw it—who will deny it?—she saw the old man's death.

"The old man's death?"

She tells me, I nod. She tells me, I close my eyes. She tells me, I can see it in my mind's eye—see the old man's death.

Old man—what old man? And why did he have to die (poor man), why did he have to go away?

***

One time (a long time ago) I was at the market. There were some stores there, there were some stalls. There was a short and ugly man: a lump on his neck, a scar on his left cheek. The man said he had a horse at home, he even had a car.

One time he took me in his car. He took me to Gdansk, he took me to New York. He took me to Paris, he took me to Rome. He took me to a small hut (he said that this is where God lived). A man was there, an old man. He was playing the piano, he had diapers in his hands.

"Kessler?" I said.

The old man did not answer me.

"God?" I said.

The old man did not answer me.

He was playing the piano, he had diapers in his hands.

The old man played the piano, he played it for a long time. But then he seemed to grow sad (or was it even weary?). He cursed, he cursed. He took the diapers, he threw them on the floor.

He took the diapers, he threw them on the floor.

The years have passed now, so many years. I think of that old man. He was good and kind. He was playing the piano so well. But why then the change of heart? Was there some meaning to it, some significance? Some significance without end?

***

My daughter comes to see me. I ask her about the man.

She does not know.

Again I ask.

She does not know.

The meaning and significance. The significance without end.

There is a man at the platform (who is he?). A man in a dress (who is he?). A man with a ring in his ear.

My daughter goes out to see them. They huddle, they whisper. They huddle, they whisper. Of what do they whisper? Of what do they speak?

They speak of Kessler, they speak of God. They speak of the piano, the diapers. Do they speak of the world that God has made (what world?). The world with the meaning and significance. The significance without end.

I ring the bell.

No one comes.

I ring the bell.

Someone comes.

They take off my diapers. (I am a baby again.) They clean my legs. (I am a baby again.) They put powder on my legs. How nice the powder feels!

The days pass, the weeks. The Jew is happy. The days pass, the weeks. The Jew is sad.

The old man and the diapers. The diapers without end.

It is dark, so dark. It is cold, so cold. But she is a good girl (he knows it). She will come and see him (he knows it).

The old man and the diapers. The diapers without end.

The father sits in his room and he waits for his daughter. Patiently, patiently.

So patiently he waits.

The Lovers in Bengal

There was a pond in the village, steps leading to the pond. People would come there to bathe. They would stand in the pond, a *lungi* or a short cloth around them. They would rub soap over their body. They would take a mug and dip it into the water. They would lift the mug, pour the water over their head.

The children would laugh; they would jump up and down at the feel of the water. The grown-up people—the parents, the old people—would make sure that their important parts were covered as they bathed. And when they were finished, they would take a towel, wrap it around themselves—wrap it as they took off the old, wet clothes and put on the new ones.

Yes, as I say, people would come to the pond to bathe. And they would also come there for a social gathering. The pond was, as it were, the meeting place for the village. They would come there to see each other; to see each other and be seen.

Girls would come. Sometimes they would come with their friends, holding hands. Sometimes they would come by themselves. Sometimes they would come accompanied by their mothers, or their fathers, or even their grandfathers.

It was there that they met—my father and mother. My father did not live in the village, but in a small town a few miles away. But someone in the family (or perhaps a friend, I now forget) had told him about my mother's family. "They live in the village," he had said. "They have such and such a daughter. She is the third daughter. The first daughter is married to a Superintendent of Police. The second daughter is married to an engineer (from a good family, Calcutta University). And this third daughter, she is virtuous, fair-complexioned. She has a good voice."

The good voice—that is what captured my father's attention. He did not care about the money. He did not care about the good family. He did not care that he himself was only twenty-five years old—without a college education, with some good experience (perhaps), but not the education, the breeding.

"I am not a nothing, a misbreed," he said. *Misbreed*: this is the very word he used.

He wanted to meet this girl—virtuous, fair-complexioned. The voice—above all else the voice.

And who would stop him?

***

The days passed. My father began coming to the pond. He would go to the office in the morning. He worked for a printing company; he dealt with papers and files, papers and files, all day. But at last the day was over. Twilight came. He would take off his shoes, put on his sandals. He would take off his formal clothes, put on his *lungi*. And he would take the bus to the pond.

The bus would stop about a quarter of a mile away. He would get off the bus and walk the rest of the distance. It was a dirt road, there were often puddles on the ground. But what did it matter? He was going to see the girl—this girl who was fair-complexioned, the girl with the voice.

He would see the girl from a distance. He would stand behind a pillar. He would sit on a bench, drink tea. He would look in her direction and cast furtive glances.

But speak to her—speak to her directly—that was out of the question. How could he do that?

One day a woman was bathing her son at the edge of the pond. The son was six years old, maybe seven. She was lathering him with soap. The boy's arms grew slippery, the woman lost her grip on the boy's hand. The boy fell backwards into the water.

"Help! Help!" the woman screamed.

It was twilight, almost dark. Who was there to hear the cry? Who was there to come and help?

My father was walking by just at that moment. He had gotten off the bus and was walking towards the pond. He was walking there for the same reason that he always walked: in hope of seeing my mother. He would not talk to her (of course not), he would not dare to come close to her. But he would see her from a distance.

He would espy her and he would dream. Dream of the day that they would be together. Dream of the day that they would be married!

My father was walking by, he heard the screams. He threw off his sandals and jumped into the water.

No sign of the boy.

My father swam and swam. He raised his head to get air. He dove down again and again.

At last he found the boy. The boy was splashing around trying to stay afloat. The water at that point was about six feet. It was not too difficult to get a hold of the boy, to drag him to the pond's edge.

A crowd had gathered on the bank of the pond. They oohed, they aahed. Some of them cheered. The adulation that they poured on my father!

"God will bless you," the mother of the boy said.

"You are a saint," she said.

The others joined in. "A saint," they said. "A saint to surpass other saints."

My father was embarrassed. For all his bluster and confidence he was still, deep inside, a timid man. He blushed. All this attention—for what?

And there, in the distance, he saw her. The girl. She had short black hair. She was dressed in a lime-green outfit: green pajamas, a green skirt. A long white scarf thrown backwards over her shoulders. She was looking at him.

Looking.

There was, he thought, a smile on her face. There was—or did he only imagine it?—a look of adulation as well.

***

This was, then, the beginning. And why drag it out—why make a short story long?

Contact was made. The relatives of the girl approached the relatives of my father. The boy and girl were introduced to each other formally. The relatives, of course, were present in the room. They all drank tea. My father smiled, my mother blushed, lowered her head.

The date of the wedding was set. Four months later they were married.

The priest said to my father, "Who are you?"

My father answered: "I am Hemant Kumar."

The priest said to my mother, "Who are you?"

My mother answered: "I am Usha."

They walked around a fire seven times. When they finished, the people smiled, asked them, "One more time."

"No no," the priest cried out. "There is no need. The deed has been done."

The deed has been done. I paused, I looked at my audience. Were the people still there? Were they still listening?

I saw some smiles. I met, directly, the eyes of a few. I was reassured.

I went on.

My father married, he was a happy man. He went back to work with joy and energy. He worked for a printing company. He worked every day.

Sometimes it would rain. You know how Bengal is, how hard it sometimes rains. My father would take my mother's hand, he would take her out to the veranda. "Usha," he would say. "Look Usha, look."

Sometimes he would take my mother's hand and go running into the rain itself.

"Stop!" my mother would call out, screaming, laughing, pulling back her hand from his pull. "Stop, crazy man, stop!"

But my father would not stop. He would take her out in the rain. He would hold her by the hand or the wrist. He would hold her and twirl her in a circle.

The rain would fall hard—so hard it would fall. My father's voice would ring out in the air. My mother's laughter—cries, laughter, cries, laughter—would ring out in the air as well.

My father was a timid and reserved man. But he was in love. And love is love. Who knows what love can do?

And my mother, was she not in love as well? Those were the old, the golden, days. What was not possible? What could not come to pass?

***

One day the war came. My father left and joined the army. The Japanese were in Burma, he was there. They were moving closer—to Bengal, even to Bengal. He was there as well.

But the war ended, my father came back.

The days passed peacefully. My sister was born. They called her Savitri, after the virtuous maiden. Two years passed. I was born. They called me Gaya—after the word cow, but also meaning mother, earth: the cow as mother and earth.

They were busy years. When you have children, you are busy, you have to be so. You have to raise the children, take care of them. There was an *ayah*—a governess—who helped out. But there was work, of course there was a lot of work. The children get sick, the children want toys. They want you to read, they want you to play.

Those days, I tell you. They were sweet and innocent days!

God was above us, he was looking after us. And why should we not enjoy them—the sweet and innocent days.

But these days, could they last? Could they really last? God has created a world, He has not created an easy world. Sometimes He wishes things to be otherwise.

The years passed and my father grew sick. At first it was just small things: he could not remember a name. The name of a person, the name of a place. It would be there on the tip of his tongue but somehow, somehow, it would slip away.

Then it would be bigger things. He would be in mid-sentence and he would suddenly stop. He would not remember what he was saying. A person would walk in, even a relative. "Who is that?" he would say.

A few minutes later—even a few seconds—he would remember. But why did he forget in the first place?

"It is normal," they said.

"It is nothing," they said.

"It is what some people do all the time."

But was it as simple as that?

Sometimes my father would go to the window. He would just stand there. He would call out to passersby.

"Hello," he would say.

"Why do you not look at me?"

"Is this any way to treat a man—a *respectable* man? Is this any way to behave?"

The people would just look at him, stare. Some of them had known him, or at least seen him, for years. He *was* a respectable man. And was this any way for such a man to behave?

My mother worried for him, she worried every day. But what could she do?

Sometimes he would lose his temper and he would push my mother. Sometimes he would hit her. Sometimes my mother had to go to the market for a few minutes. She would close the door and lock it from the outside. She did not want him to go wandering off on his own.

He would stand at the window (the one with the grilles), angrily calling out to passersby. "Open the door, you bastards," he would say. "Open the door. Don't you see that she has locked me—locked me inside?"

Sometimes my mother was home and the door was slightly open. She was busy with something in the kitchen. He would put on his robe. He would put on his slippers (or sometimes he would even be barefoot). And he would go out to the street.

He would go looking for *ladoos* (sweet cakes), "the kind that Nanaji would always bring." He would go looking for copybooks. "My teacher told me that I must write neatly. And if I do not have a copybook, how can I write?"

He would go looking for tangerines. He loved to see the tangerines at the stall, piled in a mound, one on top of the other. "Pretty," he would say, "are they not pretty?" "The smell," he would say, "do you not like the smell?"

***

One day my mother gave him his food. She locked the door. And she went to the pond. It had been long—so long—since she had been there. But something forced her, impelled her, and so she went.

It was a cold and cloudy day, not many people were there. She sat on a rock. A bird came and sat in the distance. It was a pretty bird with a long neck.

"What a noble bird," my mother said.

My mother sat there for some time. She was lost in reveries, lost in the past—who could say.

There was a fish there, a tiny fish. "How small, a *baby*," my mother said.

My mother was lost in reveries. Suddenly she was awakened—was it startled?—by a sound. She looked up and it was the bird—the noble bird. It was at the edge of the pond. And it had the fish, the baby, in its mouth.

My mother sat there for some time. It was a big world, a bird—a noble bird—had made the world. And sometimes the bird came. It was proud, it shrieked. Perhaps the sound startled you. And it took the baby away.

***

My mother rose—she forced herself to rise. And she made her way home.

The days passed, the weeks. The weeks passed, the months. My father was sick, he grew sicker. And what was there to be done?

My mother took him to all the doctors she could find. She took him to the doctors in Dacca, she took him to the doctors in Chittagong. But do you think it helped?

She gave him Teramycin (for the eyes), she gave him Borofax (for the lips). She gave him Silicia, Ferrum Phos, Natrum Mur. She gave him every medicine she had ever used—every medicine anyone had ever used on her.

The people thought she was mad. What was the point of these medicines—these irrelevant medicines? What effect could they have?

But she gave them, she believed in them. They had worked on her—worked on her when she was sick, worked on her when she was a child. Why should they not work now?

It was faith, don't you see? (Or perhaps it was madness.) They were good medicines, they were kind medicines. They had worked on her. And so why should they not work now?

But of course the medicines did not work. The illness was a big illness, the medicines were small medicines. And work—how could they work?

My father grew sicker. One day he wet his bed. My mother had to help him off the bed. (How heavy he was!) She rolled him over and she helped him to sit up. She took her arm and she put it around his shoulders. She lifted him up—he fell back; she lifted him up—he fell back. A third time she tried, a fourth.

At last she managed. She sat him up on the chair. She took off the sheet from the bed, changed it.

He sat on the chair—he was panting now, he was restless. Then his eyes closed, his head drooped. She was afraid that if she left the room, he would fall off the chair.

That night my mother sat in the corner, she turned on the low lamp. She took a pad, she took an old pen (it was the only one she could find), and she wrote a letter. She wrote a letter to God.

It was a simple letter. She wrote it in Hindi and then in Bengali. The script was small, it slanted from left to right.

"Dear God," she began.

***

The days passed, the weeks (or was it the months?). The weeks passed, the months (or was it the years?). My father went to the window, he stood there. He went to the window, he cursed. One day he said that there was a story—a story he must tell.

"A story?"

A story he must tell.

My mother told him to be quiet, she told him to get his rest.

But he would have none of it. "Rest," he said, "who needs rest? A person can rest all his life."

There was a glitter in his eye, a strange look. He took a deep breath, and then a second. He took another deep breath. His breathing was labored. He went on.

He spoke about life, he spoke about death. They were strange words—the words were jumbled, the meaning not clear. But he needed to speak. He went on.

He spoke about the past: the times in Poona when they owned the factory. He spoke about the past: the times in Delhi when he worked in the sugar mill. But especially he spoke about his childhood: the times in Dacca when his mother's father, his Nanaji, would come to visit. The *ladoos* he would bring.

"He would bring me *ladoos*—they were the best *ladoos* in the world."

"*Ladoos?*"

"I would stand at the door, you see, and wait. I would wait to see his figure, his tall figure, in the distance (the turban, the white turban at the top). At last I would see him and go running. He would be standing there, his face blank, or even stern, his arms behind his back. I would ask him if he had brought me anything.

"'No,' he would say.

"I would ask him again.

"'No,' he would say.

"A third time I would ask him, a fourth. (It was a game, you see, just a game.)

"But he could not keep up the pretense forever. At last his face would break out into a smile. '*Ladoos*,' he would say, 'only *ladoos*. You know, the ones you like so much. The ones they sell in the bazaar.'

"Or else: 'A box, he would say. Just a box.'

"But it was no ordinary box. It was the box with the picture of the goddess Lakshmi on top. There was a string on the top, brown and yellow. And there were *ladoos* inside—the best *ladoos* in the world.

"I would put the box in my left hand (or I would hug it against my chest). I would put my right hand in his left hand. And thus we would walk, my Nanaji and I, swinging hand in hand—thus we would walk towards home.

"Nanaji did not want me to open the box (not yet). 'Oh ho, wait,' he would say, 'can you wait one minute till we get home?'

"And I was a good boy, you see, I was a good boy. I did *not* open it—I did not open it till I got home."

He told the story, his breathing was labored. He would begin to sweat—you thought that he was about to choke.

But then, somehow, he would recover. He would go on. He would take a deep breath, and then a second. He would find the strength. He would go on.

My father told the story with passion. It was a simple story—a story about childhood. But it was important for him to tell it. He must tell it. He must!

***

The story was over. My father lay back on his pillow—his head dropped against the wall behind him, his arms stretched wide on each side.

The days passed, the weeks (or was it the months?). The weeks passed, the months (or was it the years?). My father was sick, he was dying. One day the bird would come, the noble bird. It would take him away.

My father lay straight on his back. His arms were stretched wide on each side. And how tired he was— how infinitely tired!

He would lie there, his eyes open. Sometimes he would speak. But it was not clear to whom he was speaking. Was he speaking to my mother? Was he speaking to the walls? Was he speaking to himself?

My mother came to see him, sometimes he recognized her. Sometimes he did not. "Raj," he said, "are you Raj?" This was his cousin brother.

"Padma," he said, "are you Padma?" This was his sister. She had died when he was a child.

"Nanaji," he said, "are you Nanaji? Can you bring me *ladoos*? The *ladoos* you used to bring?"

He lay there on his back. And he was lost, you see, he was lost to the world. He would open his eyes, he would close them; he would open his eyes, he would close them. And he was lost, you see—he was lost to the world.

***

My mother took her head and she rested it against his face. Then she was afraid—she feared that she might disturb him. She took her head and she rested it against his chest.

She was afraid of that as well. She took her head, she rested it at his feet.

She liked him. She wanted him to stay. She did not want him to go away.

He lay there, he slept. He lay there, he slept. He opened his eyes. He looked around him. But there was no one he saw—not really—no one he recognized.

"Put me on a pallet," he said. "Take me to the pond (or is it the Jumna River?)."

"The pond? The Jumna River?"

"My mother is waiting for me. My Nanaji. They are waiting—how can I be late?"

"They are waiting—how can I be late?"

On the twenty-fifth of March, at 11:06 in the morning, my father died. He opened his eyes. He looked at the walls. Some thought seemed to cross his mind (what was it?). A smile came to his lips.

He closed his eyes. He did not open them again.

My mother sat there, looked at him. She was his wife—she had lived with him for twenty-one years.

A bird came, a noble bird. People came, what people? They sobbed, they wept. They said that it was God's will.

And was it?

They said that he had suffered so much. They said that it was for the best.

And was it?

A woman came. She went up to my mother and she put her arms around her.

"Usha," she said.

My mother did not answer.

"Usha," she said again.

My mother did not answer.

The woman was not a bad woman, she meant well. But my mother was old, she was tired. She wanted to go to her room, she wanted to sleep. She was tired, you see, she needed rest. She wanted to sleep for a long time.

Ajay Bhatt

He walked into the room. It was pitch dark. There was loud music (where was it coming from?). There were a few lights. If you peered carefully enough you could see them—see the dance floors where the dancers must dance. The lights were at the base and periphery of the dance floors.

He turned to the left—darkness. He turned to the right—darkness. He needed to go to the bathroom. He saw a lighted red sign: "Men." He began to walk towards the sign.

As he walked, he heard a voice behind him. "Can we help you?"

He turned, looked over his shoulder. There—a few feet away and to the left—were two women. They sat at a small table, a radio—or music machine of some kind—before them. So this is where the music came from.

He walked towards them. "Are you open?"

"We open at six."

It was now three o'clock in the afternoon. "But I saw the sign—'Open 24 Hours.' I heard the music."

"No, we open really at six."

"I'll come back then."

He began to walk away.

"Ajay Bhatt would approve."

"Ajay Bhatt?"

"He would approve if you stayed."

Ajay Bhatt, who was this Ajay Bhatt? He was, of course, the famous linguist (and social critic). A distinguished man. But why must they bring him up now?

He looked at the women—he enjoyed looking at them. They were skimpily dressed, he could see most of their breasts. He enjoyed looking at the breasts.

He began to walk away.

"We are closed—officially closed. But we *are* open for private dances."

"Private dances?"

"Twenty dollars for each dance."

"Where are they done?"

"There, in that corner." She pointed to her left.

He looked in that direction. It was even darker there—he could hardly make out a thing. He was tempted—or was he?

"How long is the dance?"

"It is one song. As long as the song lasts. Ajay Bhatt would approve."

Ajay Bhatt—there was that name again. Ajay Bhatt, who was this Ajay Bhatt? He was the famous linguist and critic. He had been to dance places all over the world—dance places in fifteen countries, in thirty-one of the fifty American states. He had written extensively on the subject. *The Wings of the Dancer* (University of Michigan, 1973). *The Reclining Dragon* (Chatto and Windus, 1982). *Dancing in the Streets* (Bantam, 1984). *Who Am I What Am I (if I Am)* (Random House, 1990).

He had written extensively. He had looked at things from an ontological and epistemological point of view. He had seen "lacunas" here, "solecisms" there. But for the most part, yes, he had approved.

Could Ajay Bhatt help him here? He stood there, hesitated. And then: "One song—that's not very long."

The woman did not answer. And then: "You want the dance?"

He hesitated again. Another pause. "I'll come back—I'll come back this evening. At six o'clock."

He began to walk away.

"Ajay Bhatt would approve. He would, he would." Thus he heard the words behind him. It was a shrill voice, longing—shrill and longing at the same time.

Ajay Bhatt—he was indeed an important man. A sacred man. The hero Dilip Kumar admired the dancers—he did, he did. But it was getting late now, so late. Should he not be getting home?

"I will come back at six," he said again. "I promise, I promise. I will come back again."

***

Dilip Kumar was a short dark man with black hair. He wore black pants, a white shirt. A black nylon jacket on top. (He kept his wallet in the inside pocket of the zippered jacket.) He was in Cleveland right now—Cleveland, Ohio. He had been to other states—Maryland, New Jersey, Texas, Montana. He had tried to imitate the path of the linguist and critic. The scholar had studied dance, the intricacies of dance. His training was extensive. Dilip Kumar was a novice—just that. But the love of the master for the dance, did he not share that? The spirit of the master, did he not share that?

He went to the dance places, place after place. He took photographs. He had a journal—he made entries in the journal. He observed the scene, imbibed it—tried to imbibe it.

That night Dilip Kumar went to "The Tropicana." He saw the dancers there. The next day to "Club Paradise." The day after, to "The Cat's Meow." At the last place he met the famous Lucky Love. She sat at his table, spoke to him of the sunsets in Rio (she had been there once), the sunrises in Tierra del Fuego.

"Are you from Argentina?" he said.

"I miss the pampas," she said. "I miss the long twilights. You know—the sky that goes on forever and forever."

Dilip Kumar understood her words—he believed he understood them.

Lucky Love was dressed in a long pink robe. There was no brassiere underneath, no underwear. One time she took her fingers and ran them on the side of his neck. One time she leaned forward and kissed him on the earlobe.

Dilip Kumar believed that she liked dark men—was he not one of these men? She was covered with perfume, and he liked the perfume. It was flowery but not overly so.

As she leaned forward he saw the tattoo just above her left breast. He thought that it was a small train—perhaps one from CSX, perhaps one from the Northern Railroad.

***

The days passed. Dilip Kumar went to the dance places—he continued to go. The master had studied these places, studied them. Should he not do the same?

Ajay Bhatt was his hero. He had met the famous scholar in person once. It was a meeting at one of the intellectual clubs—they were very popular in those days. Ajay Bhatt was a man of medium height with a thick grey beard. He wore a turtleneck sweater, a tweed jacket on top of the turtleneck. He spoke of texts, of lacunas in the text, solecisms. He gave Dilip Kumar a copy of his seminal book, *The Grammar of Cries* (Chatto and Windus, 1968).

They went to the dark study, sat on the black leather chairs. It was twilight, the light barely filtered in through the window. Dense poplar trees stood on the other side. When there are dense poplar trees, how can the light get through? How can it dare to get through?

Ajay Bhatt spoke about many things. He spoke about the dark places, the private dances inside. "Dance is an ancient art," he said.

Dilip Kumar nodded.

"A difficult art."

Dilip Kumar nodded.

"One must admire, not mock, the dancers."

The scholar spoke for some time on his research. Dilip Kumar listened, he tried to listen. Much of it was above his head. But he leaned forward, he nodded. He pricked his ears. He tried to do the best he could.

The shadows in the room began to grow long. At one point the scholar rose, went to the corner and turned on the lamp. But how dim—how yellow—was the light from the lamp. Perhaps it was a symbol of some kind. Wisdom comes from inside, light comes from inside. The light of the world—the light of the room—what need is there for that?

***

More days passed. Dilip Kumar was troubled, still troubled. He felt that he had understood little. He felt that he had made little progress.

One day again he went to the same place. It was four o'clock in the afternoon today, not three. Most of the scene was the same: the pitch darkness, the loud music. The few lights—small bulbs really—at the periphery of the dance floors.

He turned to the left—darkness. He turned to the right—darkness. But there, in the distance, was a table. Some men were seated there. He walked in that direction.

They were middle-aged men—some bald, some not so. They were simply dressed—in simple pants and shirts. It was cool inside: one wore a flannel shirt, two or three wore light jackets.

These men, who were they? Were they disciples of Ajay Bhatt? They spoke of "grammar," they spoke of "cries"—they spoke of the "grammar of cries." They quoted from the famous one's books—they quoted again and again.

> *The dance is performed at noon.*
> *But people think it is dark—dark all*
> *around. (The Wings of the Dancer, p. 19)*

> *The world tries to seduce you.*
> *Will you allow yourself to be seduced?*
> *(Dancing in the Streets, p. 374)*

> *In those days I often wandered the streets*
> *and the alleys. Some led to walls, others led*
> *to culs-de-sac. There was a green wooden*
> *door. That was the door that intrigued*
> *me most. I always wondered where it led.*
> *(Who Am I What Am I (if I Am), p. 201)*

It appeared that Ajay Bhatt was speaking of the forbidden fruit, the mysterious door. He was speaking of something that was attractive precisely—only?—because it was forbidden.

The men read from the pages again and again. The light at the table was dim—only a small candle that flickered in the center of the table. Sometimes they leaned their bodies forward, held the book close to the candle. Sometimes—was it on a dare?—they pulled the candle closer to them.

> *The Lord Shiva set the world in motion*
> *with a dance. And these dancers, do they*
> *not* keep *the world in motion? (The Wings*
> *of the Dancer*, p. 218)

The men were disciples of Ajay Bhatt. The scholar, the linguist, dreamed. Did they dream as well?

Dilip Kumar approached the men, but he did not dare to come too close. He observed from ten feet away, fifteen. There was music all around. There was the darkness, the pitch darkness. And these men—lonely men, lost men?—at the table. These men speaking of the linguist, the great linguist. These men speaking of the important things of the world.

***

One day Dilip Kumar went to see Ajay Bhatt again. The linguist was wise. Would Dilip Kumar learn from him? The linguist saw. Would Dilip Kumar be able to see as well?

But the linguist was a demanding man. He was not always easy to impress. Dilip Kumar spoke to the linguist about the places he had seen—the clubs, the "joints."

"There are many such places," the other said simply.

He spoke to the linguist about the darkness, the pitch darkness.

"Darkness is not new to man. He has seen it before."

He spoke about the table, the middle-aged men who sat there.

"Men gather in the daylight. They gather in the darkness. They have done so since the beginning of time."

The linguist was rational—perhaps he was so to a fault. Emotion, cheap emotion, what need did he have for that?

They sat there for some time—the linguist and the seeker. They spoke about happiness, they spoke about sorrow. They spoke about the dancer, they spoke about the dance.

"Who is the dancer?"

"No one knows."

"Who is the dance?"

"No one knows."

"They gather in the darkness—they dance, they dance. Is that not the key?"

***

Dilip Kumar went to clubs, he went to "joints." One day he went back to the original dark place again. There was trepidation in his heart. He had come back—why had he done it? He had come back—had he done the right thing?

He sat there for an hour, perhaps two. Then a thought seemed to come to him (what thought?). He left.

One day Dilip Kumar sat in the corner of "The Cat's Meow." Beside him was the famous Lucky Love. It was dark, the tables had a pink tablecloth—a red candle holder with a faint candle inside.

Dilip Kumar told Lucky of the places he had been to in India, the cricket matches he had seen.

She smiled at him.

He told her of the bicycles he had ridden, the three-wheeled scooter-rickshaws he had taken.

She smiled at him.

"Are there fish markets in Calcutta?" she said.

"A few," he said.

"Are there good hairdressers?"

"Many of them are Chinese. 'Chinese hairdresser,' they say on the sign outside. 'Bridal mehndi.'"

She was intrigued by the last phrase, asked him to repeat it.

He repeated it—repeated it again.

Lucky said that she had been married and would like to marry again. She took his hand—it was on the top of the table—she ran her hand over it.

The chimes sounded, Dilip Kumar jerked his head in that direction. The door was opening. It was a tall man—he wore a dark suit, a shiny white tie that did not quite match. Was it Luciano himself, the famous mobster? Could it be?

Lucky Love took her other hand, put it on top of the first. Two hands—soft, liquid—on top of one. Was that really so bad? He was a simple man. From Calcutta. Do simple men from Calcutta not deserve a chance?

That night in some motel bedroom they lay side by side. The Bengali. The famous dancer. She had been with other men—he knew that. He had little money, he was a simple man—she knew that.

But December nights can be lonely and cold. They did not want the dawn to come. How nice it was to lie there side by side. To lie there thus and to be safe—safe.

***

One day there was a raid by the police. Who were these police? Why did they come?

One day a journalist came. He wore a tweed jacket, he had flowing brown hair. He asked some questions—too many perhaps. Lucky Love smiled,

Dilip Kumar played with the ice cubes in his drink. Luciano entered the room, asked the man what he wanted. The man spoke, Luciano was not impressed. He asked the man to leave.

One day the dancers came to the stage, danced slowly, perhaps with uncommon grace. Dilip Kumar began to speak some lines from Yeats, but thought instead of the lines from *The Reclining Dragon*.

> *The mothers cook the dark green lentils,*
> *the children play.*
> *And is the world at peace—is it finally at*
> *peace?* (p. 29)

Lucky Love was impressed, even the harsh Luciano. Sometimes the latter smirked, sometimes he guffawed. But today he seemed solemn—unusually so. "Ajay Bhatt is a nice man," he said. "Maybe I will invite him to the club. He can tell me about his books, his travels. It may not be so bad. No no, not so bad."

***

Dilip Kumar studied the books of Ajay Bhatt, he continued to study them.

> *The world is a stage. There are good people,*
> *there are bad people. Are there dancers as*
> *well?* (*The Wings of the Dancer*, p. 218)

They were accurate words, difficult to deny. Some of the newspapers—the philistines—did try to deny them. But their arguments were poor, not very impressive. Was anyone persuaded?

> *The musician was a blind man. He played the sarod, was working on his last raga. Once the raga was done—it was dedicated to the sun, to the bird bathing in the dirt in the sun—he would be ready for the next life. If he had followed the right path, he would know when his duties were done. If he had followed the right path ...*
>
> *The dancer listened to the musician. The first step, the second. The first step, the second. He listened, he listened. He began to dance! (Dancing in the Streets, p. 88)*

They were melodic words, pleasing to the ear. Not all the critics were appeased. But the truth was the truth. Could it be denied?

> *"Ask a boon," said the gods.*
> *"The boon of dance," he said.*
> *"So be it," said the gods.*
> *And thus began his life as a dancer. From village to village he went. The reason behind the dance was not clear.*
> *"Reason," said he, "must there be a reason?" (The Reclining Dragon, p. 147)*

In this way the linguist wrote. How moving his words, how sublime! But some of the critics would have none of it. They mocked him—again and again they mocked.

Lucky Love left "The Cat's Meow," went to work for "The Tropicana." Dilip Kumar followed her. She left "The Tropicana," went to work for "Club Paradise." Again Dilip Kumar was not far behind. Other dancers were there—Fifi, Desiree, some famous dancer from a village in Portugal. She was religious, perhaps excessively so. She began every dance with a prayer. "*Mon Dieu*," she began—in French, not Portuguese.

One day Luciano happened to be coming through the door. He wore a blue suit, a white shirt underneath—no tie. There was a gold bracelet on his right wrist, a thick gold ring on his left hand. He seemed to be upset about something. Was it at the police who were making more raids than usual? Was it at the dancers (was it possible?). Was it at the dance itself—at *that*?

"These people," he said. "I hate them."

"People—what people?"

"They think they can compete with me, take away my business."

"People, Luciano, who are these people?"

But Luciano was in no mood to elaborate. He said these things—every so often he said them. He had been thinking about something—he needed to get it off his chest.

Lucky Love tried to comfort the mobster—she rubbed her hand down his back. The mobster smiled, but it was a weak smile, a smile without conviction.

Dilip Kumar sat there silent; it was not his place to speak. He tried to think of lines from Ajay Bhatt— did they come?

That night in his motel room, Dilip Kumar found himself unable to sleep. He turned on the lamp, opened the book that he kept by his bedside. He opened to a page at random. It was a long and diffi-cult passage. Was this the right passage—did it help him to understand?

> *The musician played the* tala, *the* alap—
> *all according to the musical notation of*
> *the North. But then in the second move-*
> *ment he switched suddenly to the* pallavi
> *of the Southern Hindustani—a style of*
> *the native Hindus, a style disdaining any*
> *influence of the recent rulers, the Mughals.*
>
> *With what emotion the dancer joined*
> *him! A surprising change in movement,*
> *yes, but the dancer was prepared. Always*
> *he was prepared. And the musician and*
> *the dancer, how well they worked together.*
> *The music and the dance, could they ever*
> *be kept apart? (The Reclining Dragon,*
> *p. 302)*

The words of the linguist were refined, poetry even. There was distress in the world, there was tension. Things did not always go as planned. But the musician, did he give up? The dancer, the dancer—did he ever give up as well?

***

More days passed. Luciano was running a numbers racket. He moved on to prostitution. He moved on to real estate.

One day there was some shouting, some shots were fired. The police came. They locked the doors of the lounge from the inside. It was two-thirty in the afternoon—not many customers. They took everyone to a back room, made them huddle in a corner.

There were some jokes, there was some nervous laughter. But in twenty minutes they said all was well again. No explanations, no details. "You can go back out," they said.

Back out—hmm. They went out, Dilip Kumar sat at his table. The music was turned back on. Lucky Love came, sat beside him. Luciano—a little flushed perhaps—came and joined them as well.

"You say the virgins danced in the temple?"

"Yes," said Dilip Kumar. "They danced."

"You say the eunuchs danced at the wedding parties, asked for money or would refuse to leave?"

"It is so," said Dilip Kumar.

"And Ajay Bhatt has studied all this?"

"This and more—much more."

Luciano took out a cigar, chewed on the end of it for a while. He took out a match, hesitated about something. Finally he lit the cigar.

Dilip Kumar watched him. He watched Lucky Love watching them. (She had taken one hand, placed it softly—was it tenderly?—on the other's wrist.)

Luciano indulged in his cigar for some time. But he was a big man. He had eighty-five people working for him, perhaps a hundred. He drove in Cadillacs, he drove in limousines. Did he not deserve to indulge?

Ajay Bhatt had studied Luciano—or at least men like him. "Children," he had said about them. "Gods," he had said. "They make their world, make it from nothing. And God—the eternal one—did He not do the same?" (*The Grammar of Cries*, p. 471)

***

Dilip Kumar went here, he went there. Ajay Bhatt went with him—if not in person, then in spirit.

One day Dilip Kumar was in a dark place. "Sit," said the woman.

"Which chair?"

"Any one you like."

There were three chairs, he sat in the chair in the middle. He sat there, he leaned his head back.

The woman left the room. She came back, a bucket in her hand. She rested the bucket on the floor.

"Is this the dance?"

"Wait," she said.

He had already taken off his shoes, laid them to the side. She took his pants, began to roll them up. She rolled them almost to the knees, stopped.

She took the bucket, moved it closer to him.

"Put your feet inside."

He put his feet inside.

The water was warm, he liked the touch of the warm water.

"Is it warm?" she said.

"Yes," he said.

"It is not water. It is a Chinese medicine. All the way from China."

He sat there, his feet in the bucket.

"Is this the dance?" he said.

"Wait," she said.

He sat there, his feet in the water. She left the room, came back again. She left the room, came back again.

She sat on a low stool near the bucket. She lifted up his left leg, drying it with a towel. Then she rubbed the leg with her hands—rubbed it slowly. She rubbed the leg—rubbed it tenderly. The foot—she did not forget the foot.

He sat in the chair, his head leaning back. She rubbed his leg, she rubbed it.

"Is it good?" she said.

"Yes," he said.

"Do you like it?" she said.

"Yes," he said.

She let the left leg rest there, turned to the right leg. She dried it with a towel. Then she rubbed this second leg, rubbed it slowly. She rubbed it tenderly. The foot—she did not forget the foot.

Dilip Kumar sat there, resting, resting. He thought of Ajay Bhatt, he thought of Luciano. He thought of Lucky Love—the twilights, the long twilights in places far away.

"Is this the dance?" he said.

She did not answer him.

"Is this the dance?" he said.

The woman smiled at him. Perhaps it was with softness. Perhaps it was with pity as well.

The minutes passed (perhaps the hours). The hours passed (perhaps the days). Dilip Kumar sat there, sat there. He did not want to leave. Perhaps it was the darkness, perhaps it was the smells. Perhaps it was the dance—the dance as well.

What was this dance, no one could say. From where it came, no one could say. But sometimes it was there. And could one just turn away?

> *The children gather in the twilight, they like to play. They gather in the darkness, they like to dream. And the dream, the dream—or is it the longing?—is that not the greatest dance of all?* (*Who Am I What Am I (if I Am)*, p. 386)

Dilip Kumar had learned a lot from Ajay Bhatt, the master. He had learned from Lucky Love, from Luciano. He had learned from others as well. But now he wanted to just sit there. He wanted to long, to long (how the longing tormented him, *comforted* him). He did not want to leave.

The Bill

Ramesh Thakur had three houses—one in Defence Colony, one in R.K. Puram, and one in Malviya Nagar. But he was not happy.

"So much dusting, Chandar. I go to each house once a week. I dust, I dust. The sofas, the tables, the mantelpiece. I do not forget anything.

"But it is hard work, Chandar. It is not easy."

But still I was happy for him. He was retired, he needed something to do. This kept him busy. He had three houses: there was security in that. He had some place to go three days a week: this kept him busy, there was security in that as well.

He complained about the dusting, yes. He complained about the traffic and the pollution. But he had something to do.

One day he was at the DESU (Delhi Electric Supply Undertaking) office in South Delhi. There was a problem with the electric bill for one of the houses, the bill obviously wrong. It was overstated by three thousand rupees. He went to discuss the bill; they said that he was at the wrong office. He went to the second office; the girl was sick, she had not come in today. He went to the third office; there were six people in line ahead of him. He waited patiently, and then impatiently, for fifty minutes. At last his turn came. But just as he arrived at the glass window, a cardboard sign was put up behind the window. "Tea," it said simply.

"What is this?"

"The hours, sir, the hours of operation are posted."

He looked at the hours posted on the wall to the right. "Open 10 AM -12 PM, 2 PM—4 PM." At present it was 11:20.

He looked at his watch to confirm the time and looked again at the sign. "You should be *open*," he said.

"It is time for tea, sir."

"What is this?"

"A man needs his tea, sir."

Again he looked at his watch. Eleven-twenty, that is exactly what it said. Eleven-twenty, not twelve. Not even close to twelve.

Ramesh Thakur felt the blood rush to his face. "I have been to three offices already. I have received a bill. The bill is a mistake. A mistake."

"A hypothesis, sir."

"What is this?"

"You say, sir, that the bill is a mistake. That is a *hypothesis*." The host repeated the same word. He seemed to take pride in it.

Ramesh Thakur again felt the blood rush to his face. He was about to lose his temper. He should not do it. He wanted to tell the man many things. The man should be told many things. But what would that accomplish? No no, better to control himself.

"Hypothesis, sir, the world is filled with hypotheses." Thus continued the other. "Men make statements but they are not scientific. They do not verify them. No observation, sir, no testing. And so the hypothesis remains that: a hypothesis. Nothing more."

Ramesh Thakur looked at the other, aghast. The impudence of the man, the audacity. You go from house to house, you dust. You dust the sofas, the tables, the mantelpiece. You go from office to office trying to solve a simple problem. A problem that you did not create. A problem that *should* be solved. And yet, and yet …

The blood *had* risen to Ramesh Thakur's face. But what need was there for a fight? A fight, did it not turn into a war? A war led to more wars, more wars led to more wars still. No no, better to control oneself. Better to …

"Tea, yes yes," he suddenly added, "every man deserves his tea." He did not want to speak in this way but somehow the words came out. And he knew (or did he?) that it was the right and prudent thing to say.

"Every man deserves his tea. Please go and drink. Please go and enjoy. I will stand here, wait. When you come back, we will talk."

"Yes yes," the other added, more accommodating now, wagging his head, even that. "We will talk. The day is young. Men need to talk. If they do not talk …"

The sentence was left dangling there, unfinished. And the other left, left to drink his tea.

Ramesh Thakur watched him from the back as he walked away. The man walked into some back room to the right. The man greeted someone in the room— who, Ramesh Thakur could not say. Then the man gently kicked the door closed behind him. Lucky man! Impudent man!

Ramesh Thakur stood at the narrow blue counter. He tapped impatiently on the counter with his fingers. But then he realized what he was doing—he stopped the tapping. "Better to be patient," he said. "Patience is a virtue. And impatience—did not even our teacher tell us once?—is a vice."

***

Ramesh Thakur waited, waited. Five minutes passed, ten. Fifteen minutes passed. The door in the back opened a peep. Then it closed again. The blood rushed to Ramesh Thakur's face. He controlled himself. Consciously, deliberately, he controlled himself.

Twenty minutes passed. Twenty-one. Two more. The door opened again—this time more, more. Someone—was it the esteemed one himself?— emerged at the doorway, stretching wide his arms on each side.

Ramesh Thakur began to tap on the counter, then realized what he was doing and checked himself. There was some lint on his shirt, he flicked at it with his right hand. His heart was racing. A lackey—a low-class lackey—and he was putting him through all this.

The lackey—the esteemed one—was indeed making his way from the back room. He came in through the entrance to the right. He walked slowly, slowly, to the counter. The cardboard sign was there. Consciously, deliberately—slowly—he began to lift it.

The people in line behind Ramesh Thakur brushed against him. "Please, please," said Mister Thakur in some anger, turning slightly, his voice rising. "I have been waiting for over one hour. Kindly wait—kindly wait for your turn."

The others were not so impressed.

"Kindly wait. Please wait."

A few controlled themselves, but others, propelled perhaps by still others behind them, kept pushing.

"Order! Order!" called out the lackey. "Everyone will get his turn." He looked at the clock on the wall. "Only fourteen minutes before lunch. Time is precious. Control yourself. If you wish to be served, kindly—control yourself."

The voice of the lackey—screechy, loud—seemed to have had an effect. Mister Thakur had spoken up twice: nothing. But this lackey, this lackey ...

Time is precious: Mister Thakur was tempted to scream at the other, but beggars cannot be choosers. He controlled himself. Again he did it.

The other pulled up to the glass window, spoke through the metal grilles in the middle.

"What is the problem, sir?"

"This bill—as I was saying before—the bill is a mistake."

"How is it a mistake?"

"As I was saying before, before the tea break" (*tea break*: he felt the words to be unnecessary), "the bill is an error, an obvious error. It is overstated by three thousand rupees."

"Three thousand rupees?"

"The normal bill, you see—I have brought the bills for the past month—the month before that—the month before that …"

"Yes yes, go on."

"The normal bill is 300 rupees. This bill is 3,300. A computer error, I am sure. A human error. An extra '3' was added."

The other stood on the other side of the glass window, examined the bill.

"Did you have a big function?"

"A big function? No no, of course not."

"A birthday party—a lot of lights. A wedding perhaps."

"No no, there was no wedding."

"You have daughters? A son?"

"Why is that important?"

"They are young, they need to be married off. A party is held—a big party. Guests come—important guests. They come from all parts of the country. There is a big electric bill."

Mister Thakur looked at the other. "No no, no such thing."

"There is a function, yes. The people come—they like to come. From Poona they come, from Patiala. From Kanpur they come, from Karnataka. They come, they come. From Manipur, from Madras …"

Mad—was this man mad? Did he like geography—did he want to show off his knowledge of geography?

"Guests, I told you, there were no guests. Party, function, there was no such thing."

"Why then is the bill so big?"

"That is my point—exactly my point. It is a mistake, an error."

The other looked at the bill again.

"A hypothesis," he said.

"A hypothesis?"

"The bill is in error, you say. A mistake. A hypothesis—nothing but a hypothesis."

A hypothesis: was he back to that same thing again?

"I have showed you the bills from the previous months. Three hundred rupees. Now—3,300 rupees. It is a big difference. The same house: two bedrooms, two baths, a kitchen. It is a mistake—it *has* to be."

"Two bedrooms, you say, two baths. Attached baths, one to each bedroom?"

"Attached, not attached, what difference should it make?" But Mister Thakur controlled himself. "One bath attached. One not attached."

"Attached bathrooms, Mister Thakur, they have a much greater value in the market."

"Yes, yes, I agree."

"But only one bath is attached. The other is not so."

And the other seemed suddenly lost in thought. He looked into space, the thin air. He seemed almost saddened by the situation. As if attached bathrooms were the most important thing in the world. As if one bathroom not being attached was a sadness, a loss, and not just a general sadness and loss but a sadness and loss to *him*.

Mister Thakur stared at the other. Was it in disgust? Was it in awe? He had come to the office to point out an error, an obvious error. And now *this*. Had the world gone mad? Had it gone completely mad?

They talked for some time. The people in line behind Mister Thakur began to grow impatient. They had always been impatient—now they were only more so.

The lackey looked at the bill a second time. He looked at the bill for the previous month—the bill for the month before that. He took a wooden ruler and placed it under some line on the first bill. The second bill: the same. The third bill: the same. Then he lined up the bills together, again put his ruler in the needed places.

He did this for some time. At last he looked up at Mister Thakur, shook his head.

"The bills do not match," he said with some finality.

"Exactly," said Mister Thakur. "Exactly. That is just my point."

There was a pause.

"Two bills are the same, one is bigger."

"Exactly, exactly. That is just the point."

The lackey seemed lost in thought. Was he thinking of something deep? Was he about to reach a decision? Had he reached it already?

At last he looked up, he smiled at the other. "Are you sure there was no function?"

"No no, no function."

"No wedding, no party?"

"No no, nothing like that."

"We must have a meeting on this."

Meeting: Mister Thakur was intrigued by the word. There would be progress—a good thing. But this meeting, when would it be held? Where? Who would be present?

Mister Thakur was about to give voice to these questions. But the other was wise—he spoke up instead.

"Lunch!" he said suddenly.

"What is this?"

"Lunch!" he said.

There was a short pause.

"It is twelve o'clock, Mister Thakur." He pointed to the clock on the wall. "One minute past. I have already overworked. There are rules here, guidelines. I cannot contravene the guidelines."

Contravene: what kind of word was that? Was it an actual word? The man had just taken a tea break!

Mister Thakur was about to speak—to rant, to rail. But he controlled himself.

An audible sigh escaped from the people behind him. Mister Thakur turned slightly and looked over his shoulder.

"Damn it!" said someone.

"Bitch!" said a second.

"But I brought my lunch," said a third. "I am prepared. Cards—does anyone want to play cards?"

Mister Thakur was bewildered at the goings-on. But what could he do?

He turned to the important host. "When will lunch be over?" he asked.

The other had already taken his cardboard sign—a different sign this time—and put it on the glass behind the window.

"LUNCH," it said in block letters.

"When will lunch be over?" Mister Thakur ventured again.

"The hours are posted, Mister Thakur."

Mister Thakur looked at the sign posted on the wall to the right.

"But *two* o'clock!" he protested, he almost wailed. "I've been here for hours. I'm not a young man. We've spoken—spoken for ten minutes …"

The other seemed offended, genuinely so. "*Ten* minutes, Mister Thakur? I was here attending to you—*attending*—at 11:46. It is now well past twelve. Lunch hour. *Lunch*."

Mister Thakur looked at the clock. Two minutes past twelve.

"A man has to eat, Mister Thakur. Is he a servant

to all the people who come, who dare to come? Is he not human? Does he not deserve dignity, peace?"

"What of my peace?" Mister Thakur was tempted to blurt out. But he controlled himself, again he did it.

"No no, right, quite right." Somehow the words escaped from his lips. How they escaped, he could not say. Perhaps some angel was guiding him. "Two o'clock, my good sir, I will be here. Right here."

The other had heard enough. He had already turned his back and was on his way.

Mister Thakur sighed, turned to those in line behind him. "Can I go and sit somewhere? Come back at two? Will I be at the front of the line?"

The others laughed. They laughed out loud.

"First come, first serve," someone from the back of the line called out.

"What is this?"

"First come, first serve."

"But I *was* here first."

"You leave the line, Mister Thakur, you are no longer first."

There was logic to the words. Could he deny the logic? A man needs to go out and to stretch his legs. But so what? To go to the bathroom. But so what? Logic is logic: it cannot be denied.

Mister Thakur looked at the others behind him. They too had heard enough, they too had moved on to other things. They were sitting cross-legged on the floor. The floor was dirty, but that hardly seemed to trouble them. Some were opening up their tiffin boxes, getting ready for lunch. Some were sitting there eyes closed, rocking back and forth. Were they in prayer? Others were opening a deck of cards.

"Joker? You want to include the Joker in the game?"

"Yes yes, of course. There is no fun without Joker."

Mister Thakur looked at them, marveled at their patience. They looked like experienced people who had been here before.

Perhaps he should admire them, follow their lead. His back hurt, but so? His knees hurt, but so? He wanted to go to the bathroom, he wanted to go somewhere and get a bite to eat. But how could he?

***

The time passed. Slowly it passed. Mister Thakur looked at the clock: 12:20. He looked again: 12:21.

Slowly the time passed. Mister Thakur stood there, shaking his head. He stood there, fuming. "Breathe," he said to himself. "Breathe deeply. You took yoga—took it twenty years ago. With breathing, calm can come. Peace can come. Anything is possible."

The time passed. One-forty. One forty-one. Somehow, somehow, it passed. As the hour of two approached, there was hope again. There was light. The ordeal was almost over.

Two o'clock: no sign of the lackey. Five after two: no sign. Ten after two: no sign. "Where is he? Where is he?" the shouts were heard.

One or two messengers were seen in their khaki clothes. A security guard—also in khaki clothes, a baton by his side—appeared. But the esteemed one, the lackey, where was he?

At 2:13, the back door opened a peep. It closed again. Two-seventeen—it opened again. There was movement now, real movement. At 2:21 the lackey—the host and esteemed one—was back. He was back again at his esteemed place.

He stood there, shuffling some papers. There was a rubber stamp to his right. He lifted it, put it back in its former place. There was a metal stapler—he lifted that, put that back again.

His eyes were groggy and red. Had he been sleeping? Had he been drinking? Was he ill, even that?

"Next!" he shouted out with some authority.

Mister Thakur, already at the window, hunched closer.

"Next!"

Mister Thakur hunched closer still.

Mister Thakur had vowed to himself to be bolder this time. Did he remember his words? To teach the other his place. Did he remember his words?

Mister Thakur had the bills in his hand. He slid them forward to the other—slid them through the hole under the glass. The other looked at the bills. He looked at them again. He seemed confused, distracted.

"What is this?' he said at last.

"The error," said Mister Thakur, reminding him. "The *error*."

"Error? What error?"

Mister Thakur reminded him—calmly, simply— of all that had preceded. The discussion before lunch. The bills for the previous months. The bill for this month. The error, the *obvious* error.

The other was not impressed.

Mister Thakur persisted.

The other was not impressed.

"Remember, we were talking about the bill. The electric bill. In the past few months, 300 rupees. This month, 3,300. Three hundred, that is the correct amount."

"Correct amount? Who says that is the correct amount?"

"History, sir, that is the historical record." *Historical record*: Mister Thakur was surprised at his own words.

"I do not care about history."

"What is this?"

"History tells us about the past. It tells us nothing about the present."

Mister Thakur was about to argue, to put the other in his place. But he thought better of it.

"A meeting," he said calmly. "A meeting—you said before lunch—a meeting is needed."

"No meeting is needed."

"What about a supervisor? Is there no supervisor we can turn to?"

"Are you trying to insult me?"

"No no, it is just that …"

"I know what you are thinking, Mister Thakur. You think that I am an incompetent man. You think that I cannot make a decision. You think that superiors, only superiors …"

"No no, it is just …"

But the other was in no mood to listen. He ranted, he railed. He lectured to Mister Thakur—lectured on the need to defer to others, the need to let other people do their jobs.

"Each person has his duty, Mister Thakur."

"So I see."

"I know my duty, Mister Thakur."

"Indeed, indeed." And so it went. On and on, on and on. As they were speaking—back and forth, back and forth—a short dark man emerged from the back. He wore a short-sleeve checkered shirt. His hair was grey and balding, there was a grey stubble on his face. Perhaps he had not shaved in days. He went to the lackey, whispered something in his left ear.

Mister Thakur leaned forward discreetly, straining to make out the words.

The visitor stood up on his toes, cupped his hands around the other's ear. He whispered again.

Again Mister Thakur strained to make out the words.

The lackey raised his head, looked at Mister Thakur. There was a big smile—or was it a look of weariness, of infinite weariness?—on his face.

"The Committee will see you," he said.

"The Committee?"

"The Committee will see you."

"The Committee—what is this Committee?"

But the other was in no mood to explain. There was a low gate to the right.

"Through the gate," he said.

Mister Thakur collected his papers, hurried to the gate.

"The signs," said the other. "Follow the signs."

"Where do they lead?"

But the other was in no mood to answer. "Next!" Mister Thakur heard the loud words behind him. "Next!"

***

There was a low swinging gate in the right corner of the room. During the day only the two messengers and the security guard had passed through it. Now Mister Thakur hurried to the gate as well.

It was a blue gate, quite low to the ground. A young, healthy man could easily have stepped over it. But who would dare? And besides, Mister Thakur was hardly a young man. He was an old man, well past his prime. He was much closer to his death than to his birth. Much closer to his death than to his wedding date. Much closer to death … But why persist with these thoughts? He was an old man, quite old. The point is made.

Mister Thakur walked down a narrow hallway and then down another. The floor creaked beneath him and the walls were dingy—a faded green with the plaster peeling in several places.

Mister Thakur made several turns, came at last to a small room. The light was dim, a single naked bulb hung from the ceiling. There was an old wooden table, three men sat on the other side in simple wooden chairs.

They were middle-aged men, all in faded striped shirts, the collars open. Two of the men, one at each end, wore white T-shirts underneath, both round-collared. The other, the one in the middle, seemed to be wearing no undershirt. The hair, rank and gross, protruded from under the top button of his shirt.

Some bills lay in front of them. But what bills were they? Mister Thakur had brought his own bills with him. Were they not the relevant documents? But perhaps the others had already looked at the same bills. How? When?

Mister Thakur stood at the table and bowed to the men.

The others did not respond.

"May I sit down, please?"

No answer.

At last one man gestured with his hand toward the empty chair. He did not speak.

Mister Thakur sat down, hunching his body tightly, his hands on his lap. He waited for the others to speak.

Silence.

Still he waited.

Nothing.

At last Mister Thakur decided to speak himself. He tried to do so loudly and confidently. But more than once his voice cracked.

"I was speaking to the … the gentleman—the kind gentleman—in the front. We spoke for some time. I explained to him the case."

No answer.

"The bills for the past months. The bill for this month." And Mister Thakur went into the details.

The others were not impressed.

"The current bill is in error, clearly. Not three hundred but *three thousand* three hundred." Mister Thakur emphasized the needed words, waited for a response.

No response.

He spoke some more.

Silence.

One of the men—the one on the extreme left—turned towards the one in the middle. He cupped his right hand around the other's ear and whispered something. The other's right cheek twitched.

There was another pause. Mister Thakur wanted to continue, but what should he say? He had explained his case the best he could. Should not the others ask a question? Was it not up to them?

Mister Thakur fidgeted in his chair, clearing his throat.

Silence. And then: "You seem to be quite sure of yourself, Mister Thakur."

"What is this?"

"You seem to be very confident."

This was the man on the extreme right. Mister Thakur was nonplussed. He did not know what to say.

"You seem to be quite sure, Mister Thakur. Are you a philosopher?"

Philosopher: what an odd word. "A philosopher, sir? No no, I am not a philosopher. A businessman, a retired …"

"Are you a priest?"

Another odd word. "No, sir, I am not a priest."

"And yet you seem to be so sure. Why is that?"

Mister Thakur was at a loss. He was no philosopher, he was no priest. He was just a customer. A customer who had received a wrong bill. Who had come to plead his case. A good case, a strong case.

The other ignored Mister Thakur, looking at the papers in front of him. His companions leaned forward as well, looking at the same papers. They squinted their eyes. The light was not good.

"The light is dim, Mister Thakur."

"What is this?"

"The light is dim, Mister Thakur, very dim. What is one to do?"

The light was indeed dim. But were there not more pressing things at stake?

"The light is dim, Mister Thakur."

"But the case, sir …"

"The walls are dingy."

"But the case, sir …"

"But God is great, Mister Thakur. Is it not so?"

God, God, why must they bring Him into it? God was a good and kind man—of course He was. But the facts were the only thing that mattered. Should they not stick to the facts?

The others were not impressed. "Do you believe in God, Mister Thakur?" This was another man now, the one on the extreme left.

"God, sir?"

"Do you think that He is the cause of the bad bill?"

God? The cause? "It was a human error, sir, a computer error. But why bring God into it?"

The other was unmoved. "We know metaphysics, Mister Thakur."

"Metaphysics, sir?"

"We know logic. If you deserved, God would have helped you with the bill. He has not helped you. Therefore, you do not deserve."

"What is this?"

"If you deserved, God would have helped you with the bill. He has not helped you. Therefore, you do not deserve."

Logic, what kind of logic was this? It was terrible and flawed logic. If God intervened, it could be for many reasons. If He did not intervene, it could be for many reasons. How did it follow at all that Mister Thakur did not deserve?

"Logic is a good thing, Mister Thakur. Do not dismiss it. Do not dare to dismiss."

Mister Thakur stared at the others in disbelief. Words, words, empty words. He had the facts on his side, important facts. And did they care? He stated the facts again and again. And did they care?

It was dark in the room, and getting darker. There were flies in the room, humming in the corner. In the distance a lizard climbed the wall. In the corner there was—or did Mister Thakur only imagine it?—the scurrying of a mouse.

A few seconds passed. The men on each end of the table had apparently had their say. The man in the middle—the one with all the hair on his chest—now began to fidget. He had been silent to this point. Now he leaned forward and seemed distressed about something. He shook his head sadly—several times he did it.

"The light is dim, Mister Thakur."

"But the facts, sir …"

"The walls are dingy."

"But the facts, sir …"

"We are tired, Mister Thakur. Very tired. Is it not best that you go home?"

But Mister Thakur did not *want* to go home. He spoke again of the bill. No interest. He spoke of the principle of it all. No interest.

"But this is madness," Mister Thakur said at one point.

No answer.

"It is your job, your *duty*."

Silence.

It was dark in the room, it was getting darker. There were flies in the room. Were there gnats and bees as well?

The men looked at Mister Thakur—they stared. They looked at him—they grimaced. Did they laugh as well?

"Go home now, Mister Thakur."

"But my case, sir …"

"Go home now, Mister Thakur. Do not complain."

Mister Thakur was a grown-up man. He had the *right* to complain. He was an educated man. He had the *cause* to complain. And did anyone care?

"Go home now, Mister Thakur. *Go.*"

At last Mister Thakur rose and collected his bills—one bill, the next, one bill, the next. He shook his head. It was dark now, soon it would grow darker. Was it not best to leave?

Mister Thakur made his way in the darkness. The scooter-rickshaw, the horse carriage. The walk. The interminable walk at the end. Slowly, slowly, he made his way home.

The days passed, the weeks. And did anything change? The weeks passed, the months. And then? Mister Thakur went to the man at the counter: he was a busy man. He went to the room in the back: they were metaphysical men. He vowed to fight the case— to fight, to fight, to take it to "the highest court in the land."

And did anyone care?

"But it is not my fault."

"These things happen."

"But it is not my fault."

"God made the world, Mister Thakur. Accept what is."

The bill, now due, soon became "overdue." Mister Thakur protested. But to whom, to what avail? The bill soon became "in arrears." Again he protested. To whom, to what avail? Mister Thakur was not a young man anymore. Why fight the things you cannot control?

One day Mister Thakur sat in his room and he wrote a check for the full amount. Did he not do the right thing? One day he sat in his room, he prayed. Did he not do the right thing?

Mister Thakur went to each of his three houses—each week he went. He dusted, he dusted. "I am a lucky man," he said. Was there irony in his words? He dusted the sofas, the tables, the mantelpiece. "I am a lucky man," he said. Even his wife said that he did a good job, very good. He did not miss a single speck.

Pranab Roy

Pranab Roy was a short dark man, about five feet four inches. He went shopping for a new jacket at the mall. He had a job interview coming up.

He went to Raleigh's—much too expensive. He went to Hecht's, to Woodies—still too expensive. He went to Montgomery Ward, he found a jacket he liked.

"We will give you a pair of pants for free," said the people at the store.

"A whole pair?"

"We could give you two pairs if you let us. But for that you have to buy a suit."

"Don't need a suit. A jacket will be fine."

Pranab Roy emerged from the store, a long plastic bag in his hand (the brown wooden hanger peeked out at the top). He was proud of himself, proud of the purchase he had made. An interview lay ahead—an important interview—and he was bound to do well.

The interview was three days later. Pranab Roy bathed, he dressed. He put on his new jacket, he put on his favorite maroon tie.

He appeared at the interview, they smiled at him. Smiled knowingly. "A new jacket?" they said.

"Yes," he said.

"A blazer, a navy blazer."

"Yes," he said.

"But the jacket is *polyester*," they said.

"What is this?"

"Wool is fine, cotton is fine. Silk, linen, gabardine. But a polyester jacket—no no, not so good."

"It is new," he said.

They were not impressed.

"I bought it at Montgomery Ward."

They were not impressed.

They said that Pranab Roy had learned his lesson—and had he? He would go to the mall. He would wander the mall—back and forth, back and forth. But he would never buy a polyester jacket, not that. He would never do it again.

He was leaving the interview, they were walking him to the car.

"And polyester *pants*?" he said. "Are they allowed?"

They smiled at him, smiled again. Was it in pity?

***

Pranab Roy returned to his apartment. He did not get the job, not that. But he had learned his lesson.

He went to the bathroom, he washed his face. He took off his shoes and socks, he washed his feet as well. A man is tired, beaten. Does he not need to feel clean, at least that? To feel *pure*—even that?

He went to his room, he hung his polyester jacket in the closet. He had one wool jacket as well, a dark grey. It was a little frayed at the sleeve, but he would try to hide the frayed part. He would get away with it—he prayed he would.

He put on his striped pajamas (they were his favorite). He turned on the television. *The Rifleman*. A good show. *Andy Griffith*. A good show. *Superman*. Another.

"They are old shows," said the others.

"Yes," he answered.

"Why do you like them?"

"Why, I do not know. The heroes are nice, kind."

"Nice? Kind?"

"The Rifleman—Lucas McCain—is a widower (he has one son). Andy Griffith—Andy Taylor—is a widower (he has one son). Superman is not a widower, but he lives alone. And he *is* an orphan. His parents …"

"You like these kind of shows, then? Shows about widowers and orphans?"

Pranab Roy laughed. Had the others made a joke? Had they said something wise? He liked the shows because the people on them worked hard. They were *good* people. Was that so hard to follow?

The days passed. Pranab Roy stayed at home, he watched his TV shows. But was it enough? He ate pizza, he ate TV dinners. But was it enough?

He had to make a living. To pay the bills. The interviews called—all the job interviews. He put on his jacket (polyester? wool?), he went.

They asked him about his experience. He answered. Again they asked. He answered. One day Pranab Roy was at an interview. It was in a tall glass building, so many offices in the building. A tall man sat on the other side of the dark wooden desk. He was a handsome man—fair-skinned, with only a hint of grey in his hair. He looked distinguished. Would Pranab Roy ever look the same way?

The man asked questions. Pranab Roy answered. The man asked more questions. Pranab Roy answered. The man asked Pranab Roy about his experience.

"I have done systems design," he said.

"What else?"

"Data modeling."

"What else?"

"I have worked, I have worked."

Too general. The other was not impressed.

"Systems integration," said Pranab Roy at last.

The other's interest was piqued.

"That is important here, Mister Roy, very important. The systems integration, that is. Could you give us an example? The systems, the subsystems you worked on?"

Pranab Roy was at a loss. He had done systems integration, of course he had. But on what? This was an interview, for God's sake: he should have been more prepared. The system—the world? The subsystems—work, home, happiness?

He stuttered, he fumbled. At last he tried again. "We were developing a new system, sir."

"Yes?"

"The design, the development, the QA—all that was done."

"Yes?"

"But we needed to look at the whole system. To see if it worked. To see if we could do things to *break* it."

The other smiled. He smiled again. "And what was the system?"

"The system sir, yes."

"The system, Mister Roy, what was the system?"

"God, sir," he said. But no no, that was not the system. "America, sir," he said. But no no, that was not the system. "Happiness"—what of kind of system, answer, was that?

The other did not look impressed. "The system you worked on, Mister Roy, the subsystems?"

Again Pranab Roy was at a loss. His mind was blank. Was it the TV shows he watched all the time? Was it his jacket, his polyester jacket?

"The visa system, sir. Yes yes, that is it. Immigrant visa. The Immigrant Visa System (IV). Yes yes, *that* is the system I worked on."

The other still didn't look impressed. "And why didn't you say so?"

"Sir?"

"You hesitated—why didn't you just say so from the very start?"

Pranab Roy was at a loss. Why indeed didn't he say so? Why didn't he get to the point—right to the point?

"I am sorry, sir," he said at last.

Sorry: what a strange word it was. A word of weakness, not strength. Why did he say it? Was it necessary to say it?

"This systems integration that you worked on, what kind of tools did you use?"

"Tools, sir?"

"You did systems integration, you didn't do it by hand. Tools—what kind of tools did you use? Mapping? Interface protocols? Methodology—was there a methodology?"

Again Pranab Roy hesitated. Tools, of course he had used tools. Methodology, of course there had been a methodology. But what were they? What were they exactly?

"I know a few things, sir."

"What is this?"

"One time, sir, the TNS name file was not up-to-date. I fixed it."

"Was it a problem related to the integration?"

"We needed a remote connection, we did not have it. I fixed it—I established the connection."

"And this problem, was it related to the integration?"

"The integration, sir?"

"This problem that you fixed, good, very good. But how was it tied to the integration?"

"The performance was bad, sir, we needed to partition the data sets. I came in on a Sunday—a Sunday I tell you, sir …"

And then Pranab Roy went into some detail about the Sunday. It was an overcast morning, a brisk wind in the air. "You know how the weather is, sir. The cold wind, it comes in from the sea ..."

"The sea, what sea?"

"The bay, sir, I mean. The bay nearby."

"The bay? What bay?"

"The Bay of Bengal, sir ..."

The Bay of Bengal, what kind of talk was this? The Bay of Bengal was far away, ten thousand miles. They were talking about integration, systems integration. The project he had worked on at his most recent job. The job in America, in *Ohio*. The Bay of Bengal—nonsense, all nonsense—what did it have to do with systems integration?

The other looked at Pranab Roy, he sighed. He sighed again. This Pranab Roy may be a good man, a decent man. He may be a smart man. But he was not right for the company—that much was clear. Was it not self-evident?

The other rose from behind his desk, he held out his hand.

"Thank you for coming, Mister Roy."

Pranab Roy was at a loss. He remained there seated. Then at last he rose—weakly, limply—he held out his hand as well.

"We will be in touch with you, Mister Roy."

Pranab Roy was silent.

"Let me walk you to the door."

The tall man walked around his desk and began

walking to the door. He opened the door, held it politely for the other.

Pranab Roy was at a loss (or was he just numb?). They walked out the door. The tall one walked, he followed. The tall one walked, he followed. They walked past the open door and down the hall. They walked past the cubicles on both sides. (Cubicles, cubicles, where did all these cubicles come from?) The host pushed open a door with a steel handle and they were out in the lobby. There were six elevators there (or was it eight?). The host pressed on a button. A bell sounded. The host looked up. "Wrong direction," he said.

He stood there quietly, confidently. How tall the other was. Why was Pranab Roy not the same way?

Another bell sounded.

"That's for you, Mister Roy."

"For me?"

Never send to know for whom the bell tolls; it tolls for thee.

The other held out his hand. Pranab Roy returned the gesture.

"We'll be in touch, Mister Roy."

"Should I call, sir? If you give me your number, your direct number? Is it all right if I …"

"No need, Mister Roy. We will be in touch."

***

And that was it. The other turned, he walked away. Such a tall man he was. So confidently he walked away.

The door closed and Pranab Roy went down the elevator. Down, down. Where was he going? To heaven? To hell? He emerged in the lobby downstairs. People, all these people. People who already had a job. How lucky they must be. How lucky indeed.

Pranab Roy arrived home (it was almost an hour later), he took off his clothes. He washed his face, his feet. He looked at his face in the mirror: too dark. His hair: balding, not enough. He had his pizza (to-day with Coca-Cola and also some breadsticks). He watched his TV. He watched it again.

Lucas McCain worked on his ranch. Did he go to job interviews and worry about systems integration? Andy Taylor worked as sheriff. Did he? And Superman, what of him?

Pranab Roy lay on the sofa, the TV running in front of him. He lay in bed, he pondered his life. Who he was, why. He had had a bad interview. His heroes, how would they have handled it? Lucas McCain, would he have taken out his rifle? Superman, would he have made a hole in the wall? Andy Taylor, would he have used his charm, just that?

The days passed. Pranab Roy went to his interviews—again and again he went. And was there progress? Again and again he went. And was there success?

One day Pranab Roy was at an interview. There were cubicles all around. (Cubicles, cubicles, where did all these cubicles come from?) There were corridors as well. All these corridors and corridors. Where did they lead?

Pranab Roy wanted to sit down—to sit down right there on the floor. To clasp his palms, to pray. To sing a song from an Indian film. *Teri Pyari Pyari Surat Ko. Duniya Mein Hum Aaye Hain. Aaj Mausam Bada Beimann Hai.* There were so many songs he could sing.

Or if not these popular songs, then the hymns. There were so many hymns in India, so many sacred songs.

"I am a good man, sir."

"What is this?"

"I am an empty man, sir."

"What is this?"

"You go ahead with your meetings, sir, I will sing quietly, softly. I will not disturb."

They listened to the strange man—and did they understand? Were they impressed?

The days passed. Pranab Roy did not give up—not so easily. He rose, he brushed his teeth. He shaved, he bathed. He put on his jacket and his favorite maroon tie. And he went out for his interview. One interview and then the next. One interview and then the next.

A tall man sat on the other side of the dark wooden desk. He asked Pranab Roy about his experience.

"I have watched *The Rifleman*."

"And how does that help?"

"I have watched *Andy Griffith*."

"And how does that help?"

"I have watched *Superman*."

The other was not convinced. "A nice show, Mister Roy. If you say so, fine. But what is the relevance to us?"

"Lucas McCain, the Rifleman—he is a good man, sir. His son is Mark. The sheriff is Micah. All *m*'s in the show."

"Is there symbolism in that?"

"The gospel of Christ, sir. There was Matthew, Mark, Micah. More *m*'s as well."

"Is there symbolism in that?"

It was a good question. And did Pranab Roy know the answer?

"I am a good man, sir."

"What is this?"

"I am a decent man, sir."

"What is this?"

"I am looking for an opportunity, sir. I *seek* it."

Seek: what an odd word to use. What an odd word to emphasize. As if the word were self-explanatory, as if it explained all.

The other looked at Pranab Roy, smiled. "The people you mention, Mister Roy, they are strong characters, all of them. The Rifleman. Andy Taylor. Superman. Are you a strong character?"

"Me, sir?"

"Sam Peckinpah directed the early episodes of *The Rifleman*. Not many people remember that. He was a good director, a fine director. And you, Mister Roy, do you see yourself as a director?"

"Me, sir?"

"Directors are good men, Mister Roy, strong men. They lead, they lead. Good for the company. And you, Mister Roy, do you lead? Do you see yourself as a leader?"

Leader: what an interesting word he used. Was Pranab Roy a leader? Had he led anything? When? Where?

It was a good question, a perfectly legitimate question. And what was the answer? Did Pranab Roy have an answer?

But the other had heard enough. He was even beginning to lose patience. He rose slightly from his chair, he held out his hand.

"We will be in touch, Mister Roy."

"Sir?"

"We will be in touch."

"Can I call you, sir?"

No answer.

"Your direct number?"

No answer.

They rose all the way now, they walked to the door. They walked past the door and down the hall. They walked past the cubicles on both sides. There was a narrow alcove there, a sign. "Men," it said. Pranab Roy wanted to go there—to follow the sign.

But the host had already walked him to the elevators. "We will be in touch, Mister Roy."

"Sir?"

"We will be in touch."

And that was it.

Pranab Roy was left there standing by himself. The elevator door was closing—he rushed, he squeezed his way in. The elevator was so clean, yes. But was it not small and box-like as well? A tomb—was it like a tomb?

Pranab Roy stood inside the tomb, shaking his head. His briefcase was heavy—he rested it on the elevator floor. Why didn't he go to the men's room upstairs? He should have spoken up, he should have. That was his problem—he didn't speak up when he should. When he shouldn't speak up, he did. And when he did …

But why go into all that? The interview had not gone well. It never did. But he would try, he would try. He would get better. Of course he would.

***

The days passed. Pranab Roy was not doing well in his interviews, that much was clear. His clothes were bad—was that it? He was not a leader—was that it? He needed a job, just a job. He needed to pay the bills—so badly he needed to pay them. Things would pick up, they would get better. Of course, they would.

Pranab Roy reviewed his notes—all the projects he had worked on, all the accomplishments. "Bullet points," he said. "I should speak to them in bullet points. Bang, bang, bang. Be crisp. Do not dally. Lay it on the line for them—give it to them straight."

He stood in front of the mirror, he combed his hair. And did he feel better? He practiced his sentences. And now? He noticed that there was a twitch in his right cheek. Where did it come from? From watching Lucas McCain? Andy Griffith? Superman? But there was an actor on television who did have a twitch. David Janssen—the Fugitive. Had he learned it from him? Was he himself a fugitive as well?

"I am running, sir—running from the law."

"Did you commit a crime?"

"A crime, sir?"

"Did you kill someone—a wife, for example? Were you accused of so doing?"

No, he had never killed a wife. Never been married (alas). But perhaps he *was* running. Running from what? From work? From himself? From the world?

But he needed a job—that was the main thing. How much longer could he live on his savings—one month? Two months? He needed to get better at the interviews. He did, he did. It was as simple as that. Was it not as simple as that?

There was another interview in three days. It was a position in finance. Pranab Roy had some experience in finance—of course, he did. He would try to emphasize the experience. He would.

The day of the interview came. The tall man sat on the other side of the dark wooden desk. He was fair-skinned, a nice complexion. He used cream on his face—Pond's Dry Skin Cream. It was a good cream, reliable. Was it not the best?

Pranab Roy had rehearsed his experience in front of the mirror. At the first chance he brought it up.

"It was a project for a bank, sir, a big bank."

"And where was this bank?"

"In New York, sir, a major money center bank."

Money center bank: he emphasized the words, he let them sink in.

"The bank wanted to expand its business to other states, but didn't want to reveal its identity. I went to several states, sir—Florida, Texas, North Carolina. I spoke to the State Banking Commissioners. I spoke to banking executives. We wanted to find out the environment. We wanted to ..."

"You went to these executives? You spoke to them yourself?"

"How is that, sir?"

"You went to these executives? You spoke to them yourself?"

"We went in groups of two, sir. There was a Team Lead, I went with the Team Lead."

"How many people on the team?"

"Two people, sir."

"A Team Lead, a person who was not the Team Lead. Is that it?"

"Yes, sir."

"The other was the Team Lead, you were not?"

"That is correct, sir."

"And why not?"

"Why not what, sir?"

"The other was the Team Lead, you were not. Why didn't they make you the Team Lead? Was it a deficiency of some kind?"

"A deficiency, sir?"

"You were too short, you wore polyester jackets?"

Polyester jackets: where did that come from? Why did he have to bring that in?

"A moral defect of some kind?"

What was all this strange talk? He was short, he was dark—was that a moral defect? His hair was balding, turning a little grey even—was that a moral defect? A physical defect, perhaps, but moral?

Another man would have spoken up, taken umbrage. And Pranab Roy?

"It was an important project, sir. I learned a lot. Dealing with people. Analysis, sir, *strategic analysis*" (he tried to emphasize the words). "Penetration, sir— market penetration."

There was a long pause.

"A deficiency," said the other again.

"Sir?"

"A deficiency of spirit, Mister Roy, don't you think so? A deficiency of the soul?"

Moral defect. Deficiency. How the other repeated the words. Seemed to take pride in them. And was there any truth in them at all? Pranab Roy was a good man, a decent man. (Short, perhaps, but was that a sin? Dark, balding, but was that a sin?) He was a follower, not a leader. But do followers not have a purpose in the world as well?

Pranab Roy spoke about the bank again—he spoke for some time. "The travel, sir, it was paid for." "The per diem, sir, it was good, quite good. The hotels were nice. I saved a little bit of money every day." "And the bank, sir, an important bank. *Money center*, sir …"

But the other had heard enough. Enough, enough—was it not always the case? He held out his hand.

"Thank you, Mister Roy."

"Sir?"

"We will be touch."

"Sir?"

"Thank you for coming, Mister Roy. I will walk you to the door."

The other was an important man. He was running a business, not a charity. Charities are nice places—commendable—but this was not a charity. The other walked, Pranab Roy followed. He walked, Pranab Roy followed. Past the door and past the cubicles. Past the steel-handled door and past the restrooms. The elevators, the bell.

Never send to know for whom the bell tolls; it tolls for thee.

Pranab Roy had witnessed the scene before—of course, he had. A "repeat," they said on television. A "rerun." But each time it surprised him (or did it?).

319

Each time it struck him anew in the face (or did it?).
Each time it left him sad, infinitely sad.

***

The days passed. Pranab Roy sat in his room,
he pondered. (And did it help?) He looked out the
window, he looked at the bare trees outside. (And
now?) He went to the mall, he paced back and forth.
Weakness after weakness, sin after sin. It was a mira-
cle that he was able to get up in the morning at all. To
brush his teeth, to cook. To watch his shows—even
that.

And he did watch his shows. *The Rifleman. Andy
Griffith. Superman. The Fugitive*—even that. And did
they comfort him? Did they help?

Money, a job, that is what he needed. And this
job, where was it? Where would it come from? He
was running out of funds. How much longer could
he hold on? A day? Two days?

Pranab Roy was not stupid, he had done many
things. Systems work, he had done that. Financial
work, he had done that. Energy—even some work on
energy.

"The EIA surveys, sir, I helped to design them."

"EIA—what is EIA?"

"Imports into the country, sir. I looked at the imports over a period of twenty-five years. Crude oil
imports, motor gasoline imports …"

"And the results?"

"A time series analysis, sir. It was quite sophisti-
cated."

"And the results?"

"It was snowing in the country, sir, the weather
was bad. The imports were severely affected."

"And the *results*?"

Pranab Roy answered—he tried to answer. But
his mind wandered. Had he not moved on to other
things?

Rejections, rejections, all these rejections. A man
loses confidence. Is he the Rifleman? No. Is he Andy
Taylor? No. Is he Superman? Can the man even focus—can he focus at all?

Pranab Roy sat in his room, he pondered. He
went to the mall. He paced back and forth. It was
raining in the city—it was overcast, the clouds grey
and sad. Was he sad as well?

One day he was at an interview. A fat man sat on
the other side of the desk. Most of the people who interviewed him were tall, but this man was short and
fat. Was there some meaning in this? Was there some
symbolism?

They spoke, they spoke. They spoke for some time.

"I am a good man, sir."

"What is this?"

"I try hard, sir."

"What is this?"

"But the world is hard, sir, it is hard as well.
Sometimes you win, but most of the time you lose. Is
that not the way?"

The fat man looked at Pranab Roy. And was he impressed? He himself was fat, there were blotches on his face. The world laughed at him—laughed every day. Was the world easy for him?

"It was raining in Kanpur, sir. The people lived their lives. I looked at the monsoons, sir—the effect of the monsoons on the people."

"The monsoons? And what effect did you find?"

"Some people danced, sir, some people cried. Some people lost their homes—their possessions, their families, all they had. They lay down on the ground, sir—right there they did it—and they began to cry."

The other looked at Pranab Roy. Was it in awe? Was it in disdain—just that?

"They cried, sir, they cried. Did they not do the right thing? They prayed, sir, they prayed. Did they not do the right thing?"

The fat man was at a loss. He was a manager, not a philosopher. How was he supposed to know these things?

"I am from India, sir."

"So I see."

"I am a short man, sir. Dark, balding."

"We all carry our cross."

"Cross, sir, indeed it is so. My heart is broken, I believe I left it back home."

There was a short pause. "I seek, sir, I seek."

"What do you seek?"

Pranab Roy spoke, he spoke. His voice rose, it fell. It rose, it fell. He spoke of his youth—the kites he had flown, the songs he had sung. He spoke of the job interviews—this interview, that. This interview, that.

The other's eyes grew small. Was it in boredom? He lowered his head. Was it in sadness? Did he not have problems (too many) of his own?

"This is a business, Mister Roy, not a charity."

"Yes, sir. So I see."

"One must be strong."

"Yes."

"To the strong go the spoils."

"Indeed."

"We are looking for strong men, Mister Roy. Strong men, not weak."

In the distance the dawn began to break. The lightning flashed. They said that a storm would come. And would it? They said that it would clean the office building. And would it? It would clean the building, the ground, the world. The world—yes yes, even that.

When would it happen? When would it come to pass?

The other had apparently heard enough. He looked at Pranab Roy, he smiled. He looked at him, he held out his hand.

"We will be in touch, Mister Roy."

"Sir?"

"No need to call us, we will call you. We are good people, Mister Roy, decent people. We will be in touch."

Pranab Roy rose, bowed to the other. He lifted his head, bowed again. And again—was it for the thousandth time?—he made his way to the lobby. There were elevators there: so many. There was a bell there: *it tolls for thee.* The inside of the elevator: a tomb.

"I am a sad man, sir."

"So I see."

"I am an empty man, sir."

"So I see."

"You go ahead with your meetings, sir—please, please. I will sit on the carpet—sit right here. I will sing quietly, softly. I will not disturb."

Acknowledgments

ABOVE ALL, I WOULD LIKE TO THANK Joel Aurora. Joel has read all the stories in this collection and consistently taken them to the next level. He has made detailed edits, turned the stories inside-out, and offered invaluable insights. He has done so without trying to superimpose his own style. For me, Joel is the ideal reviewer and editor. He has consistently made the stories more polished, "publishable." Without his help, this collection simply would not exist.

I would also like to thank John Robbins, a person who has read most of the stories in this collection and offered important insights and detailed analyses. Our writing styles and approaches are quite different, and that makes his comments especially useful. John's insights began decades ago when I first began writing, and they have continued over the years. John has also been a close friend for several decades. I value both his insights and his friendship.

Finally, I would like to thank my brother, Rajive Aurora. Rajive has read several of the stories in this collection and offered useful comments. Just as importantly, he has been a supporter—quiet, sustained—of my writing over the years. In the Indian community, where writing is often considered a silly and/or frivolous endeavor (a "hobby"), he has been a steady source of support.

To Joel, John, and Rajive, my deepest thanks.

Some of the stories in this collection have appeared, in slightly different form, elsewhere:

"Munnu Shunnu": *Quarterly West* (Fall 2008/Winter 2009)

"Krishna": *The Chattahoochee Review* (Vol. 34, No. 1, Spring 2014)

"My Father Is Investigated by the Authorities": *Epiphany* (Fall/Winter 2009-2010)

"A Small Market": *Harpur Palate* (Vol. 10, Issue 2, Winter 2011)

"The Servant": *The Common* (Summer Fiction Issue, August 2012)

"Gurmeet Singh": *Michigan Quarterly Review* (Vol. 51, No. 4, Fall 2012)

"Mother of Gulu": *Crossborder* (Vol 2, No. 2, Fall 2014)

"D.K. Choudhary": *Quiddity* (Vol. 4, No. 2, Fall/Winter 2011-2)

"The Lovers in Bengal": *Nimrod International Journal* (Vol. 57, No. 1, Fall/Winter 2013)

"Pranab Roy": *Western Humanities Review* (Vol. 58, No. 2, Summer 2014)

About the Author

BIPIN AURORA WAS BORN IN DELHI, INDIA, and came to the United States when he was nine years old. He has worked at all kinds of part-time jobs—cashier, stock boy, waiter, salesman—and then, more "professionally," as an economist, an energy analyst, and a systems analyst. His fiction has appeared, or is forthcoming, in *Glimmer Train*, *Michigan Quarterly Review*, *Southwest Review*, *Nimrod International Journal*, *Witness*, *The Chattahoochee Review*, *Western Humanities Review*, *Puerto del Sol*, *The Common*, *Southern Humanities Review*, *South Dakota Review*, *New Orleans Review*, *The Carolina Quarterly*, *Confrontation*, *Grain*, and numerous other literary publications.

MARQUIS

Québec, Canada

RECYCLED
Paper made from
recycled material
FSC® C103567

Printed on Rolland Enviro, which contains 100% post-
consumer fiber, is ECOLOGO, Processed Chlorine Free,
Ancient Forest Friendly and FSC® certified
and is manufactured using renewable biogas energy.

PERMANENT

100%